TALENTED BOOK TWO

A DASH OF FIEND

AMY HOPKINS

Cover by Valerie Chambers

This book is a Spellscribe Press Production

Amy Hopkins

50 Eudlo Road

Mooloolah Valley, Q, 4553.

Print ISBN: 978-0-6489761-1-0

Chapter One

Tork was possibly the most intimidating creature I'd ever seen. Nine feet tall with a horned nose and bony carapaces covering his shoulders, he dominated my tiny shop. The two gnomes who'd been here when he arrived had long since fled, leaving me alone with the short-tempered troll.

"I say THREE chips!" His fetid breath washed over me and a speck of spittle hit my cheek. I didn't flinch.

"Four. I don't haggle Tork, you know that."

"Was three chips last time. Tork pay three. Give me now or I crush you like bug." His hand squeezed shut in front of me as if to demonstrate what would happen if I resisted his demands. Perhaps he realised how bad his English was and wanted to make sure I understood the message.

"Four. My costs are up, and so is demand. If you don't want it Tork, I'm happy to sell it to Obar. I'm sure he'd *love* this blend." My heart sped up as I said that. It was a big risk to threaten a half-troll, but I'd been dealing with Tork a long time. He was all bluster... I hoped.

Perhaps I was wrong. I could almost see the steam coming out of his ears as he processed what I'd said, then his giant arm reached out and he tried to grab me. Heart galloping, I skirted out of the way.

"SQUASH!"

"Come on, Tork! If you squash me, who's going to make the next batch? You'll never have your special tea again." Despite my spike in anxiety, I kept my voice level. I stole a quick glance to the side where Lenny was lying on the floor nonchalantly ignoring us. Some guard dog he was.

Tork hesitated. His brow wrinkled as he considered his options.

"No more... tea?"

"No more tea. If you want more tea in a month, you can't squash me. And you have to pay four chips, like we talked about last time. Without fighting, Tork. If you threaten me again, I'll tell Gibble you're not allowed back."

"Tork no threaten!" A trembling smile stretched over his crooked teeth, somehow making him look even scarier. "Tork just haggle. No haggle with tea-lady, is ok. You not tell Gibble, Tork be good. Four chips! See, Tork pay four chips like tea-lady say!"

Using Gibble as a threat was something I tried to avoid, but I didn't want to have to deal with this every moon-cycle. Not that Gibble minded – he'd appointed himself my protector, and if he'd been here, would have evicted Tork long before he'd gotten this aggressive.

Gibble was a big, scary boggart, and he was mine, bonded to me after years spent with my family. He would do anything to keep me safe, so I felt comfortable offering up his name during my negotiation. Still, I was a little proud that I'd gotten my four chips without getting squashed.

I placed the chips into the box that held my otherworld currency and handed over Tork's tea. It was a complicated blend. I'd had to overlay a mind sharpening spell with one that would also calm him. Usually, the two would cancel each other out but I'd found a way to make it work by focusing the calming aspect to work on a purely emotional basis.

As he left with his precious packet I wondered, not for the first time, what he was using it for. He'd come to me with the request some time ago; to have a tea that would make him able to think better, but also control his rage.

Maybe I need to juice up that calming spell, I mused as I watched him go.

His departure was noted and within minutes my shop was full again. A kobold, two piskes and a half-blood Talent like myself were easily taken care of with regular orders. A half-giant and a hobgoblin were both sent away with instructions to return in a few days for custom orders and two mortals came in to browse the selections of teas. Gibble had arrived by this stage and was helping to serve customers, tidy the shop and generally keep things in order.

When the tiny bell above the door tinkled again I looked up and was surprised to see DCI Charlie Greyson. He gave me a respectful nod, then waited in the corner as I finished wrapping a parcel for one of the mortal customers – a party pack for the weekend, consisting of an energy and libido blend along with the world's best hangover cure, if I may say so myself.

I wished the customer luck and he gave me a cheeky grin.

"You want to see the results?" he asked, winking. "I don't have a date for Saturday night yet."

"I'm... good, thanks. Have fun!"

The guy gave me a wave and took off. A piske slipped through the door before he closed it and I raised an eyebrow at Gibble, then tipped my head towards Greyson. Gibble nodded to indicate he'd take care of the shop, so I grabbed Greyson's arm and pulled him towards the door.

"I didn't expect to see you today," I said once we were outside. "Is everything ok?"

Greyson had taken to dropping by every couple of weeks. Not as a customer – I don't think he'd ever tried my tea – but to talk. After taking the position as head of the Otherworld Crime Unit, he'd made a conscious effort to maintain his connection to the community – Talents, half-bloods and Otherworlders.

Part of that involved visiting me regularly. I'd become something of a touchstone for the community as a whole, a place where people would meet, pass messages and share the latest news of gossip. That wasn't an accident; after the incident six months ago, when a Talent Lord had gone on a killing spree, I'd realised how hard it was to be a part of a community that was so fractured. I'd set to work building relationships and encouraging others to do the same, providing my shop as a place of neutrality and safe haven. I'd met Charlie Greyson during that time, and had come to trust him over the following months.

Despite one date and Greyson's frequent visits, it had never progressed past friendship. Still, things were comfortable as we strolled along the bust street. We'd taken to walking while we talked to avoid the constant interruptions in the shop.

"It's not, actually. Did you hear about the damage last week?"

"The vandalism over at the supermarket you mean?" He nodded. "You think it could be related to the damage to the zoo this morning, don't you?"

Greyson stopped walking and looked at me, surprised. "You heard about that already? Cripes. Your network is almost as good as mine. Yeah, we think both incidents were related. It's got to be an Otherworlder but no one's talking."

"I'll tell you anything I can. Can you share what *you* know or is it under wraps?"

"We don't know enough to *put* under wraps yet. We think it's some kind of creature. The supermarket manager said he didn't think anything had been taken, just destroyed. The doors were forced open, looked like they'd been rammed. Whatever is was ripped apart the produce aisle, ate the fresh flowers and then hacked it all up before leaving through a window." I glanced at him and he snorted. "Yeah, smashed it out. All we got from the scene was some grey gunk and a pile of puke."

"And the zoo?" I prodded.

"Damage to the front gate. Greasy trail through to the exotic amphibians' enclosure. They think there's a missing platypus and some eggs were destroyed. The babies were near ready to hatch – none of them made it, but they don't think it was deliberate."

"Wow." My mind raced, trying to quickly assemble all I knew about animals and wildlife from the Other. "Well... it won't be any of the sentient creatures, unless a troll went on a mating display. Trolls don't eat plant food though, they're strictly carnivorous... well, meat and rum anyway. There are a few herbivores in the Other but the ones I can think of are all either really gentle, or never come into the city. I'm sorry, I don't think I can be much help on this one."

"It's fine," Greyson said with a quick grin. "I didn't expect you to be a walking Otherworld directory."

"Oh." I wondered why he was here then. I enjoyed it when he dropped by but he was a cop – social visits during work time? No, there was something going on here. As if he knew I could sense his hesitation, he grimaced and took a breath.

"I want you on the case. As a consultant, you know? You can talk to people that we can't. We can't pay you but-"

"No." My voice came out louder than I intended, but he didn't seem to notice.

"Oh. Well, I mean, I can try and rustle up some funds-"

"It's not that. I'm not a detective, I wouldn't know the first thing about questioning people. This... it isn't something I can get involved in. Not now." I wrapped my arms around myself as we walked on in silence. The hum of passing cars seemed muffled against the sound of my heart thundering in my ears.

"You're still having nightmares." He said it as a statement, not a question, though his voice was gentle.

"Yeah." I hadn't spoken about that for ages.

"I'm sorry, Emma. I didn't realise. I shouldn't have asked."

This time it was me who stopped. Eyes on the pavement, I cursed myself for being such a coward. Greyson had done so much for me, and I wanted to help.

"No, it's ok. I'll keep an ear out and tell you if I hear anything."

We headed back to the shop. Greyson caught my arm before I went in, then pulled me close for a friendly hug.

"Take care, ok?" he said. "And don't worry about the case. I've got other contacts; we'll figure it out."

I gave him a tiny smile, and went inside, leaving him alone in the cold.

Chapter Two

Gibble looked up when I entered.

"You look sad," he said matter-of-factly.

"It's nothing, Gib." Guilt biting at my stomach, I tidied up, waited until the last customer left, then flipped the little door sign over to 'closed'. I didn't bother locking it, instead ducking upstairs to get changed while Gibble sat down with a book. When I came back down, he was waiting by the door for me. I threw my purse into a handbag and we left.

"Do the lessons be helping, Lady?" Gibble asked as we walked to the port-gates.

"No. Maybe. I'm more aware of what I can do, but I still have no control over it."

"It be taking time, Lady. Do not be getting discouraged."

We reached the port-gates and I spoke the word to take us to the entrance to the Inner City. Flashing my papers to the guard on duty, we hurried through the streets as the sun started to dip behind the tall buildings. Gibble had taken to walking me to my lessons with Mergime, but was always eager to leave for the Otherworld by sundown. He never spoke of why, or where he went, and when we were running late one day he did stay until after the sun disappeared to make sure I reached my destination safely. He'd seemed anxious though, so I tried not to let that happen again.

We arrived at the house of Lady Mergime Dumass. When I turned around to see Gibble off, I gave him an impulsive hug. He chuckled and waved as he left. Before I had the chance to knock, the old oak door swung open. I took a breath, set my shoulders and stepped inside.

As soon as I passed through, I was assaulted by a cacophony of noise. Beethoven's Fifth screamed at me while birds screeched in the background and thunder boomed. I flinched but, try as I might, couldn't engage my blocking Talent to stop it. The noise intensified, piercing my ears and making my head throb. Then, a physical attack. Not pain, but the pattering of a thousand butterfly wings on my skin, beating me with tiny flicking sensations. I reflexively tried to wave it out of my face, squeezing my eyes shut and holding my breath to stop myself inhaling imaginary insects. Abruptly, it ceased.

"Were you born in a cave?"

Flushing at the reprimand, I turned and closed the door behind me. Mergime was old, a strong Talent and a legend in the Talent-tutoring field. She also had the compassion of a bedpost. How Harrod had convinced her to take on a student like me was beyond my imagination. Mergime snorted loudly at my inability to block her spells. Every visit followed the same pattern. She'd coaxed me, bombarded me, surprised me and used some pretty coarse language. My blocking ability was sporadic at best, absent at worst. Today was one of the worse ones. Halfway through the lesson, she stopped.

"As fascinating as I find it to wonder what depths of uselessness you'll reach every day, I really do wonder why I bother." Her wrinkled face scrunched up around her monocle. It was easy to believe the rumour – that she'd declined healing after the loss of an eye simply because the healer in question hadn't studied beneath her.

"I'm sorry, Mergime, I'm trying my best." I tried to keep the words respectful but they came out through gritted teeth.

"In which case I wonder why *you* bother."

I muttered something nasty under my breath and she raised an eyebrow at me.

"I've spent the last six months using every technique at my disposal. Today, you haven't even managed a simple rebuff of the most basic spell." She flicked her wand up as she spoke, and I flinched from an attack that didn't come. She sneered.

"I'm *trying*." My nostrils were flared and my face hot, not embarrassment this time. "I don't enjoy being assaulted every time I walk through the door. If I could snap my fingers and engage the block, I would. If I knew of something, anything that would help, I'd tell you. Are you sure *you've* tried everything?"

My mouth clicked shut and my heart started racing. What had come over me? Speaking so disrespectfully to a Talent—especially one ranked as highly as Mergime – was *not* a good idea. Mergime looked at me, her pointed expression telling me how well she appreciated my question.

"There is nothing left to for me to try. I've even employed methods used by less qualified tutors who have need of cheap tricks to bolster their meagre reputations. At some point, one has to wonder if a student is simply unteachable." She folded her hands and stared me down.

Rather than feeling cowed, anger rose within me. "Even if progress is gained by cheap tricks, it's better than six months of going backwards."

"Perhaps." She stared me down, unmoving.

"It's useless!" I said. "It can't be controlled. Surely if it could I'd have found a way by now, even just a hint."

"Perhaps," she said again. "And yet, you've just completely shut down a three tiered attack on all the senses without batting an eyebrow. Ah. I see from the surprise on your face that you hadn't even noticed."

My body seized, rigid with shock. She was right – my gift pulsed through my body, the ever-so-light touch of spells slithering off my skin. This wasn't the first time I'd embraced it unknowingly. The frustrating part was that instead of getting easier to tell when I'd done it, it was getting harder. Mergime shook her head disparagingly.

"Harrod was right to bring you to me, despite your shortcomings. You may just be the most unique student I have ever encountered; that is the only reason I persist. It's certainly *not* due to your dedication to your work, or the respect you show to your superiors."

And so our lessons went. It seemed the only way I was consistently able to use my gift was when I was angry, or in fear of my life – a training technique I'd vetoed after the first session. Mergime would taunt and prod at me, until I finally got fed up and my anger fed into my gift to trigger it. I was no closer to figuring out how to control it consciously than I was the day I first used it. Harrod insisted that despite her prickly demeanour, Mergime was the best Talent trainer he knew; that she was an expert on training Talents with gifted abilities like mine; and that above all, we could trust her.

This last was key, as a gift like mine could be dangerous to have if it became general knowledge but Harrod swore up and down that she wouldn't tell a soul. Unfortunately, 'trustworthy' didn't mean 'nice'. Mergime treated me like dirt and I was pretty sure it didn't have anything to do with a tactical effort to trigger my gift through the anger she caused. No, she was just a curmudgeonly old bat with a strong prejudice against half-bloods. To her, I was nothing more than an experiment.

As if to drive that point home, she rounded on me after my block slipped yet again.

"Do you have any idea how many students wish I could give them the attention I've given you? I have nobles demanding my classes who spend every moment in study and practice, who do nothing but work on the improvement of their skill. Your dedication leaves much to be desired, no matter how impressive your raw ability is." She pursed her wrinkled lips and snorted. "This lesson is at an end. If I see no convincing sign of improvement three lessons from now, I will need to seriously consider whether I shall keep you on as a student."

I wasn't angry anymore, I was mortified. My face burned and tears pricked my eyes. How would I tell Harrod? He'd bent over backwards and put his reputation on the line to even get me an audience with Mergime. The only half-blood she'd agreed to train before me was incredibly gifted and done great things. Me? I'd failed before I'd even got out of the gate. Mergime threw the door open with a flick of her wand and I hurriedly gathered my things. As I passed her, she caught my shoulder in a painful grip.

"Don't think tears will engender my sympathy, girl. I have students undergoing far worse trials than mere laziness. You *will* return having trained and improved, or you will not return."

As soon as she let go I bolted out the door and into the dark street. Rain pattered on my head and I threw my arms up in disgust. My lesson had ended early; normally Harrod would be here to drive me home – he didn't like me wandering the streets of the Inner City alone any more than I did. Glad for a short space of time to gather my thoughts and calm down, I sent him a text message and started walking. Ok, it was more of a sodden stomp. When the Bentley slid up behind me, I was shaking with cold and sniffling miserably. Letting out a sigh of defeat, I climbed into the car, ready to face a barrage of questions. To my surprise, Martin was in the car instead. I shut the door and he gestured to Davoss, the faske who worked as Martin and Harrod's driver, to head home.

"You look like you've had a wonderful time."

I didn't grace him with a reply, sinking back into the leather seat and staring out the window.

"That good? Don't worry, I won't ask. I imagine you'll be thrilled to hear my next bit of news though – Harrod's not here because Abnett popped by for a meeting. When Harrod said he was on his way to get you, Abnett insisted on sending me, to bring you back. He wants to talk to you."

"You can't be serious," I groaned, covered my face with my hands.

Martin looked at me closely. "Are you ok?" All trace of his usual smart ass self was gone from his voice.

"I'll survive. Just... Can we go back the long way?"

"Sure."

Martin sent a quick message from his phone, then leaned forward to say something to Davoss. The faske grunted, then nodded. Martin's phone beeped and he fired off another text. I paid little attention, settling back with my eyes closed and trying to will the puffiness from my face. It was still early, but fatigue made my bones ache as it often did after a lesson. Despite the lack of Talent I'd displayed for my tutor, I *had* used some magic, and the effort of trying to grasp at something I couldn't find had left me drained. When the car came to a halt and the engine switched off, I looked about, confused.

"I thought you said Abnett was waiting for me at your place?"

"I told them to reschedule. Oh, don't look at me like that – I just said you were tired from the lesson, that's all."

"Thanks Martin. I owe you." I was glad Martin had come instead of his brother. Though Harrod's heart was in the right place, sometimes he could be a little blind to the needs of others.

I climbed out of the car but before it drove away, Martin's window slid down.

"You know," he said. "You don't have to keep doing it. Harrod suggested the lessons because he thought they'd help. You won't be letting him down if you stop."

"I know. It's fine, the lesson just didn't go as well as I'd hoped." A lie, followed by the understatement of the year.

Despite Martin's assurance, I knew Harrod *did* care about the lessons – he'd been on my back from the very first one, grilling me about how it went. He'd constantly asked for updates and though he was always kind and encouraging, it felt like I was failing him. I was failing him, myself, and everyone around me. Why couldn't it be easier? If I could just figure out the how, then I could work at it. Mergime telling me to practice when she wasn't there was like telling me to practice a symphony without an instrument.

I slunk inside like a cowed, wet dog. Lenny greeted me with a whine and a cuddle and I took myself up for a shower and bed.

Chapter Three

The next morning was bright and sunny. The weather, along with the knowledge I wouldn't have to face Mergime for another week, lifted my spirits and I started the day in a far better mood than I'd ended the last. Opening the shop, I greeted my first couple of customers warmly and when Abnett arrived, I managed not to let on that anything had been wrong the night before.

"Emmeline, so good to see you again. I trust you've recovered from your exertion yesterday?" The High Seat was, as always, cheerfully polite. He certainly had the charm required to run the Council without treading on toes, and the energy he'd invested in turning that charm onto the mortal and half-blood population hadn't been wasted. He was becoming as popular outside the Inner City as he was inside it.

"Good morning, High Seat. I apologise for not coming to see you last night. Martin didn't– "

Abnett waved his hands, cutting me off. "Nonsense, it was a spur of the moment visit and I hadn't expected you to be there. I'd intended on seeing you today, so here I am, no trouble at all."

"Thank you. What was it you needed to see me about?"

He smiled and shrugged. "Oh, just the usual I suppose. Exchange of information, keeping up with the local gossip, that sort of thing."

Abnett had begun visiting much like Greyson did, to touch base with the population this side of the Wall. As the High Seat of the Inner City, he was trying to introduce new agreements that would be more inclusive towards mortals and half-bloods. The new Council positions had been filled, meaning there were now mortal representatives, and several other new initiatives had been introduced, such as the Council's official endorsement of the Talented healing centres in the outer city.

Abnett had decreed that in addition to the Talented volunteers who normally manned them, young Talented students with an eye for the healing arts would now serve as apprentices in the centres for one year of their training. Senior healers who had never stepped outside of the Inner City were being pressured to offer time as well.

This had had the unfortunate effect of causing riots by the mortal medical professions, who were against these centres serving as anything but a stop-gap for London's homeless population. They worried jobs would be lost, or that harm would inadvertently be done by the students. Several other initiatives had come across the same problem, so Abnett had pulled back to re-evaluate and keep an eye on things for a while.

I passed on the information Greyson had given me about the damage to the supermarket and the zoo.

"So you'll be working with him on that, I take it?" he asked. An uncomfortable feeling settled in my gut.

"I don't think I'm quite qualified to lead an investigation, my Lord. If there's a Talent who can help, though, I'm sure he'd appreciate it. His superiors won't give him the funding to pay a consultant, but could the Council... er, donate someone?"

"We can, we can. Pay them handsomely, set up a fund perhaps. The problem is getting someone to do it. Tension is high right now and volunteers are scarce." His brow wrinkled in thought, jowls quivering as he nodded to himself.

"With all respect sir, you're the High Seat. You could order someone to do it. Even the Talents and half-bloods this side of the Wall would obey an order from you."

I wasn't entirely sure why I was pushing the matter, except that I felt a strong urge to help Greyson out, even if it wasn't how he'd intended.

"Yes, quite right. Well then Emmeline, I order you to assist this Mr. Greyson in his investigation. You will of course be compensated for your time and if there is a specific accommodation you need, the Council shall supply it." His teeth flashed in a self-satisfied grin and he clapped me on the shoulder. "That was easily sorted, yes?"

Wincing at the contact, my stomach dropped into my boots. Well, that was my day gone to hell. Oblivious to my discomfort, Abnett spent the next hour chatting about Talent politics. I didn't absorb much of it - I didn't know many of the players and much of what he spoke about had little to no impact on those outside the wall. Then, he gave me a discerning look that made me squirm under his gaze.

"I suspect this won't be the last time your Mr. Greyson requires assistance," he said. "I shall have to see about that."

"What's Greyson after now?" Harrod entered the shop, dropping his hat on a coffee table. At my glare, he hastily picked it back up and fiddled with it, as Martin followed him in.

"Ah, Harrod, my friend! Hope I didn't keep you up too late last night, eh? Jolly good time that was, but I must be off now. People to see and all that. Goodbye, Emmeline. Let me know how you go with that other business, won't you?"

I gave him a tight smile and he left, waving jovially as he strode away. As soon as he was gone, I dropped my head into my hands. Harrod stood in front of me, waiting patiently for me to speak. Martin wandered over to examine a shelf of tea. Peeking through my fingers to see who was in the shop - there were two unfamiliar piskes - I gestured for the two of them to follow me upstairs, leaving Gibble behind to deal with the shop. I didn't want to rehash this in public; I didn't want to do it at all.

"So... Greyson? I thought you said you weren't... err..." Harrod said as we filed up the narrow stairs.

"How's he doing?" Martin asked. "Bloody good fellow, but he'll drink a man under the table in thirty minutes if you're not careful."

Harrod turned to Martin, agape.

"What? We went out for a drink after that ruckus with Opius. He asked me to keep an eye on Emma. I told him *she's* keeping an eye on *us*." He winked at me and I laughed.

"He's doing great, Martin, he's just been busy. He drops by every few weeks to check up on things. We haven't been out again though." I narrowed my eyes at Harrod's disapproving expression. Was he... *jealous*?

"Checking up on you? You're fine. Why is he checking up on you?" Harrod said, his tone sounding a bit discomforted. Martin eyed him as I tried not to chuckle.

"Harrod, he's checking up on everyone. He comes here because he knows I hear everything that goes on."

"Does he come by often?" Harrod persisted.

"Oh, every so often. Why?" I watched him closely for a reaction. It was too hard to resist baiting him gently.

"Got a bit of the green-eyed monster there, Harrod?" Martin snorted.

"What?" Harrod's eyes widened in consternation. "I don't know of any monsters with green eyes. Have one of the Otherworlders been causing trouble?"

"Gods, sometimes I'm embarrassed to say I'm related to you." Martin shook his head disparagingly.

"Actually, Martin, that's sort of why he was here. Greyson came by to ask for help on a case - some kind of creature causing damage to property. He hasn't got any leads, so he wants me to ask around."

"You said yes, of course?" Martin asked, just as Harrod said "I hope you told him no."

"I told him no, but *now* I have to call him and tell him yes." I sighed, all trace of humour gone. "Abnett just ordered me to."

"What?" Harrod's voice was loud enough that I had to shush him. "Look, I'll take care of it. You're not getting involved, it's too dangerous."

My skin itched at his tone. It was one thing to not want to do it on my own terms. To have someone else *forbid* me?

"Harrod, don't you *dare* go to Abnett. I've already given him my word that I'll help. Greyson wouldn't put me in any kind of danger, he just doesn't know who to talk to. I have contacts he needs, that's all. I'll be perfectly safe." My stomach quivered at the last bit. Was I trying to convince Harrod, or myself?

"Of course you'll be safe." Martin gave a wolfish grin. "I'm sure Greyson will take *very* good care of you."

"Shut up, you." I punched Martin in the shoulder.

"I'm not comfortable with this. You're overstretched, and this detective-"

I cut Harrod off. "What do you mean I'm overstretched?" I snapped.

"Martin said you were tired after your lesson last night, that's why you couldn't come to see Abnett. You've been working hard and training - I know Mergime rides her students, it's why she's so good. You can't afford any more on your plate."

I looked at Harrod, eyes narrowed.

"I'm fine." I said flatly. "And even if I wasn't, *you* don't get to decide where I spend my energy. I told Abnett I'd help Greyson and I will. In fact, I'm about to call him right now."

Harrod's brows furrowed. He was clearly unhappy with my decision and I wasn't sure it was a good one either. Unfortunately, I had little choice. To go against Abnett's wishes probably wouldn't have devastating consequences right now, but it would make it less likely I could count on his help if I needed it.

Harrod saw the man as a puppet, controlled by those who helped to put him in power. I saw a man who, while he relied on the usually good advice he was given, knew he had been granted an incredible gift and was determined to use it well. He was set on improving the relationship between mortals and Talents and he wouldn't look kindly on anyone who seemed to be getting in the way of that.

Harrod ran his hands through his hair, turning away in frustration.

"You're doing that thing again," Martin said to him.

"What? What thing?"

"The thing where you try and boss her around because you think you know better. You know, the thing you told me to tell you not to do if I saw you doing it?"

"Not in *front* of people!" Harrod flushed, then raised his hands in defeat. "Fine, I'm doing the thing. I'm sorry."

Martin gave me a mock bow for his service and I laughed, letting go of my anger.

"Really, Harrod?" I asked.

"Yes, alright. I know you hate that and I know I do it a lot... not just to you." His eyes slid to Martin and I wondered what they'd argued over.

"Yeah, he does it to me all the bloody time, only he doesn't listen to *me* when I tell him to stop." Martin said, confirming my suspicions. Neither of them seemed to be harbouring hard feelings over it though.

"What is this, crucify Harrod day?"

Martin just laughed.

Harrod turned to me, apologetic. "Look, I fully support your decision and I'll help in any way I can." His eyes narrowed. "I'll even bring my brother, even if he's only good for wise cracks and cooked lunches. If nothing else, he might get eaten. Might save us both a world of trouble."

Martin socked his brother in the arm and Harrod winced. My nerves flared again at the reminder of what I'd agreed to do, despite having their support. I didn't know what Greyson expected of me, or Abnett for that matter. My biggest fear was that trying to track down an Otherworld creature would inevitably involve a trip to the Other. There was no real way around it. A trip to the Other meant potentially running in to the Guardians, a prospect that made me sick with fear. They'd taken an interest in me and I didn't know why. I wasn't sure I wanted to...

Martin looked at his watch.

"Sorry to love and leave folks. I have to run. I'll see you tomorrow Harrod; Emma, keep me updated on the new case, and the new beau." He gave me a sly wink and dashed out the door.

I glanced at Harrod, who was looking at the now closed door with concern.

"What is it?" I asked.

Shaking himself out of his reverie, Harrod assured me everything was fine. Martin had dated several Fae over the last few months and Harrod had made his disapproval clear. He was trying to stay out of it, but I understood his concern for Martin's safety. Though most Fae who lived and socialised with mortals meant no harm, their very differences could make them a little unsafe. Few mortals survived a long-term relationship with a Fae without being changed in some way.

"I know you're worried, Harrod, but he's a grown man. You have to let him make his own choices." Without thinking, I touched his shoulder. He turned away.

"He's mortal. He doesn't know the danger like I do, and he won't listen when I try to explain."

Oh boy, this was going to be delicate.

"Harrod, do you understand what you're saying? You're telling Martin that because you're Talented, because you were born with power and he wasn't, that makes you more competent than he is. You're telling him that because he had the bad luck to be born Talentless, you think he's unable to fend for himself. You do it to me too and... well, to be honest, it's a little insulting."

"What? That's not what I mean at all. He just... he hasn't had the exposure to things that he would have if he'd been raised inside the City." His eyes searched my face, trying to convince me of his words.

"No, he *wasn't* raised in there, he grew up out here. There are Fae on this side too, remember. We grew up alongside them just fine and Martin didn't have any Talent to protect him - no magic, no title, no council. Don't you think that maybe that's enough?" The blank look on Harrod's face said no, it wasn't. "When you keep nagging him like that, all you're doing is rubbing it in his face he missed out on your privileged upbringing. Just because you had expensive tutors, it doesn't make you better than us." He opened his mouth to protest, but I cut him off. "Oh, I know you don't *mean* it that way, but how do you think it feels from our end?"

Harrod shifted uncomfortably. "It's not the same. Living a few streets away from one of those blasted creatures isn't the same as dating one. He doesn't know the risks."

I knew he didn't see it the way I did, but he really was acting like a clueless jerk. Even though his heart was in the right place, it stung that he thought so little of us. He blew out a breath and looked down.

"Fine. I'll leave off the both of you and I'll try to think a bit more before I speak. Damned if I'm going to let either of you walk into a dangerous situation alone though; I won't let you get hurt."

I shook my head in exasperation. The guy just didn't get it, and I didn't think he ever would.

"Ok. I suppose that's better than nothing. I have to go down and check on Gibble. Are you staying for a bit?"

Harrod nodded - I suspected he felt a bit lost now Martin's social life had taken off. Since Harrod moved in with his brother, they'd been close, Martin giving Harrod the company he craved when he left the society he'd been raised in. Now, he was like a lost puppy.

He trailed behind me as I walked downstairs, wondering if there was anything I could do. Despite Harrod's bossy streak, he'd become a really good friend over the last six months. So had Martin.

The brothers were as different as chalk and cheese, but they fit together like they'd been raised together. I didn't want them to lose that closeness, but I was wary of trying to fix their relationship - meddling with other people's problems was Harrod's department, not mine.

Chapter Four

Downstairs, I found Gibble cleaning the counter down in between customers. He looked up and grumbled good-naturedly as I entered, Harrod and Martin jostling each other behind me.

"Where's Lenny?" I asked, frowning.

"Ah. The hobgoblin did be taking him for a walk." He shook his head ruefully. "Gibble did not be thinking what might be happening when I did ask him for one small favour. He and Lenny-dog be good friends, but Lady, Barg be a lot of hard-working when he does come."

I laughed. 'Hard-working' didn't begin to describe one of Barg's visits. The tiny Otherworlder was a pocket rocket of energy and mayhem, and he'd taken to Lenny like a duck to water. After I helped clear the few customers that were waiting, I told Gibble to go take a break.

"Gibble not be needing a break, Lady. It be almost time to close the shop."

A quick glance at the clock showed he was right - time had flown. We closed up, Harrod helping to tidy away the day's mess and set everything in order. Lenny returned, Barg riding atop him like a horse with one hand grasping his collar and the other flying in the air like a rodeo cowboy.

The dog had grown since his strange Fae healing by the Otherworld animal healer and he carried Barg with ease. The two of them galloped up to the door, then skidded to a halt, walking in sedately and looking for all the world like they'd just been out for a gentle walk. Lenny's stomach growled and Barg's followed suit. It reminded me I'd skipped lunch.

I turned to Harrod. "Stay for tea? I don't think I've got anything to make but we could walk down to that new fish and chip shop near the port-gates?"

"Sure." Harrod looked pleased at the prospect of a warm meal.

"Sorry," Martin said. "Must run. Places to go, people to do and all that." He winked salaciously, eliciting a groan from his brother.

"Don't believe a word out of his mouth," Harrod said. "He's meeting with a tailor for a suit fitting, not a woman."

"I'll tell her you said that," Martin said before scooting out the door with a wave.

"Ahem." Barg cleared his throat delicately, then looked away disarmingly. "Barg has delivered the Lenny-dog back safely, Lady!"

"Thanks Barg." I tried not to chuckle, waiting for what was coming next.

"Lady, Barg is forever your faithful servant! As long as Barg does not have other duties to attend to first, of course. Barg gives this service freely, Lady!"

I raised an eyebrow and waited for him to continue.

"Ah. Lady. Barg, your poor and ever-so-loyal servant, is ever so loyal. And, well, Barg is also ever so hungry, you see... would this fishenjips be a sort of food by any chance, Lady?"

Harrod chuckled and I told Barg he was more than welcome to accompany us to dinner, as long as he didn't steal any cutlery or try to sit on the table again.

"Yes, Lady! Barg will be the uttermost epistome of decorative decorum!"

"I think you mean epitome?"

"And Barg will be an epitome also, Lady!"

The weather was perfect for walking, so we took advantage of it. We left together, Barg vaulting back on to Lenny's back, much to the dog's joy. The walk was a short one and the sun had only just set when we arrived. The shop was new - small, but trendy, and a line had already formed. The tables were all taken so after a short discussion we decided to order our meals to go, then take one of the portgates to a small park I knew of for an outdoor picnic. We had to wait for our order while Lenny and Barg performed for the waiting customers. Watching a hyperactive hobgoblin who thinks he's a medieval knight on his noble steed isn't the most peaceful way to spend an evening, but it's fun. The eager duo paraded up and down the queue, entertaining the other customers while Harrod and I watched on in fits of laughter. We finally got our meal, much to the relief of the shopkeeper, and headed for the park. The light had just begun to fade into the chalky tones of dusk when we found a table. Using his wand to trace a globe of light, Harrod chased away the darkness. Then he enclosed the small picnic area in a warm bubble to ward off the night-time chill.

An hour later, we were full, tired and happy.

"Barg is *most* grateful for your sustenance, Lady!" Full tummy bulging, Barg saluted me. Lenny wagged his tail in agreement.

"As am I, Lady," Harrod said, with a mock salute of his own.

I stood and gave a formal curtsy in the style of the High Talents. "Lady is most-"

A threatening growl made me stop mid-sentence. Lenny jumped to attention, tail straight up and ears forward. His hackles were raised and the sound coming from his chest seemed to vibrate all around. Fumbling for my wand, I looked around to see Harrod had his out already and was scanning the park for danger. Barg threw himself on to Lenny's back and leaned forward to whisper in his ear.

"Danger comes, Lady. A disturbance in the Air-Force. Lenny-dog suggests we leave, now."

Harrod scooped the leftover food into the paper and we hurriedly collected our things, Lenny and Barg standing guard all the while. An almighty crash erupted from the darkness. I jumped, and Harrod shot a globe of light in the direction it had come from. Lenny let out one deep, loud bark. A skittering, shuffling sound in the distance indicated that whatever it was, it was going in the opposite direction.

Something moved in the shadows and I thought for a moment that a pair of orange eyes looked back at us, reflected in Harrod's light. We fled.

The port-gate wasn't far and we dashed through as soon as Harrod spoke the word to activate it. On the other side, I looked up to find we'd gone to the one closest to his house.

Catching my glance, he said, "I thought this would be safest. We're only a minute from my place and I can drive you home from there."

I accepted without a second thought, happy to take the safest option. We didn't quite run, but it wasn't a leisurely stroll, either. After we were safe inside, door locked behind us, I felt silly. We'd run from a growling dog and a clatter in the park? It had probably just been a stray cat. As for Barg's melodramatics, there was no way I believed he could actually communicate with Lenny.

"Barg," Harrod said as he took off his coat off. "How long have you been able to communicate with Lenny?" My skin shivered at the way he had echoed my thoughts, and how he asked the question - as if it were perfectly reasonable that a hobgoblin and a dog shared a language.

"Well, quite for some time, I am supposing. Lenny-dog and Barg have many deep and complex speakings, on topics such as the virtuous nature of sausages, and what the Darth Lord Vader might say if he could be tasting one."

"You talk to my dog. About Star Wars... and sausages?" Well this was turning out to be an informative night. "Barg, have the two of you always understood each other or is this... different?"

"Ah, Lady, this is... well, not a this-world occurrence. Lenny-friend is of the believingness that the tree-god did occur this change in the Lenny-dog, for it was after he was healed with Otherness that he did begin to speak to Barg of such things."

Lenny whumped his tail on the ground and blinked at me.

"Were you going to tell *me* at any stage?" I directed that at the dog, who gave a guilty whine, sneezed, then let his tongue loll out with a dopey grin.

Barg's explanation made sense, if talking dogs made any sense at all. Olfred, the healer who had tended Lenny after an attack, had imbued him with magic from the Other. That could have all sorts of unintended consequences and to be honest, I'd been surprised to only notice him eating more and growing a little.

I asked Barg if he knew what had come upon us in the park, but he said neither of them were sure - just that it had, I guess, the Other-world equivalent of bad vibes about it. It hadn't *seemed* like a sentient creature; the shuffling sound it had made put me more in mind of a bear, if a little more... vigorous. Harrod was frowning in thought; I was certain he was thinking what I was.

"We could go back," I suggested tentatively. "Quietly, just for a look. If we can catch a glimpse, we'd at least have some idea of where to look for answers."

"What? You're joking, aren't you?" His face fell as he looked at mine. "You're completely serious. We just ran hell for leather away from a giant creature stalking us in the dark, and you want to go back for a *look*?"

I waited, expecting him to say no. Despite all my earlier thoughts of rebelliousness, I wasn't brave enough to go on my own and honestly, I didn't want to go at all.

"Fine. But you promise to stay behind me and if I say run, you run. Ok?"

Crap.

Barg insisted on joining us, saying Lenny would never speak to him again if he let any harm come to me. Lenny himself pressed against my legs as if to suggest I should stay. It seemed like a really *good* suggestion, but I was knee deep in this now. I'd given my word to Abnett and if I was going to track this creature down, I had to do it properly. This time, we set out on guard and watching for danger.

We passed through the port-gate near the park. The short walk seemed to take forever, and the night wrapped around us, stifling us with its darkness. Harrod traced a globe, but positioned it off to the side - that way it wouldn't blind us, and it would draw attention away from our actual position. We moved slowly, and stayed close to each other as we approached the park. My ears strained over the sounds of distant traffic and buzzing, chirruping insects, trying to pick out a noise that didn't belong. I placed a hand on Lenny's back for reassurance. He gave his tail one quick swish as if to comfort me.

We reached the table we'd sat at and my heart jumped into my mouth. Ragged claw marks had gouged deep scratches across the wooden table and a greasy film covered the area. Lenny whuffed quietly but he didn't seem to be picking up any imminent threat.

Harrod threw out some more globes, lighting the park in full. There was a bin lying on its side, contents strewn over the ground, and a tree had been attacked. The old elm had claw marks at its base, similar to those that had destroyed the table, and the ground around it had been torn up as if the creature had been digging for something.

Lenny nosed around the area, and found a short trail that ended before it really went anywhere. The park was open; there was nowhere a beast this size could hide. Where had it gone? I shuddered to think what damage it might do if it came across a person. That made me wonder what it would have done to us... Swallowing, I forced that thought away.

"I'm going to call Greyson; he'll want to send someone out tonight, I think."

I pulled him up on my contacts and dialled, cursing as it kicked through to voicemail. The message I left was short, simply telling him where we were and that we'd seen the creature he was looking for. After I was done I looked at Harrod, unsure what to do next.

"Do you want to wait here for him to call back?" he asked.

"There's not much point. The creature's gone, we didn't see much. I'm kicking myself for running now, dammit."

"We don't know what it is, or how dangerous." Harrod's eyes darted around nervously, as if expecting it to pop out of thin air, right next to us.

"It hasn't hurt anyone so far," I pointed out.

"*So far*. So far, it's been in secluded places with no one around to antagonise it."

"Fair enough." I wasn't going to argue the point. A sudden yawn erupted from my mouth. "Let's go back to yours. Lenny and I can head home from there. That is, if that lift is still on offer?"

"Of course," Harrod said.

"Ah, little-man?" Barg gave Harrod a short bow. "Barg would be most appreciating of the driving also."

"Sure."

Harrod left the globes up until we were well on our way back to the port-gate. We reached his house to find Martin just getting in from his date, or suit-fitting or wherever he'd been.

He looked... odd. He gave us a dreamy smile, then headed in without speaking. Harrod huffed irritably, giving me the impression that Martin had come home in a similar state before.

Confirming my guess, Harrod whispered, "Damned if I know who he's been seeing, but I bet she's not human. Not entirely."

"Do you want me to talk to him?" I asked.

"You told me to stop ordering him around. Why do you get to do it?" Harrod's question seemed genuine, so I answered.

"I'm not going to tell him to stop. I'm going to ask him how he's been feeling, if everything is ok, and how on *earth* he puts up with you on a daily basis. Then, I'll tell him you're not being a jerk intentionally, that it's somewhat genetic and a little due to an upbringing deprived of reality... and I'll see if he wants to talk about it."

"Oh." Harrod glanced my way. "That seems nicer than the grilling I'd planned to give him."

"There's more than one way to express concern, Harrod. It's not always about telling them how to live their life."

He grunted and fell silent, but I could see the wheels turning. I hoped Martin would talk to me - there was an element of truth in what Harrod had said. Martin hadn't spent enough time around the Fae to really grasp the danger.

Opening the door of the car, I stepped back to let Lenny and Barg through. Davoss was nowhere to be seen, Harrod explaining he would likely be asleep. Rather than wake the faske, Harrod took the wheel himself. Lenny draped himself across my lap in the back seat, Barg snuggled into my side. We reached my house and went our separate ways. Barg set off into the night and Harrod drove away. Lenny and I trudged upstairs, both wearied by the evening's events.

I slept poorly that night, tossing and turning, dreaming of hideous creatures chasing me through a forest.

Chapter Five

Greyson called to tell me they'd examined the park and taken the trace in the morning, but I didn't see him again for two days. He'd been caught up in the investigation, along with meetings with his superiors.

When he arrived forty minutes late, brows furrowed angrily, I guessed those meetings hadn't gone well. I answered the door to his loud rapping and rather than our usual walk, I suggested we stay in.

"The place looks bigger when it's empty," he said.

"I think I'm going to have to extend my days," I replied with a grimace. "The shop's getting busier, and people are complaining that I close Sunday and Monday."

"You won't get a break at all then." Greyson sounded horrified at the prospect.

"I'd need to take on help." I shrugged. It was a topic I'd been mulling over for some time. "I know it's just a matter of finding the right person, but Gibble and I have been doing this alone since we started. Bringing someone else in... it'd be strange."

"Sounds like you won't have a choice, soon," Greyson remarked.

I locked the front door of the shop and we headed up the narrow stairs. "It'll be a big adjustment, but I don't see a way around it. Even during the week, there are days I can barely keep up with the stock. An extra person would mean I can go and trace the spells during the work day instead of trying to get it all done after hours."

"I see," he said, sounding like he really didn't.

I allowed myself a small smile. In some ways, it was refreshing to be with someone who wasn't tied up in the world of Talent magic. Our conversations always started on topics relevant to the work we both did, but usually veered towards the mundane – new movies, music, places to eat and things we'd done.

It was a new feeling for me – because so many mortals weren't comfortable around Talents, even half-bloods, my friends were almost exclusively Talented in some way, or were Other. The fact that my best friends included a boggart and a hobgoblin made me an anomaly even in my own circles.

"How did your meetings go?" I asked as I clicked open the door to my living space.

"The usual," Greyson said.

It occurred to me he hadn't been up here before when he scanned his surroundings curiously. His eyes quickly noted the entry and exit points – doors, windows and the fire escape next to the kitchen – then examined the room.

The tiny open plan living space was sparsley, but comfortably furnished. Most of my waking hours were spent downstairs in my shop, working and being around people. For this reason, I treated my living space as somewhere that privacy and comfort took precedence – the over-stuffed lounge, soft throws, pillows and cushions. Heat rose in my face as I looked around. If I'd known he was going to come up, I'd have tidied the place first. It didn't seem to bother him though.

He flopped into the couch; it was a garish orange, but the sort that made you feel like melting when you sat down in it. A tiny groan of appreciation escaped his lips when he sank back, and he closed his eyes for a moment, savouring the comfort.

"Tea?" I offered.

"Don't suppose you keep any coffee around, do you?" he asked hesitantly, as if afraid I'd take offence. I laughed.

"How do you think I drag myself out of bed so early? Of course I have coffee!"

He looked like he'd been living on it for days. I thought for a moment, then rummaged in my cupboards. Ah, there it was. Though coffee beans were notoriously hard to enchant, I'd managed it. This was a blend of nourishment I'd traced into the whole beans, made to get me through my incredibly busy Christmas period. I threw them in the grinder, then made two cups of hot, black coffee.

Taking his coffee and a handful of biscuits, Greyson wolfed down a few bites and a swallow before he started talking.

"Alright, so you know I got your message about the park incident? Well, we managed to get some samples of the grease. It's definitely Other – our lab is making some real progress analysing some of the substances from over there, but this one's still unknown. It seems to be animal in nature but they can't tell us any more than that."

"Meanwhile, the shit's hit the proverbial fan as far as the public goes. This morning, someone released a video clip online of the... thing, whatever it is. The guy who uploaded it claims it was from the night the monster was at the zoo, and we've confirmed the time and date it was taken coincides with that. There's been an outcry, people demanding it be caught, shot and burnt, and the rest insisting the damn thing should be rescued and protected. It's like Greenpeace versus the Gun Club, they're getting nasty. We've got to catch this thing, or scare it off for good before some fool decides to go after it, and gets themselves hurt in the process."

"Or starts a war with the Others," I said without thinking.

Greyson winced. "I was really hoping you wouldn't say that. Is it likely to get that far?"

"Hard to say." My knowledge of Otherworld politics was spotty. "If it's a creature under the protection of the Fae, it could get nasty. Worst case scenario would be if they thought the creature was attacked unprovoked, and that it was sanctioned. They may have signed a treaty, but I'd bet my left foot that it's riddled with conditions to cover situations like this."

"So we're hoping it's not one of their pets?" he asked dubiously.

Shaking my head, I explained. "If it's not, then it's nasty. We're pretty sure this thing is just lost, right?"

Greyson nodded. "It hasn't gone after any people, seems to be scared off if someone approaches. I can't see any sentient creature doing the kind of damage this thing has – it's random, messy, and unproductive from a criminal point of view."

I bit my lip, thinking. "The Fae have claimed guardianship of pretty much all the non-sentient creatures in the Otherworld, especially the gentler ones. There are some exceptions, but they don't fit with what we know."

"So if someone goes after this thing, we're screwed?"

A breath hissed out through my teeth. "Maybe. Probably. The best thing you can do is release a statement, telling people that the department is taking a non-violent approach. Make sure anyone with any kind of official standing knows the risks. What are the guys at the top telling you to do? You said you've been hauled into meetings over it all week, I imagine they want it dealt with a certain way?"

"Yeah, they want it dead. I tried telling them that may not be appreciated by our new Council-mates, but they don't seem to care." Greyson gulped down the last of his coffee.

"Has anyone approached the Fae on the Council to see if they'll help? Everything I've heard seems to indicate they have an interest in making things good between all parties."

"Have you met any of the top brass?" Greyson let out a loud snort. "They expect the Fae to come to us, so we can do them the favour of letting them help. Bunch of blowhards, they are."

"So, what are you going to do?" I asked.

He was staring into the bottom of his cup, so I took it and busied myself making a second brew for him. "Honestly? I don't have a plan, other than to stay one step ahead of the beast, the Fae and all the damn people who think it's better off dead. I don't want to hurt the thing, Em, but if it's a choice between taking it down and letting people get hurt?" He left the question hanging, but looked at me quizzically. "For someone who told me quite clearly she didn't want to get involved, you're asking a lot of questions."

"Yeah, about that... I'm now involved. I asked Abnett to put someone on the case for you – bastard picked me." I smiled ruefully. "It's not that I don't want to help, Charlie, I really do. I'm just... scared."

It cost me a lot to say that aloud, but I trusted Greyson enough to admit it. I knew he wouldn't use it against me, or use it to hold me back.

"Abnett said he'd spring for any costs. I don't need money for doing this, but it's there if you need it for the investigation. I think he wants to set something more permanent up."

"Oh Em, I'm sorry." The look of regret on his face deepened my guilt and I almost wished I'd just said yes to begin with. "I didn't mean to drag you into this all unwilling. You let me know as far as you're comfortable going and I'll take care of the rest, right?"

"Thanks." I gave him a heartfelt smile.

"I'll need you to fill out some paperwork, is that ok? It'll grant you access to the precinct house and you'll get a login for the police database. I made sure to organise all that before I asked you, so it won't take them long to set it up for you once they have your information. Is there anything you need from me?"

"To be honest, I have no idea what I'm doing," I admitted. "I mean, there's one person I can talk to; he works with animals, so he might at least know what sort of creature it is. Do you have the footage from this morning?"

"Of course," He fiddled with his phone for a moment, went to hand it to me, cursed, and fiddled a bit more. Finally, he handed it over, video ready to play. The footage started rolling as soon as I tapped the screen.

A muffled voice said "There's something trying to get into the zoo!"

"Don't be stupid. Animals break out of the zoo, not into it." Another voice, this one slurred.

"Look at it mate, it's trying to go in!" The speaker laughed.

The camera wavered constantly and the shadows made it hard to see, but there was definitely a creature visible and it definitely wasn't from the world we lived in. It stood about seven feet tall. Heavily built, it seemed to shamble around both on all fours in a fat, waddling manner, or up on its back legs like a bear. I heard a metallic grinding, scraping sound – that would be the gates. One of the voices said, "Oi, it just ripped through those metal bars!" The creature looked up, orange eyes shining directly at the camera pointed at it.

"Sam, it's looking at us. Sam?"

"Nah, it's turned back. Look, it's... oh my God, it just ripped the gates off!"

True to his words, the video showed the giant creature shaking, then pulling down the iron gates to the zoo. The image swung to the ground and bounced around for a moment before shutting off.

"That's all they got?" I asked.

"Yeah. We've taken it down for now, but it had almost a million hits by the time we got to it. It'll probably pop up elsewhere if it hasn't already. Bloody internet. Does it look like the thing you saw in the park?"

"As far as I can tell. It was so dark; all I can really verify is that the eyes were the same. Can I get a copy of this? I'll show it to my contact, it might help."

"Sure, sure." He took back his phone and frowned at it, pressing the screen, cursing it, then pressing again.

"Uh, do you want me-"

Looking relieved, he passed it back and I quickly figured out how to email it. After tapping in my address, I hit send and passed it back.

"I've saved my email address in there for you too, in case you need to send me anything else."

"Cheers. Damn things, just can't work them out. Handy, though." He smiled.

The coffee was kicking in and he looked a little less ragged around the eyes. He'd slumped into the chair a little, losing the tired, buzzing energy he'd come in with.

Leaning back into my own chair, I contemplated the man on my sofa. He was good looking, kind and enjoyable to be around. Our one date had gone well, but ended suddenly when he was called out to work. We'd talked about doing it again, but between his job and my shop, we never seemed to be able to find the right time.

"How long have you been on the force?" I asked on an impulse.

"Too damned long." He gave a wry chuckle. "Somehow, I've ended up in a position that has me working more hours than I ever have, I've taken more meetings this week than I did last year and the idiocy I deal with from above and below makes me wonder how the human race has even survived this long."

"That bad, huh?'

"I'm bloody loving it." The smile that crept over his face showed the truth of his words. "I'm finally doing something to make a tangible change, something that no one has succeeded in doing ever before. There's gotta be some fun in that, right? Half the O.C.U. are now people I trust, people who've moved over because they believe in what I'm working towards. Another year and I think I'll have dispelled a good lot of the stigma around the position; then, I can start attracting even more talent."

"Sounds like you've got it sorted then." His hope was infectious and my heart lifted at the prospect of having a police force that worked for *my* people.

"Feels like it. Of course, that's usually the cue for it all to go to shit." He laughed. "Always the way, isn't it? Look, we've got all the samples and photos of the scenes down at the station. Why don't you and your boys come down for a look? You can fill out this paperwork while you're there."

"My... boys?" I asked, bewildered.

"Yeah. Harrod's rank gives me some leeway in regards to security clearance. Bloody stupid rule, but I'll use it if I need to. If you want to bring them, you can. I know they helped you with that other thing last year. I mean, if you'd prefer to work solo that's fine too, or I can provide you some backup from one of my men – can't deny I'd feel safer if you had someone working with you, but that's up to you, of course."

And that, I reflected, *is how you get someone to do what you want.*

"Sure." I said. "I'll give them a call. Is first thing tomorrow a good time?"

"Perfect," he said. "I'll let the crew know to expect you, they'll let you straight through."

Greyson tipped his cup up to drain it, looking disappointed that it was empty. The lines around his eyes weren't as deep and he had a spark back that he'd been missing when he came in. Smiling, I offered him another cup. His shoulder dropped and he declined.

"I wish I had time, I really do. You'll come by soon though? To the station, I mean."

"Of course, I'll let you know when to expect me." I took his cup over to the sink, then turned back. "Charlie?"

He looked up, pausing in the act of picking up the coat he'd draped over the back of the chair.

"Thank you. For not pushing me into this, and for... well, being there, I guess."

A couple of quick strides and he'd enveloped me in a hug. "Anytime, Em. Anytime."

Chapter Six

Harrod and Martin were both eager to join me the next day. Greyson met us at the entrance to the building - it was small, run down and pretty much embodied the way the department viewed the Otherworld Crime Unit.

As we traipsed past the dead garden bed out the front, I traced a small spell of nourish on the area. It wouldn't do much, but might give some of the local wildflowers a fighting chance. Harrod saw what I did and his lips twitched into a smile.

The inside was as dismal as the outside. A window was cracked and looked like it had been that way for a while. The front desk was dated and had little accommodation for computer equipment and the computers themselves probably had less processing power than my phone.

The officers - seven of them present at the time - seemed divided into two camps. Four were well dressed, polite and working. They must be part of the team Greyson had brought over. The other three sat in a corner, leaning back in chairs and glaring at us as we passed them. Their wrinkled shirts were untucked, badges lying loose on a nearby desk. I imagined these were the last of the dregs that had been assigned to the department as a form of punishment.

A small room out the back held the evidence that had been collected. As Greyson unlocked the door, I noticed the lock was newly installed, and heavy duty. I waited until we were inside and the door had closed before I asked about it.

"New locks?"

"Yeah." Greyson looked away. "Just want to make sure nothing gets... compromised in any of our cases."

I had a strong suspicion that things had been compromised in the past, and that it had come from inside the department. He pulled out a plastic box and dumped the contents on the table. Sorting through sealed bags, he set them out for us to examine. The small table felt crowded with the four of us clustered around it. Martin stepped back to give us more room.

"So," Harrod said leaning back. "Exactly how much progress has your department made? Do you know what we're dealing with yet?"

"Not yet," Greyson admitted, nonplussed by the bluster in Harrod's tone. "That's why you're here. We have an idea of what it looks like and where it's been, but not where it goes afterwards, or where it's coming from."

"You need to put officers on the port-gate that leads to the Other. That's the only thoroughfare, if the beast is moving between worlds, it would *have* to pass by there," Harrod said.

"Actually, it's the only *legal* thoroughfare. We've got it under surveillance, don't you worry about that. The other access points are watched as best we can, but that's spotty at best."

"Wait," I interjected. "Other access points? I thought there was only one way in and out, except through brute magic?"

"There is," Harrod said confidently. "If there were other port-gates the Council would know about them. Whatever information you've been given, it's wrong - something like *that* couldn't be kept a secret, not from us."

"I suppose it could if it were set up by someone who wanted to avoid Council notice - and clearly, it has been." The slightest note of irritation was creeping into Greyson's voice, though he didn't look up as he spoke.

"*What?*" Harrod snapped. "Then why haven't the council been notified? And why isn't it being watched twenty-four-seven? *Any* manner of business could be passing through a gate like that."

"We did." Greyson folded his arms and stared Harrod down. "The Council member assigned to liaise with us seemed neither convinced, nor concerned. I'm not sure whether he thought we were wrong, or if it just didn't matter because it was being used by mortals, not his own kind."

"Right." Harrod had his hands on his hips, nodding sarcastically. "So you're just letting people pass through this secret gate willy nilly, without any kind of surveillance?"

Greyson took a breath and blew it out through his nose, mouth settling into the same kind of tight line I imagined he'd been using through a lot of his recent meetings.

"We can't *watch* the gate it if we don't know where it *is*."

"You said-"

"This passage isn't like a port gate." Greyson cut Harrod's words off, raising his hand. "It moves. It's a temporary setup that disappears a short time after we get on to it, then pops up somewhere else. Seeing as the almighty Council doesn't seem to want to help shut it down, we're on our own. As much as I'd like to, I can't have a man standing on every corner waiting for a gate to pop up." Harrod raised his eyebrows but didn't speak. "Our surveillance tools are limited as well. Some of our watching officers have noticed goings on that'd suggest that even when we can see the gate, we can't see who's passing through. We're doing our best but I'm sure you'll appreciate the constraints I'm working under, especially considering the lack of support from other parties."

Greyson's tone dared Harrod to say another word. A smart man would have backed down. Unfortunately, Harrod wasn't feeling very smart that day.

"Clearly you need to get a better handle on your department, then. Lodge more funding applications, train your men better - those three I saw out there, they aren't doing anything productive-"

"Now you listen to me-"

"Harrod, *stop*." I couldn't take this anymore. "You *know* the state this department was in before Greyson took over, and far as I can see he's done a bloody wonderful job of getting it up to scratch. I know it smarts to hear your precious Council dropped the ball, but *don't* take it out on him."

"I was only suggesting-"

"Oh Harrod, just shut up, will you?" Martin broke in irritably. "You're making yourself look like an idiot. Pipe down and let the man do his job."

There was a tense silence for a moment.

"You have my apologies, detective." Harrod said abruptly.

Greyson just nodded, leaving it be. He tossed me a bag with a small, plastic jar in it. The jar had a glob of grey stuff in it.

"This is a sample of the grease?" I asked.

"Got it from the park last night," he confirmed, then held up another one with black gunky residue. "This is what our older samples look like; I thought you might have more luck with the fresh one. You know anyone who could take a look at it?"

"I can do it right now." Harrod plucked the small jar out of my hand and I struggled to hold back from growling at him. What was his problem?

Harrod traced a light spell. At least, he didn't show any effort while doing it. I couldn't see what he was doing but assumed he was laying a revelation type spell on it.

"It's from a kind of Otherworld animal," he said proudly. "Something large. This is a coating on its skin."

"Yeah, we knew that Harrod." I'd have let it slide if he hadn't been acting like a jerk, but I wasn't going to let him think he could crow over Greyson for something we'd already established. "Greyson told me the other day his trace lab had already confirmed that. You didn't find anything else?"

"Oh. Err, no, I didn't."

"It's ok, I know someone I can show it to." I looked at Greyson and he nodded to indicate I could take the sample. I slipped it in my pocket. "What else is here?"

There were photographs of the scenes - pictures of the damage wrought by the monster, some blurred, muddy footprints and other strange marks in the dirt. I couldn't make sense of the markings. It was as if the creature had been dragging a heavy, flat object behind it. There were swirls where perhaps the creature had turned around, and deep indents in soil where long claws had dug in. The grease had smeared over surfaces where it had pushed against things - trees, the zoo gates.

The police had taken pictures of the park where we'd seen it, and in another area, similar damage. A second huge old elm tree, some way from the one we'd been sitting near, had been flayed and dug up around the roots.

"This damage," I said, flipping the picture around to show him what I was talking about. "Has it done this at any other tree, or just these two?"

Greyson took the picture off me, and picked up the other one from the park.

"No. They're both the same kind of tree, aren't they? You think it's worth looking into?"

I shrugged. "It could be."

My hunch would probably turn out to be nothing; I was new at this and had no idea what I was looking for, didn't have Greyson's training or experience. Still, if I said nothing and it later turned out to be relevant, I'd feel like an idiot for not speaking up.

"Do you have a map of the city?" I asked.

"In my office. Anything else you need in here?"

After I shook my head, we packed up the boxes. Greyson pulled out his jumble of keys and locked the doors behind us. Three pairs of eyes followed us as we walked over to his office.

It took him a moment to clear a space in the small, crowded

room. His desk was littered with papers, coffee cups and rubbish, and the filing cupboard in the corner sat ajar, so overstuffed it had no chance of closing. He scrambled to tidy it and pull up a couple of chairs. Excusing himself, he dashed out to dump the cups in the small kitchenette outside. While he was gone, I eyed Harrod.

"Best behaviour," he promised, raising his hands in supplication.

When Greyson returned he motioned us to a large map across one wall, littered with flat markers of various colours. On it was marked the three sites that had been attacked along with some blue marks and date ranges. Other spots were marked in red with notes, scribbles of dates and codes I didn't understand. As my eyes scanned familiar street names, I noticed some of the markings corresponded with the killings from earlier in the year.

My fingers reached out to gently touch a little green pin. That was my friend, Carmel. Another was Keely. Other green pins were scattered about - more people I knew, who'd been killed.

It had been six months, the man responsible was dead... why did my heart still stop every time I thought of it?

"The map tracks everything," Greyson said behind me. I jumped and snatched my hand back. "I've an online version you'll be able to access through the system. You can filter out the labels you don't need, so it only shows the attacks or the gate locations, but I wanted to show you this first. It shows every major instance of Otherworld or Talent related crime or reportable activity over the last twelve months, along with every reported sighting of a gate, and the dates we know it was active." His fingers slid to the blue markers, each one marked with dates and scribbled notes. "Looks like a dog's breakfast, but I keep hoping *something* will throw light on when and where these damn portals are showing up."

"The map tracks all the Talented activity outside the wall?" Harrod sounded impressed.

"As much as we can. There's a... where is it... oh, here. This overlays it with the residences and port gates, along with other general places of interest." A large, clear sheet rolled down to superimpose new marks on the existing map, littering it with new marks. "Does anything stick out?"

"Well, yes," Harrod said immediately. "These portal locations - they're all on ley lines."

Martin, Greyson and I looked at him. When he didn't clarify, I asked.

"Ley lines?"

"Yes. The strongest ones, too." His eyes roved the map as he nodded to himself.

"Harrod, what *is* a ley line?" I asked impatiently.

He looked at us, surprised. "You don't know? Oh right, of course you don't. They're lines of magical energy, where our world rubs up against the Other. It creates a weak spot. Tracing magic along one can be a bit unpredictable. The Others who don't need to use port gates usually flit through along the lines, it costs them less energy."

"So you're saying someone's tapping into these ley lines and using it as a conduit?" I asked.

"Well... it makes sense." He shrugged. "The way lines fluctuate through the moon cycles. I bet if you tracked that, you'd find the gates are being constructed when they're strongest. That's why they don't stay in one spot. Three days... Yes, sounds about right."

"Harrod, can you get us a map of those?" Greyson asked.

"I could. I'll have to tell the Council about the gates you realise?"

I looked at Greyson, who shrugged.

"Go ahead. Like I said, I've already told them. They just didn't do anything about it."

"Well, perhaps I'll have a quiet word with Abnett about that, too," Harrod said.

"I'd appreciate that." Greyon gave him a polite nod. "We have no way of knowing if our information gets through to him, or if it's filed away before anyone's passed it on. If Talented bureaucracy is like ours, it wouldn't surprise me."

I frowned at the map. There didn't seem to be any connection between the crime scenes and the gates.

"OK," I said. "I think I have everything I need. These samples might shed some light on the beast we're hunting, and if Harrod gets that map of ley lines, I can see how it lines up. Unless you'd rather do that yourself?" I queried Greyson, wary of stepping on his toes.

The feeling of discord among his team wouldn't be helped by a half-blood nobody sticking her nose into more than was needed.

"I've got a good data analyst who'll take a look at it for me." Greyson's voice was distant as he mulled over the new information. He snapped back into the present and added, "Take a look at it anyway. You might come up with something he doesn't, and the gods know we need all the help we can get on this one."

"Sure. But you can get me access to the online version?" I prodded.

"If you fill out the paperwork today, I should be able to hand over your login details by lunch time tomorrow. Is that soon enough?"

At my nod, he pulled out a slim folder and slid it over the desk towards me. I flicked though - it was an application form to allow me to access department resources, along with the appropriate legal and confidentiality clauses. Looking for a place to sit in the crowded office, I cleared some paper off a seat and perched on the edge, leaning the documents on a corner of the desk that seemed a bit flatter than the rest.

"We can wait outside," Martin said. "I've got a call to make. Harrod?"

Harrod looked up, startled. He'd been off in his own little world, absorbed in the map on the wall. He nodded and the two left, leaving Greyson and I alone. Typical for any kind of governmental application, the form was laborious. My personal details, references, travel history and Talented lineage was all asked for, along with a police check that Greyson had already done. When I finally had it done and signed, I handed it over.

"Look, I'm really sorry about before. Harrod's just been under a bit of stress lately. Personal stuff. He's not normally that..." I trailed off, not quite sure how to describe his earlier behaviour. Greyson had no hesitation in helping me out.

"Arrogant? Stuck up? Insufferable?"

Sighing, I just nodded.

"It's fine," he said, and grinned at me. "He's just used to being the biggest fish in the room. Under the new agreements, I outrank him out here. Don't worry, I know he's a good bloke; you wouldn't be friends with him otherwise. He'll settle down before long."

It had felt like there was more to it, but I didn't say anything. Instead, I ran my eyes over the map one last time, settling again on the little green dot. Ever perceptive, Greyson wrapped an arm around me.

"I should have warned you about the map. They're pins on a board to me, but they were your friends. Sorry." He squeezed a bit tighter and I had to swallow hard to stop the well of emotions over-flowing.

"It's fine," I said with a too bright smile. "I have to deal with it sooner or later, right?"

"You're human. It's right to grieve and it's normal for that to take time."

Something broke inside of me at his words, letting out a grief I didn't know I was still holding on to. My chest was tight and tears pricked at my eyes as I turned to bury my face in his shoulder.

"Thank you for understanding," I whispered. He held me for a moment in a fierce hug, then stepped away as someone cleared their throat at the door to his office. Blinking, I raised my head to see Harrod standing at the door, looking at us. His cheeks were fiery red, and his eyes darted away as soon as he saw me lift my head.

"Ah. Martin's just - he's gone. Out." His voice was hoarse and he cleared his throat roughly. "He's late for a date, apparently. I just… came to tell you. I didn't meant to interrupt you."

He turned abruptly and walked back out of the building. Suddenly, everything made sense. Oh hell. What had I gotten myself into?

"Time for me to go," I said to Greyson. He turned to me and gave a reassuring smile.

"You take care, Em. I'll come see you tomorrow?"

Nodding, I headed for the door. Before I stepped outside, I pulled out my phone to send a quick message. Harrod waited for me in his car, staring gloomily out the window. Just as I hopped in, my phone beeped. I pulled it out and read it quickly.

"Hey, would you mind dropping me off at Melanie's?" I asked. " She just sent me a message and asked me to drop by." It was only a little lie.

"Sure, of course." Harrod didn't look at me, and I didn't know what to say. I resolved to keep my mouth shut until I worked out what I wanted to say to him.

CHAPTER SEVEN

It was only a fifteen-minute drive, but it was the most awkward one I'd ever endured. We rode in silence, Harrod twice looking at me as if to speak, but changing his mind at the last moment. Finally, we arrived, and I let out a breath of relief. Melanie coasted down the driveway in her wheelchair to greet me.

"Emma!" she called enthusiastically.

"Hi, Mel," I replied quickly. "Harrod was just driving me home when I got your message, so I came straight over."

"I'm so glad, Emma." Without missing a beat, she said to Harrod, "Sorry for pulling her away. I'm having a small emergency. Ciao!"

We turned and hurried inside, leaving Harrod to take himself home. Closing the door behind me, I twitched the curtain to make sure he'd left. Mel clapped her hands in glee, grinning wildly.

"Go on, spill the beans. I've never had a text like *that* from you. I feel like your knight in shining armour! Is it Harrod that's got you all in a tizz?"

"Sort of. Maybe. Oh I don't know how I got myself into this mess, Mel!" I threw up my hands and sank down onto her couch. "Greyson and I still haven't moved any further, we're just friends.

Only, Harrod's suddenly gone all jealous and I don't even know what brought it on! It feels like they've both gotten the wrong idea and I have *no idea* what to do about it."

"The both of them? Oh, don't tell me yet, we'll need to break open the stash for this one."

Fifteen minutes later we were settled on her couch sharing a bottle of red, some soft cheese and a packet of biscuits. Mel didn't stand on occasion when I was around - the biscuits were straight out of the box and the wine was poured into two water glasses. I loved her for it.

"I think... I think Harrod might have a thing for me," I confessed.

Melanie snorted into her wine and raised her eyebrows at me as if to say 'you're only figuring this out now?'

"Oh, *don't!*" I chided. "We're just friends, it's never been anything more than that. Then, today, he was acting like such an ass around Greyson and-"

"Wait, you put him in a room with Detective Tightpants and expected him to roll over and play *nice?*"

Rolling my eyes, I ignored her pet name for Charlie. "Yes. How was I supposed to know it'd be such a problem? Anyway, Harrod left and I thought he was outside, but he saw Charlie giving me a hug. The look on his face was a dead giveaway. I didn't know what to say!"

"So you came straight here?"

I nodded.

"Good. So the first question is: what is it *you* want?" Melanie gulped the last of her wine and held out her glass for a refill. I obliged, buying time for my response.

"Nothing. I'm happy, Mel. I like spending time with both of them but that doesn't mean I want it to go further."

"Em, are you trying to convince me, or yourself? You said things were going well with Greyson, what happened?"

I heaved a sigh. "There's just too much going on, for both of us. It doesn't help that we're working together now." I filled her in on

Abnett's little arrangement, along with my suspicion that he'd want to make it a long term agreement.

"And you're not interested in starting anything with Harrod..." Melanie raised her eyebrows as if sceptical.

"No. We're just friends, that's it."

"Truth, Emma!" She pressed a hand down on my arm to stop me taking another gulp of wine.

"It is!" I protested. "He's too overbearing, and he already treats me like a porcelain doll. You know me, Mel. I *hate* being treated like that."

"So, tell him you're not interested in anything more than friendship. I know it's awkward but it can't be any worse than it is now, right?"

"I guess so. He does try - I mean, he's slowly figuring out what a jerk he can be sometimes, and he's trying to change." I hesitated, mulling over how much Harrod really had changed in the time I'd known him. "Mel, what if I tell him no and then change my mind?"

"Then change it, you goose! You're not signing a binding contract and if he turns around and says no, it's not the end of the world, right?"

It wasn't that simple and she damn well knew it. But then, it also *was* that simple. Heaving another sigh, I buried my nose in my glass. I wasn't sure what I wanted, just that I was comfortable. Comfortable isn't exciting but it's a damn good place to be sometimes. *Why* did he have to go and complicate everything?

"Speaking of your bevy of gorgeous blokes, how's Martin?" Melanie didn't meet my eye.

"Oh he's ok, I guess. Every time I turn around it seems he's got a new Fae dangling off him arm." I grimaced. "It's not safe for him but ever since he came to the Other with us it's like he's obsessed. Harrod's been trying to make him step back a bit but you know how he is. Martin's probably just doing it to prove a point now."

"Do you think they did something to him?"

"You mean the Guardians?" My stomach twinged like it did

whenever I considered that possibility. "It wouldn't surprise me, but I don't know if I could do anything about it if they did."

"Damn. Well you tell him if he ever needs a human body..." Mel offered up a cheeky grin.

"I thought you were the one who broke it off with him?"

"Oh, I was. Girl can change her mind, can't she?"

CHAPTER EIGHT

Olfred agreed to meet with me, as long as I went to him. Gibble knew the old god and they were friends, of a sort. Unfortunately, that friendship didn't make Olfred agreeable to meeting at a time of my choosing, so that Wednesday, I had to close up early.

This was getting ridiculous. There were several protests as I ushered the straggling customers out, despite the very obvious sign on the door that I would be closing at two. Perhaps it really was time to start looking for someone to help run the shop.

I'd asked Harrod and Martin to join me but to my surprise, Harrod declined, saying he had a prior engagement. He didn't say what it was. So, as I was locking the door, it was Martin that emerged from the old Bentley alone. Davoss stuck a furred hand out of the window to wave goodbye as he pulled away, and I waved back. After I locked the door, Gibble, Martin and I set off on foot to the port-gates.

We were meeting Olfred in the Otherworld, something that scared the pants off of me. Gibble, sensing my mood, offered me an arm to hold.

"It be different this time, Lady. We be going to meet one with purpose, not be seeking audience with *them*." He spat the word out venomously, making it clear how he felt about the Guardians. "They will have no hold over you and it be an easy trip, Gibble does promise that be true."

Comforted by his words, I felt some of my anxiety settle. He would never let harm come to me, in either world. I felt braver than I expected as I reached out to grasp Martin's hand, then stepped through the gate. After my last trip through to the Other, I knew to expect the strange sensation of being turned inside out as we passed between worlds. Still, I wasn't quick enough to avoid being dumped on my behind when a gust of wind, followed by a whooshing pop dropped us at our destination. Martin landed on his feet like a cat and held a hand out to me, trying not to laugh.

We'd arrived in what looked for all the world like a small village on a bright, sunny day. Gibble glanced around and nodded, satisfied that we'd come to the right place. Our path cut right through the centre, a road made from nothing but pressed mud, lined by tiny thatched houses.

There was no one in sight, despite signs of inhabitants. Washing hung on a rope, a pie sat on a window sill and fresh hoof prints dotted the ground before us. Without stopping to look in any of the buildings, Gibble led us straight past the cottages and towards a stand of trees that bordered the small town.

It was an easy walk and the day was beautiful. The sparse smattering of trees soon condensed into deep woods, cool and dark under a tight network of branches and leaves overhead.

After a short, easy walk, we emerged in a small clearing that took my breath away. It was like in a story. A parting in the trees opened onto a small pond, fed by gentle falls. Sun peeked through the leaves, gently reflecting on the rippling water to throw sparkling light in the forest. The water was pure and fresh and the fish that swam in the pool were like rainbow darts, shooting around in circles. Birds sang amongst the trees and the occasional rustle suggested other small animals were close by.

"What is this place?" I whispered. "It feels like home... but better somehow"

"It's the Other," Martin said. "It's not a copy of our world, it's more. *So* much more."

His voice was soft and he had the same look in his eyes that he did after a date with a Fae. Had they been bringing him over here?

"Olfred did be making this place to remind him of where he be born." Gibble whispered. "The druids did be summoning him in a place like this, though I don't be knowing if it be a true copy, or one he be making to suit his own self better."

"It's a true copy, ye big git, an' don't ye be tellin' otherwise."

With a clatter of noise, nearby leaves shook violently as Olfred emerged from the underbrush. "When folk be summonin' a god, they be doin' it in a place that be worthy of such things, hear? And this do be that place."

"Olfred, Gibble be meaning no harm." Gibble's voice was steeped in affection for the little tree god. "It be a beautiful place you have made, and it be suited well for a god."

"Aye, well, I'm no' a god now, am I? Just a wee old man lookin' for some peace. Peace that's been interrupted by ye friends. What do they be wantin'?"

"We need your help to identify a creature that's been escaping through to our world," I said carefully. "It's been destroying property and my people are afraid. We need to find it and return it to its home before one of the mortals take matters into their own hands. I'm worried someone's going to get hurt."

"Ay, well if one of yer mortal fools get himself speared by a collywobble, that be none o' my doin', is it now?"

"And if the mortal fool takes to it with a shotgun? Olfred, I'm afraid the people in charge are going to go after it. I don't want anyone – or any*thing* – to get hurt. Will you help, for the sake of whatever it is?"

"Ye don't even know what ye fighting?" he asked, bushy eyebrows shooting up his face. "That be foolish indeed."

"We were hoping you could help us identify it. We have a photograph and some samples of a substance it left behind." Martin spoke respectfully to the small ex-god, lowering his head respectfully as he handed over the pictures and the sample jar Greyson had given me.

Olfred squinted at the images, then took the jar. He opened it, gave it a sniff. Sticking his finger in to scoop out a smear of the greasy stuff, and before I could stop him, he stuck it in his mouth. Then, he spat violently and made a choking sound.

"Ack, pah, ye fed me poison? Argh." He wheezed horribly, and fell to his knees, heaving. "Ye did be coming te kill old Olfred? After... all I done... for ye?"

"Oh Gods, Gibble, *do* something!" I screeched. "Olfred, I'm sorry! We just took that sample, we didn't think you'd-"

Olfred erupted into hearty laughter. Startled, I looked at him, then Gibble, who was trying very hard to keep a straight face.

"Ye think a bit o' barrow goop could hurt me? Ye silly lass! Oh, but it was worth the look on yer faces!" He dissolved into laughter again. Smiling myself at the joke, I tried to get him back on track.

"Barrow goop – does that mean you know what the creature is?"

"Well o'course, nowt makes this stuff but a barrow fiend." He squinted at me, sobering. "Ye do know wha' a barrow fiend is, don't ye?"

"It lives in a barrow – or under one... and it's a little fiendish?" Martin said sardonically. Olfred burst into laughter again.

"Nay laddie, they flatten barrows. It do be fiendish, I'll give ye that. They be havin' blunt horns on a bony head, and sharp diggin' claws at their front. Flat back feet an' tail for swimming and pushing mud. The grease, it coats the fur to protect its skin from the acids it produces. It's a buildin' animal. It flattens the barrows, then builds 'em up back how they want them. They eat water nymphs, the cheeky buggers, but tha's about the worst of it, other than they be messin' around with the flow of creeks and streams at crossroads. Cause all sorts o' trouble for them Fae bastards, it do." He chuckled again at the thought of the barrow fiends ruining one of the famed Fae crossroads.

"So it's like a giant beaver? That's adorable!" Martin said

"Pah. If beavers could burn through yer skin with a touch, and rip yer innards out wi' the flick of a paw..." Olfred nodded slowly. "Aye, I suppose they're a wee bit the same."

"Ah. It just got a whole lot less adorable, didn't it?" Martin wrinkled his nose in distaste.

"Olfred, please, what else can you tell us about them?" At this stage I thought any information would be of help.

"Well, the fiends live in herds and they do be liking the dark and the wet. They do be blinded by light and the sun in yer world would dry its skin. I dinna think a barrow fiend be able to survive wi'out help outside the Other."

"Why is it in the city destroying parks, why did it try to get into the zoo? Where is it going?"

"Och, ye be askin' a lot o' questions, lassie." His gnarled, tree-like features twisted into a look of concern. "The poor beast should'na be outside o' the Other. Creatures like that have no reason to pass through to the land of mortals. They be gentle by nature and they no' be leaving the herd."

"Could there be more than one coming through?" Martin asked.

"No' likely. If it were a full herd o' beasts, ye'd have more than a mite o' damage done, ye can trust old Olfred on tha'. Summat's amiss, lass, and I no' be likin' the feel of it."

"Tiny god," Gibble said deferentially. "What of the takers? Do you be thinking they be involved?"

"Takers?" I asked.

"Atch." The mere mention of the word seemed to offend Olfred and he spat on the ground. "That do be likely, boggart. They do be causing more problems here of late. Filthy scum."

"The takers be humans who be taking the creatures from the Other to sell." Gibble's eyes were full of pain as he spoke, and he shook his head sadly. "There do be a market for it. It be a sad thing, that a creature may be taken from here... It be a very sad thing."

"You mean... people are smuggling out Otherworld animals and selling them on the black market?" Martin asked, his eyes flashing dangerously.

"Aye. And if I do catch one of them at it..." Olfred's words failed him at this point, his tiny fists screwing up in rage. "Gah, I do think they be involved. The poor wee fiend mebbe lost, or perhaps it be a young 'un that be taken and it be his mam that be passin' over te look for it. Sweet things, but they dinna be clever."

"Wee beast?" I asked. "Olfred, the thing we're looking for is about this high when it stands." When I raised my hand about two feet over my head, Olfred snorted.

"Aye, a wee beast. If ye be thinkin' tha' be anything but, ye nowt be seein' the creatures that dwell here of a regular, lass."

"Right," I said, a little disturbed. My skin crawled and I had to resist the urge to look around, lest a not-so-wee beast was lurking in the trees around us. "So, we need to track down any known dealers and try to find out if a barrow fiend has passed by them."

"Ye be finding them takers and ripping the innards out o' their skin an' settin' them alight wi' your magic," Olfred said in a low, hissing voice. "That's what ye be doing. Then, ye be finding the poor wee creatures an' setting them free. Ye be doin' this for the love o' ye doggy – ye know if he were taken from ye' and sold te some rich mortal for his collection, that's what ye' be doin'. I charge ye' wi' this duty lass, for these creatures be mine as ye be Lenny-dog's."

My insides cramped. Me? Shut down an illegal trade in Other-world creatures, run by who knows what kind of people – or even what kind of creatures? Olfred's eyes blazed in righteous anger and I remembered the day he'd saved Lenny's life. He was right. He loved every one of these animals just as much as I loved my dog.

I kneeled to look him directly in the eye. "I'll do my best, Olfred. I'll try, I will. I'll try as hard as if it were Lenny they held captive, but I can't promise I'll win."

Olfred returned my gaze, taking my measure. "Aye, lass. That ye will."

He turned and left, just like that. As he disappeared into the forest, Gibble gave a small bow to his retreating figure.

~

"You did be making a promise, Lady. You be knowing that be a heavy weight to an Other."

"I know, Gibble." I was locked in now, no turning back. Yet, try as I might, I couldn't make myself want to take back the words. They'd been said with all the intent that any promise to an Other-worlder should be. Seeing how much Olfred cared, and knowing I was the only one who might be able to stop them made that impossible. Oh, he'd manipulated me by mentioning Lenny, that was obvious. He knew the dog was family to me, and that I felt I owed a great debt to him for healing Lenny.

Martin shook his head.

"Harrod's going to kill me, you know," he muttered to himself. "Keep her safe, he said. Don't let her do anything stupid, he said. Sure, like I had any chance stopping *that* from happening."

Gibble led us away from the clearing and a few moments later, we were back at the public port-gate in the centre of London. I looked at Martin, who was still grumbling away under his breath. He caught my glance and raised an eyebrow.

"Don't get me wrong, I think you're very brave," he said. "It just so happens I also think you're incredibly stupid. Do you know *anything* about smuggling rings? Have you got any idea how *dangerous* they are?"

"And I suppose you have first-hand experience?" I asked pointedly.

"I watch television!" He looked at me, daring me to argue.

There was no point. He was right, I'd just made a promise to a very dangerous creature to do a very dangerous thing.

We walked back to my place and as I opened the door, Martin sighed. "Like I said, I think you're brave. And you already know Harrod and I have got your back, even if he's... well, you know. He's Harrod."

Without asking, Martin followed me inside and up to my living space. The ease with which he did that made me momentarily sad that I didn't have the same comfortable relationship with his brother, but I knew Harrod thrived on manners and formality. Without those... well, he wouldn't be Harrod. Steeling myself, I asked the question I'd been dreading. I didn't want to broach the topic but I'd rather ask Martin than Harrod himself.

"He, um... didn't say anything about yesterday, did he?"

"What, about finding you in the arms of a ruggedly handsome police officer, and reacting so badly his unrequited feelings are now completely exposed?" Martin collapsed into the couch and grinned at me. "Not a word!"

"Ah, hell." I flopped down next to him. "That bad?"

"Not really." He shrugged, seeming unworried. "It's Harrod, he's always been a bit melodramatic. Look, he spent so much time inside the walls working towards political goals, it didn't leave a lot of time for romance. Outside, he just plain didn't know anyone. I know crazy old hermits with more of a social life than my brother. He just got a bit caught up in all the attention, that's all. He'll come round eventually."

"You know you don't sound the slightest bit convincing, right?" I told him.

"You can't say I didn't try." He gave another frustrating shrug.

"Besides, I'm not *dating* Greyson, we went out one time! What happened yesterday was nothing. He said something that touched a nerve, I got upset and he gave me a hug – that's all." I was on the defensive for no reason. Trying to calm my voice, I continued, "Look, I like Harrod. We're really good friends, all three of us are. He's done so much for me since we met, and he's fun to hang out with. That's all it is, though. I'm not looking for anything else."

"You mean you're not looking for anything else with *him*." Martin's tone was easy, with no trace of judgement. My shoulders dropped.

"Maybe? I don't know! Greyson's just... I don't know. If I had a thing with him, that's all it'd be, you know? Just 'a thing', not a lifetime commitment. It's different with Harrod. I'm not ready to start something I can't walk away from."

"Oh, he's different alright. Don't give me that look, you bloody well know he is. You're saying he wouldn't settle for a fling, and you're right. He knows it too, which is why he's not here now. He figured you both need a breather before tomorrow night."

The blood drained from my face. "Tomorrow night?"

"Oh dear," Martin said, wincing. "You forgot about tomorrow night, didn't you?"

The look of horror on my face made that fact *very* clear. I'd agreed to it weeks ago – an invitation from Dyson and Columbine Undridge for an intimate dinner.

Like the other invitations we'd received, Harrod had been very clear it was me they wanted to see. Since my appearance at a Talented gala some months ago, all the gentry wanted the opportunity to meet me.

My father had been important when he was alive, and had involved himself in several political movements, including the progression of right for mortal and half-bloods, like myself. Those who'd worked with him wanted to meet me and to perhaps persuade me to join their political cause. Others just wanted the social recognition of netting me for a meeting.

Harrod had been vetting each one, telling me who each person was, why they'd likely want me there and helping me to choose which ones to accept or decline – each answer made a statement politically and I needed all the help I could get juggling that.

Tomorrow's meeting was one of the few I'd looked forwards to. I'd already met the Grand Master and his Duchess, and had somewhat enjoyed their company. They seemed genuinely interested in meeting me for the sole fact of getting to know me, the daughter of a man they'd known as a friend. Rather than having a political agenda, I hoped this dinner would be a chance to find out more about my family. Of course, that was before yesterday's awkwardness.

"Look," said Martin. "It's not that bad, I promise. He'll be fine!"

Somehow, I doubted that...

CHAPTER NINE

Bee surprised me by dropping by the next morning. Usually, I would only see her if I needed a new gala dress. and I was more than fitted out for those now. Despite being the most highly esteemed dressmaker in the Inner City, able to charge small fortunes for each one of her creations, she had always insisted on dressing me for events at no cost.

For a human, that would be unusual. For a Fae like Bee, it was downright strange. She insisted it was because my position as the half-blood child of the Talent Lord who fought hardest for my kind, meant all eyes would be on me. Free advertising, she called it.

I snorted softly to myself as she sailed gracefully into my shop. She, of all people, didn't need cheap marketing tricks. Bee smiled serenely at the hulking giant she passed, and proceeded to step right up and interrupt my conversation with a customer. The customer, a young man who'd come in asking for a nerve tonic, nearly fell over himself when he saw her. Stammering an apology - apologising to *her* for interrupting *him* - he stood patiently by while he waited for me to speak to her, cheeks flushed and mouth hanging slightly open as he watched us.

"Emma, dearest, just thought I'd wander past and see if you needed anything?"

"I'm good thanks, Bee. You've supplied me well, and my schedule isn't as thick as it was a few months ago." My gaze flitted to the customer, who gave no sign of wanting to interrupt.

"Nonsense." Cherry lips formed a pout. "You haven't had a fitting for weeks, and anything you own will be *well* out of season. My reputation hinges on you, you know." She eyed my simple pants and blouse with distaste. "There's a gala coming up in three weeks and you'll need something new for that, so perhaps I'll do a matching set. And a little something for your shop?"

Her eyes slid to Gibble, who looked back at her in alarm. Surely she wasn't considering dressing Gibble as well? His entire wardrobe consisted of basic linen pants and shirts, and he'd worn nothing but for as long as I'd known him.

Last time she made me a 'matching set', it included six outfits of varying complexity for attending small and large events within society, along with more practical clothes for day to day errands within the Inner City. I'd only used three of them.

"Bee really, it's too much. I don't need anything, the blue set you made will be just-"

"Blue? In this weather? Don't be obscene. I'll have it to you in a fortnight." She leaned in to kiss my cheek.

"Serracuse," she said in a low whisper, then directed a cautionary glance at Gibble, who'd turned to greet a piske coming through the door.

"What-"

"Farewell my pet, I shall see you with new accoutrements by the new moon." Waving, she breezed back out of the shop and turned a beatific smile on the young man, leaving him practically drooling on my floor.

I sighed. "Here," I said and thrust a cup of hot tea into his hands. Luckily, the samples I had out for the day were for clearing the mind. "Drink this, it'll wear off faster."

"Wear off? No way, love, I want this to last forever." Completely forgetting what we'd been speaking about earlier, he wandered out of my shop and off in the approximate direction Bee had left in. *Bloody Fae.*

After we closed that afternoon, I asked Gibble about Serraceuse.

"Where you be hearing that name, Lady?" he asked, voice rough with alarm and the fine hair on his body standing on end. "Do not be saying that name out loud! It be a very dangerous name to know."

"Who is he though?" I pressed.

"Lady, he be a very bad man. He be mortal, but be doing many deals with Others who..." His ears twitched and he blew out a short breath. "They not be the kind you be meeting, Lady. That man be having power, but not like Talent magic."

"Bee whispered his name in my ear earlier. Could she know about our meeting with Olfred? Maybe he's connected with the smugglers he told us about."

"Stupid Fae woman." His ears twitched again and he snapped his teeth in a feral manner. "Gibble be speaking to her of this. The man be a part of most bad things that be happening between this-world and Other. He not be someone to go against, Lady. Forget promise to Olfred. Gibble be talking to little tree-god, telling him it be too dangerous for Lady *and* for him."

"No way, Gib, I gave my word. What Olfred said, about Lenny? I'd go up against anyone for him, or for you. I don't like it and I'm scared as hell, but I have to do this."

He made a low humming sound, as if he wanted to argue but was forcing himself not to.

"I'll be careful, I promise. Now, I have to go and dress for tonight."

~

The car - not the Bentley, but a larger one I hadn't seen before - arrived on time. Harrod, Martin, and a gorgeous Fae woman were inside. Harrod darted around to open my door as I approached. As he put his hand on it, he looked at me and started to stammer an apology. I gave a quick shake of my head and he stopped. Careful not to let my pale yellow dress touch the ground, I slid into the car across from Martin's date.

"Emma, meet Graenn." Martin spoke to me without taking his eyes off his stunning date.

"Emmeline, it is so wonderful to meet you." Graenn put a slender hand out to touch her palm to mine, a formal greeting amongst the Fae.

It was sign of great respect to be greeted this way and I did my best not to fumble the motion.

Graenn settled back in her seat and placed a hand on Martin's leg. He looked at her, completely enamoured. I could understand that - I was finding it hard not to stare myself.

Her eyes were green. Not human-green, but the colour of dark leaves. Her hair had a tinge of it too, not in a sickly way but in a manner that made her look like a forest nymph. A charcoal dress set the colours off vibrantly and made me feel plain in comparison. That was fairly typical of being around the Fae and I chided myself for allowing it to affect me.

Graenn started up a lively chatter about the latest fashions within the City - it seemed that darker colours were in, and sunset hues. Open backs were out and shoes were getting flatter which was, she said, an absolute relief. The men looked about awkwardly - though both of them could brush up well themselves, they had a fairly normal appreciation of the finer points of fashion. That is to say, they were bored out of their brains.

Talk moved to rumours of a planned visit from *Ashik* Farun, a renowned musician born of both Talent and Fae blood. It was very rare combination and the product was one to behold. He not only held the stunning looks, grace and musical talent of the Fae, he'd perfected the art of combining Talent and Fae magic to enhance his musical performances.

Harrod joined in on this conversation - he'd heard the *Ashik* play once before, several years earlier. He told us of a trip to Germany that had coincided with the musician's tour of the country, and conversation moved on to Europe's success in abolishing the divide between Talent and mortal.

"What is it that makes your people so reluctant to accept their differences?" Graenn asked, all wide eyed innocence. Her act was almost convincing... however, the simple fact that she was Fae meant she was, more than likely, playing some kind of political game.

"Oh, I think we're making good progress," Harrod said, eyes refusing to meet hers. A soft snort escaped me.

"You disagree, Emmeline?" Graenn turned her green gaze to me.

"Yes." Not wanting to sound rude, I explained further. "As a half-blood, I still don't have the basic right of protection. No, don't you dare." I shot Harrod a warning look as he opened his mouth to protest. "Greyson has made that his mission, but it's not law. He doesn't have the ability to protect us from people like Opius. If he leaves the department, people like me are back to square one, with no one to turn to. If a mortal is in trouble, there are laws they can call on to seek help. Talented are the same. We half-bloods are still stuck in the middle of a fight between the two that exists beyond rhyme or reason, and certainly has nothing to do with us."

"If the mortals wanted integration, they'd have agreed-"

"To give up all autonomy?" I cut Harrod off, my voice rising. "To submit to a *superior* race?"

"No one said we're a superior race, we just have access to better facilities. Having Talent allows us access to knowledge and power that-"

"That allows you to act like you own the place, with *no* regard for the needs of others." I stopped for a breath but couldn't keep the words from tumbling out. "When are you going to get it out of your thick head that you don't know everything? That maybe, just *maybe* people like me are the best judge of what people like me really need?"

Throwing myself back into my seat I glared out the window, face flushed with anger. Out of the corner of my eye, I could see Martin awkwardly look away while Graenn watched me with appraising eyes. Her glance slid to Harrod and I felt him shift in the seat next to me.

The rest of the journey passed in silence.

The short drive finally ended and we arrived at the manor. Martin attended to Graenn while Harrod helped me out of the car and pulled me aside.

"Look, I know we don't see eye to eye on a lot of things, but I don't want to fight. I have a lot to learn, I *know* that." His voice was sincere, but didn't quell my anger.

"You can't keep using that as an excuse, Harrod." I stared at the ground like a petulant child.

"I know. It's just… maybe I don't *want* to believe it's that bad. I worry about you enough, Emma. Imagining you being attacked on the street just because of who you are, unable to defend yourself, not being able to help? That's my worst nightmare."

Breathing in deeply, I looked up at him. "Harrod, I'm not a helpless child and it's insulting to-"

"Dammit, I know. I'm making it worse again." He looked away and ran a hand through his hair. "I know you don't need me. I understand that, I do, but maybe I want… no, gods I'm making a mess of this. I wish you didn't have to go through what you do, I wish I could just make everyone get along and accept you and your kind like they should. It's what I spend every day fighting for. I see some of the worst of my society, and of the mortals, and it's not pretty. Egos big enough to fill a room and everyone so sure that they're right. If they catch a hint of weakness, they pounce. The only way to deal with them is to sound like I know what I'm doing, even when I don't."

"And you think it's fine to treat me like that, too?" I tried to keep the heat from my voice.

"No. I've done poorly by you, and by Martin. I'm sorry, Emma. All I can promise is that I'll keep trying."

I sighed. That wasn't much of a promise. Still, there was no use arguing about it now. Harrod took my arm and we walked to the door, Martin and Graenn waiting patiently for us to catch up. I flushed, wondering how much of our conversation they'd heard.

The Duchess Columbine greeted Graenn and I with a kiss on the cheek, while the men clasped hands and offered the usual formal greetings. We retired to a sitting room to spend the time before dinner was served. The room was small but well laid out, in a way that let the two groups split off for separate conversations. Columbine tinkled a tiny bell and a piske appeared.

"Flyss, we're ready for the refreshments now if you please?"

Her tone was more respectful than most Talented gentry when they spoke to their house staff. The Duchess and her husband were friend's of Harrod's so I'd expected this - Harrod was vehemently against slavery even of the less sentient creatures that served. Piskes and faskes were commonplace in larger households. They couldn't survive without some kind of servitude agreement, and many generations of Talents had taken advantage of this.

It was good to see that more of them were placed in houses where they were treated with respect, and shown gratitude for their service. Not all of them were treated so well, but progress was picking up and I had a strong hope that soon, they'd have their own protection directly from the Council agreements.

I glanced at Graenn and saw that she too had noticed the short exchange, and approved. Fae were reluctant to intervene in matters not of their own, but I knew they disproved of many practises the Talented indulged in.

"My dear Emmeline, it's so good to see you again. I'm sorry it took so long to extend an invitation to you. Dyson hasn't been well, so we've been keeping to ourselves a little more than usual. And of course, you yourself have been quite busy fielding requests for appearances." The Duchess smiled gently. "I can't say I envy you that. I imagine it's quite a chore after the first few?"

"Yes," I said before realising how that might sound. "I mean, I was really looking forwards to tonight, but it's the only one so far. Thankfully, Harrod has helped me avoid some of the... less accommodating houses."

"I'm glad to see he's taking good care of you dear. The two of you have been well?"

"Ah... yes, we have."

Flyss returned with two trays of delicately presented hors d'oeuvres, saving me from having to answer further. That was the biggest drawback of these dinners - most of the Talented community believed Harrod and I were a couple, and we'd done nothing to dissuade that view, worried that some of our hosts would take any opportunity to exclude him from the invitations offered to me.

Though most of the hosts were simply after the social prestige that came with having a new celebrity come to visit and others hoped to secure my help to further their political position, I couldn't be sure they all had such innocent motives. We hadn't actively encouraged the rumour, but Harrod's attentiveness to me and the fact that we were so often seen together cemented the assumption in most people's eyes.

"There is much afoot inside the Wall these days. You've been kept informed?"

"I've been busy," I said. "I'm barely keeping up with my own work at the moment."

"Ah yes, that business with the police, I assume." Duchess Columbine noticed my surprise and said, "Abnett made it known you were working with them. I trust it wasn't supposed to be kept confidential?" She heaved a sigh in response to my horrified face. "The man means well, but he wouldn't see the need for discretion if it thumped him in the head. No matter, it's done now. Are you making progress?"

Swallowing down my unease, I said, "We think so, but there's still a way to go. We think smugglers of some kind may be involved."

"You mean... Oh, my dear *girl*." The colour drained from Columbine's face and her hands trembled. "Child, those that dabble in that sort of trade with the Others are not to be reckoned with lightly." She shook her head at my expression of dismissal. "No Emmeline, I mean it. This is not the first time these vile people have surfaced and there have been casualties in the past. Mark my words, this is a dangerous, *dangerous* position you're now in. Promise me you'll tread lightly?"

"I promise," I said, relieved that she hadn't asked me to drop the case. It felt like I was making an awful lot of promises lately.

"With your permission, I shall have a quiet word to Dyson about it later. Abnett approached him to assist in the development of a task force to assist Detective Greyson's team on a permanent basis. It's being discussed, but with no real urgency. We'll see if it can't be streamlined, so you may have at least *some* assistance. You have others helping now?"

"Yes. Gibble - that's my boggart - and Harrod and Martin of course. Detective Greyson is giving what help he can and we've reached out to one of the Others, an old god who has taken it upon himself to act as protector to the creatures of our world and theirs."

Columbine looked at me sadly and a niggling feeling of worry settled in my gut. "I fear that will not be enough... not to deal with this." She brightened with a quickness that suggested it was false. "However, there's not a thing we can do about it tonight. Let us leave this unsavoury discussion and move on to more pleasant things." She picked up a glass of sparkling lavender wine and took a large gulp. Giving me a brittle smile, she gestured to our companion. "Graenn, my dear, we've been neglecting you. Would you tell us how you found that scallywag over there?"

The talk did indeed move on to lighter things. Graenn told us how she had met Martin through a mutual friend and been instantly enamoured with him. His name had become quite popular amongst the Fae. This concerned me greatly, and the knowing glance our hostess gave Harrod suggested I wasn't alone. She and Columbine moved over to the topic of fabrics - it turned out Graenn was an apprentice dressmaker. Among the Fae, those with a trade such as this were highly respected amongst their peers. Fae artisans spent many years perfecting their craft to earn a higher place within their society and often received high acclaim even amongst the Talented, not that the Fae put much stock in that.

Graenn shifted her attention to me. "I know you are a close friend of Bee. I'd be *most* grateful if you could mention my name when next you see her. Training with her would be the utmost honour, but she hasn't taken on a student in decades."

"Of course," I said, wondering if she knew Bee had also briefly dated Martin. "Though, I don't know that I have any influence over her decisions."

"Oh truly, that alone would mean a lot to me," She clapped her hands in glee as we settled back into conversation.

The sitting room door opened and a faske bowed to the Lord and his Duchess to signal the dinner was ready. We headed into the dining room - a magnificent chamber with tall windows along one wall looking out onto a small courtyard. A grand chandelier hung from the ceiling and twinkling lights drifted down from it, winking out a few feet from the table. The effect gave the room a truly magical feel.

The table itself was laid with fine bone china and beautifully crafted silverware. Though I'd attended dinners like this before, and though I was far more comfortable with these people than others I'd dined with, I still felt a rush of nerves as I approached my seat. As always, Harrod sensed this and gave my arm a gentle squeeze.

I was getting much better at the formalities of dining with Talented nobility, but there was so much to remember. Before sitting, we each gave a small bow or curtsy to our hosts, who returned the gesture in kind. I sat and waited patiently for the table attendant - a small, waist-coated piske - to lay a cloth over my lap. Then I folded my hands in my lap until our hosts thanked us for our presence and sat.

The Duchess, highest ranked in the room, took the first mouthful, her husband the second. Then, it was permitted for guests to eat. The bevy of piskes hovered back and forth, serving food and topping up drinks. I managed the order of utensils without too much difficulty, though had to wait and copy the others when it came to dessert, which was a crispy, sugared pastry shell that looked impossible to pierce with a knife or fork without causing it to crumble.

Harrod simply picked his up between thumb and forefinger and ate it carefully. I followed suit, trying not to let any fall. It was harder than he made it look, as it crumbled at my touch, sending fine dustings of powdered sugar puffing away. When Dyson fumbled his and cursed as it crumbled on his lap, I relaxed a little. He noticed and laughed.

"Damned chefs. Why can't they serve normal bloody food, food a man can eat without making a cursed mess?"

"My Lord knows quite well that he personally requested the pastry, forgetting that he makes this same complaint every time." Duchess gave him an exasperated look.

"Ah, yes. I did at that. No matter, at least it tastes ripping wonderful." He grinned wolfishly.

"Dyson, I do wish you'd stop trying to sound like you're twenty." Columbine shook her head fondly. "I'm not saying you're old, but you *are* supposed to be a distinguished gentleman of the court."

"But my dear, I simply like to keep up to date with the latest terminology. It helps me to adequately communicate with the younger constituents of the gentry."

"It would if they weren't too busy laughing at you behind your back to pay attention to what you're actually saying." Though her words had bite, her tone was soft and affectionate.

The two were clearly close, even after all these years amongst stuffy nobles. Most Talents married for station or magical ability rather than love; though Dyson and Columbine were well matched politically, it was clear there was genuine affection between them.

After dinner, we retired back to the sitting room, this time sitting as a group. Dyson asked me about the general feel outside the Inner City.

"It's getting better," I said, choosing my words carefully. "The half-bloods are starting to have some hope that things will improve. The mortals seem... well, they're still divided and the recent attacks have caused some panic. The small faction that wish to oust the entire magical community are trying to use it as leverage, but as long as no one's actually been hurt, it doesn't seem to be getting much traction with anyone outside their own circles."

"And how are police dealing with the threat?" he asked.

"Dyson, dear," the Duchess spoke up. "You know Emmeline likely can't answer most of your questions, yes?"

"It's alright," I said. "Sounds like most of what I have to tell has already gotten out anyway. There's a possibility that the creature escaped a smuggler, who was transporting creatures from the Other-world to sell on the black market. We're short on leads, but we're following what small clues we have."

"Smugglers, eh?" He looked as worried as Columbine had when I'd mentioned it to her. "Horrible business, that. You're certain there's no one you can hand the case over to? I can speak to Abnett-"

"Oh for goodness sake Dyson, she's not a porcelain doll *or* one of your children," the Duchess gently chided. "She's quite competent and she knows enough to step back if it's too much for her to handle."

Reddening at the chastisement, Lord Dyson grunted and buried his nose in a glass of whiskey. Harrod's cheeks also had a hint of colour, knowing that he'd said exactly the same thing. Giving her a grateful smile I wondered why she'd come to my defence, after her words to me earlier. Maybe, just maybe, she understood.

"Really, dear," Columbine continued. "I'd think after all these years of marriage you'd know better than that."

He gave a resigned sigh. "Have you told them about your little escapade with smugglers back in the day? Unless, Emmeline, your father filled you in on *that* debacle?" He looked at me questioningly and I shook my head, bewildered. Columbine examined me closely, eyes narrowed. She gave a small nod, as if satisfied by what she saw.

"I suppose you should know then," she said. "So you can decide for yourself if it's a risk you're willing to take. It was about thirty years ago - no, a little more than that, before you were born dear. Your father, myself, and a couple of friends had been working towards abolishing the slavery of the brownies, faskes and piskes."

"I'm sorry," I said, aware I was interrupting but unable to stop myself. "You knew my *father*?"

"Of course, dear. Dyson and I worked with him closely." Her face softened. "If we'd known you were back in London, we would have reached out, I swear it. Your... status doesn't matter to us."

I pressed my lips together and dropped my eyes, trying not to think of how much easier the previous months might have been if I'd had someone like her watching over me. She took the hint, and continued her story.

"As I was saying, at first we tried to work through all of the legal channels. Clearly we didn't get far with *that*, though I hope to live long enough to see it happen. At any rate, there certainly were laws regarding the demi-fae. There was a risk of it coming to war between some of the Otherworld factions, so it was heavily enforced." Columbine took a steadying breath. "We discovered there was a smuggling ring, operating in the Other. They were poaching creatures from the Otherworld, bringing them here and selling them for ridiculous prices. We found the man responsible. A terrible person, the sort that would give you chills just running into him on the street." Her voice dropped as though she were talking to herself. "Serraceuse was more story than man, a monster to scare children into staying in their beds."

His name made me flinch, but all eyes were on the Duchess as she spoke, hanging on every word. This time, I didn't dare interrupt.

"We went after him, of course. We weren't officially sanctioned by the Council, but they knew of our work. In this rare case, they actually approved of it. We found out where he was bringing them though and went to shut the port-gate down. Someone had tipped him off though. Well, we think so. At any rate, he knew we were coming. The five of us - your father, myself and the friends we worked with - came up against twelve Talents, some of whom I'm sure had a touch of Fae. We took down two but... Daniel and Sarah were both killed." Columbine stopped and looked out the window, cleaning her throat before continuing.

"The rest of us ran, tails between our legs. We eventually stopped the smugglers with the help of the Fae and some of their allies. All of them except Serraceuse. He hunted us for a time, the bastard. Dyson had an entire stable full of thoroughbred horses, all slaughtered simply because he was courting me at the time. Your father woke one morning to find the house alight and the door to your sisters' room warded shut. They got out of course, I believe your boggart had somewhat to do with that. Other attacks - family pets, threats, tokens left in bedrooms. We were all terrified. Then... it just stopped. It took months to believe it, but the threats, the attacks, all stopped." She unfolded the small lace napkin she'd been twisting in her lap and smoothed it out with shaking hands. "Our hope is that someone he crossed eventually caught up with him, but we can't be sure. It truly was the most terrifying time of my life."

"That is why you must take the utmost care, my dear." Dyson had no trace of condescension in his voice. "That bastard might be gone, but we don't know who's taken his place. If the ring is still operating, or if a new one has sprung up to take its place, you can be sure it's being run by a hard, hard man. It takes a cold heart to go against the Fae, and a lot of firepower if you expect to live through it. Don't underestimate them, don't think you can out-best them alone."

I was sure my face was as white as a sheet. I'd told no one of Bee's mention of Serraceuse to me. Could she have simply been warning me of this past ghost, or did she believe he had come back? There was no way to know without talking to her, and no point terrifying the nobles if it was merely the former. *Please, let it be that.*

"Oh my sweet, I didn't mean to frighten you." Columbine reached out to clasp my hand.

"No," I said, voice husky and dry. "I'd rather know what I'm up against."

Graenn had watched the exchange with interest.

"You were one of the gaiscedach?" she asked the Duchess.

"Yes," she answered simply.

"I thought the gaiscedach were just a story," I said in awe. "You – and my *father* - really did those things?"

"Your deeds are still celebrated amongst the Fae." Graenn said, then turned to Martin who was looking rather lost. "The gaiscedach were a band of warriors, masked heroes that used subterfuge and cunning to free many creatures that were held in terrible conditions. They alone had the bravery to confront the worst of the Talent Lords and take from them that which they did not deserve to have." Graenn turned back to Columbine. "I hadn't realised the connection. Your true names are not well known, I'm afraid"

"Oh, that was by design, my dear. We didn't wish for fame or fortune, just to do our work and hopefully make a little progress."

Conversation drifted after that, to matters of little import. After some time, Lord Dyson caught me trying to stifle my third yawn, and insisted we wrap up for the night. We said our farewells, with promises to meet again soon. I really did feel comfortable in their company and, despite the dire warning it had contained, I'd enjoyed hearing about my father's exploits in his younger days.

Martin requested to be dropped at the port-gate with Graenn, to

Harrod's displeasure. That meant Harrod left first, saying a stiff farewell to Graenn and Martin, and an awkward one to me. When we reached my house, Graenn whispered something in Martin's ear and exited the car to speak to me.

"Martin believes his brother does not approve of his choice of lovers, and he feels you share that view. Is it true?"

Taken aback by her bluntness, I stammered before answering. "I... it's not that - Look, I like those of the Fae I've met, and I have the utmost respect for your people. I'm just... worried. Mortals can have bad reactions to spending too much time in the Other, or with full blooded Fae. I don't want to see him hurt, or changed."

"Then let me put your mind at ease my dear." Her smile should have been reassuring. It wasn't. "He is one of the most important people to your success. As such, he has had a certain level of protection placed upon him by the Guardians themselves. His time with us will not cause him to be altered and he will be free from the addiction that plagues many of your kind. It's because of this - and, in truth, because he's quite simply delicious - that we so love to spend time with him. It's so rare to be with a mortal and not have to guard from the kind of harm you speak of."

"What do you mean, my success?" I asked warily.

"Your quest." She said the words with a serene expression, as though expecting me to know exactly what they meant. At my blank look, she paled. "You don't know, do you? Oh dear. I'd assumed that after your meeting with the Guardians, they'd..." She cleared her throat and darted a look over her shoulder, as if to check if anyone had heard her slip of the tongue. "Perhaps I shouldn't say any more, though in truth I don't know much of it myself. They guard their secrets well."

"Please, tell me." Desperation shone through in my voice. "Please - I know they have something in store for me, and it terrifies me. What do you know, how does it involve Martin?"

Graenn studied me carefully. "I can tell you this - your destiny was not set by the Guardians, simply foretold by them. They shall give you tools, but they won't interfere in your destiny other than that. They have an interest in keeping you and your friends safe."

"There *must* be more than that." My insides quivered, wanting but not-wanting to know.

Graenn leaned closer, her voice dropping to an urgent whisper. "There was a prophecy child, before you were born. I know they'd been looking for you for some time. You are a catalyst to great events that may lead to the golden age of the Other, or to its total demise. Martin and Harrod will play a part, though I don't know what. You must keep your friends close, Emmeline, you *must*."

"What else?" I begged, sick of the vagueness of her explanation.

"I can't." She shrugged gracefully, eyes wide and earnest. "I just don't know. There is truth and there is rumour, and I doubt it will serve you well to have too much of either right now. Take care, and know that Martin will be well taken care of."

She kissed my forehead and slipped into the car. *Dammit.* The Guardians were terrifying and I hated knowing I was blipping on their radar.

That night, I coaxed Lenny into my bed and together, we curled up and went to sleep.

Chapter Ten

The next morning found me standing in the freezing cold dawn, banging on a shop door in the middle of the Inner City. A window in the street slammed open and an irritated Talent Lord poked his head out to see what was happening. He pulled his head back in and snapped the window shut. Hitting my fist on the door again, I cursed when it made no sound. Bloody Talent. He'd traced a silencer on it.

"Bee? Dammit, open up!"

The sound of a latch being lifted on the other side choked off my next angry yell. The door swung open and a small brownie bowed, then motioned me inside. He led me to a pink curtain at the back of the room, and pulled it aside to reveal a rabbit warren of hallways branching out from a small sitting room. Bowing again, he waved at a chair and I sat, tapping my foot impatiently as he darted off again, the curtain swaying shut behind him..

"Emmeline, it is so wonderful to see you." Bee came gliding out of a doorway, dressed in a white silk pantsuit. It was belted with a silver cord and a posy of blue flowers was tucked into it, matching a hairpiece made of the same.

"Bee, tell me about Serraceuse. Is he back? What do the Guardians have to do with this?" I stood as I spoke, tilting my chin up in a bid for confidence that I didn't feel.

Bee coughed delicately. "Max, we'll be opening late today. Please put a note on the door, and bring Emmeline some refreshments shortly?"

The brownie, who had popped out of nowhere, nodded and disappeared back through the curtain. Bee sighed. "I knew I shouldn't have gotten involved. Come, best we speak upstairs."

She led me down one hallway, then another. Despite not actually seeing any stairs, the room we entered had a window that looked out over the street. A small table perched by it, with two chairs. We sat, and I peered out the window. It didn't look out on the street I entered from, but I banished that from my mind. I'd come here for answers – getting side-tracked would make that all but impossible, with the way Bee often twisted conversations like a pretty ribbon caught in the wind. I could see it in my mind's eye. Purple, and long, floating on the-

"Stop it," I snapped, and the vision dissolved. Bee gave me a wry grin.

"I apologise. It's a reflexive habit, one that's very hard to break. You know this really isn't a conversation I want to have, don't you?"

"Then why come to me in the first place?" I asked.

"Because I *care* about you, Emmeline! Do you remember the first time we met?" Max darted into the room and deposited a tray of biscuits and tea on the table.

"When Harrod brought me for a dress fitting. I remember it." Was she trying to divert me again?

"No, dear. It was your father who brought you to me, when you were seven."

Memories flashed through my head, of a trip to the Inner City long ago. The City had seemed bigger then, more exciting. Father had taken me to get a special dress fitted for a gala we were to attend.

The woman who'd seen me was fuzzy in my memory, but I remembered the beautiful gowns. I'd begged Father to let me have something more grown up, more glamorous than the simple child's dresses he'd made me wear. He had refused.

It was a short visit and three days later, my dress had been delivered. Rather than the bejewelled masterpiece I'd hoped for, it was, as always, simple. A dress of bronze silk, adorned only with gold clasps at the throat and sleeves. It had fit perfectly and the cut made me look taller, the colour giving life to my normally pallid complexion. Despite it being exactly what my father had ordered, it was somehow more.

My sisters, several years older and of a station that demanded full gala attire, had waltzed into the room in elegant dresses dripping with lace and pearls. Both were of the current style and worthy of a Lord's daughter, but somehow, my dress had outshone them. Something about its simplicity made theirs seem overdone, almost cheapened by their adornments.

Aveline, my oldest sister, had glared at me in pure hatred and muttered something about a potato sack under her breath. Myr, always loyal to Ave, had wrinkled her nose at me in distaste. Another memory nagged at me – later in the night, Myr had approached me quietly. "I think your dress is pretty, Emmeline." Simple words, that shouldn't have meant what they did. It was perhaps the only compliment Myr had ever given her unwanted half-blood sister.

"You made that dress? The bronze one?" I whispered.

"Yes, dear. You so badly wanted to look like the other girls at the gala, but your father was adamant. He wanted you to stand out, and the best way to do that was with simplicity. I do hope you liked it."

"I... always thought he did it to make me invisible. It was beautiful, Bee." My voice was thick, my mind buzzing with resurfaced memories, but I pushed past that. "Tell me about Serraceuse."

Bee's face whitened and she took a sip of tea. "He was a monster. Preyed on my people, and on our beautiful children. He hurt people, innocents and those who tried to stop his nasty trade. He was... dealt with, but only temporarily. Not long before the Otherbeasts started to disappear, a rumour came to me that he was back."

"What do you mean he was dealt with, Bee?"

"The Fae took him. Oh, they wanted to kill him but they couldn't. He has Talented blood, and we'd already signed the treaties by then. And, he is Fae. A terrible pairing, that. When such a coupling turns out well, it creates a beauty like you've never seen. Sadly, he took a darker path. So he was ensorcelled, made to forget his desire. It's not a nice spell, Emma, and it takes an awful lot to maintain. For years he lived with no desire for anything at all, not food, nor love, nor death. And yet somehow he broke free. Those watching him failed and now... Emmeline, I'm *sure* he's back. A darkness is coming and he's a part of it, a small one, but a part nonetheless. You must stop him, but you *must* be careful." Bee's hand shook and the tea she held slopped onto the table. Gasping in dismay, she blotted up the spill with napkin, then stared at the wet spot left on the tablecloth.

"What about me? Bee, when I met the Guardians, they said things that didn't make any sense."

"That, I cannot tell you. You know how future-seeing works, dear. If you know, if you expect it, the outcome can be altered... and that's rarely for the best."

I stood. By the set of her face she wouldn't say any more, but she'd confirmed my suspicions.

The Guardians were planning something and it involved me.

"Take care, my dear." Bee rose and pressed me into a gentle hug. "I shall do what I can to help, you know that?"

Later that day, I met with Greyson to discuss the possibility of Otherworld poachers. To my surprise, he'd already followed that track some way. Shuffling through the papers on his desk stacked beneath a wrapped sandwich, he stabbed a finger at one.

"Yeah, we've got a contact who deals with the Fae. They knew about the previous history of these guys and entered it into our records, unofficially of course. I'd only come across it a few weeks ago, so it was fresh in my mind. Far as we know, Serraceuse hasn't been heard from in years. We'd discounted him, but not the possibility that smugglers are involved in some way."

"Why didn't you mention it at the beginning?" I asked.

Greyson picked up the sandwich as if he'd just discovered it. He unwrapped it, sniffed it, and took an enormous bite. He chewed for a moment before answering – he looked like he hadn't eaten in days. "I didn't want to throw you off. It was only a hunch and so far, we don't have anything to suggest it'll pan out."

"Fair enough. However, one of *my* contacts has suggested Serraceuse is still around. I didn't really get the chance to ask any questions – all I got was his name, and that he's no longer... well, wherever he was before."

After I filled Greyson in on what I'd learned over the last two days, we discussed our next plan of attack. I decided to go back to Olfred. He might be able to get me a glimpse of the creatures, and I wanted to ask him about Serraceuse and the 'takers' he'd spoken about. Greyson was still waiting on the maps from Harrod, so he was going to talk to the contact who'd informed him about the smugglers. With luck, he'd get a chance to speak to the Fae who'd been the source of his information.

As we talked, we walked along the river. I was in no hurry to get back as it had been a quiet morning and I was sure Gibble would handle the shop, though I felt a pang of guilt at that. I'd been leaving him there far too much lately.

"Oh, damn," I said, thinking aloud. "If my father was involved in busting the smuggling ring then Gibble must have the details. That's how he knew the name Serraceuse." *And why he was so worried about that name,* I added to myself.

I hadn't gone into details of the retribution that had been taken on those involved, assuming Greyson already knew. If he didn't, then I didn't want to risk being taken off the case, not now. Greyson stopped walking and touched my arm, halting me mid-stride. He looked at me, then looked away.

"Look, I just wanted to check in with you about all this. You're ok? I don't want to be pushing you into this. It's getting more dangerous than I expected." His voice was steeped in concern.

"Please, Charlie, don't take me off the case. I know I was reluctant to start but I made a promise to Olfred. Now that I know my father was working to stop these people, it means even more to me."

"I wouldn't pull you off, not if you want to keep going. Just keep me in the loop, alright?" He grinned. "I know I'm only a mortal but I have resources that can help, and I don't want you doing anything crazy without touching base first."

"Oh c'mon. You do pretty well for 'just a mortal'. You took down that rampaging orc a month ago and you shut down a goblin fighting ring before that. You hold your own." I nudged him in the side as I spoke and he chuckled.

"I did do that, didn't I?" A corner of his mouth twitched up in a smile.

"You're even getting a bit famous for it. My customers have been talking, DCI Greyson. They're impressed by the work you're doing. Dyson told me Abnett's working towards getting you more help from his end, and he wouldn't do that if he didn't think your team was effective."

"Don't suppose you'll be part of that help?" he asked, looking at me hopefully.

"Me? I couldn't hold my own for a moment against the Talents he'll have working with you. You won't have to settle for a half-blood who runs a tea shop anymore."

"Oh, now who's being modest? You took down one of their Lords remember. And besides, you make damned nice tea."

It was my turn to laugh. Despite my reservations in the beginning, and the constant gnawing in my gut that reminded me that what I was doing could very well put me in danger, I enjoyed working with him.

"Look, you might not have the magical brute strength of your boyfriend but you're smart, quick on your feet, and that counts for more in this line of work. You also have connections my people could only dream about."

"What? Harrod's not my boyfriend." I shot him a sideways look and caught him grinning.

"Just checking," he said. "Sorry. I shouldn't poke fun. You know he has feelings for you though, don't you?"

I rolled my eyes and groaned. "Apparently the whole bloody world knows. It's not the *slightest* bit awkward, not at all!" I glanced at my watch. "My time's almost up, I have to get back," I said reluctantly.

"Right-oh. You'll do what I said though, won't you?" he prodded.

"Of course. You'll let me know if anything else comes to light?"

"Of course." Greyson smiled and as I turned to go back to work, said, "Maybe next time we can do this over dinner?"

"You're on," I called back with a wave.

When I entered the shop, I was surprised to see it had gotten busy again. Dashing behind the counter to help, I called a quick apology to Gibble, who just shrugged and continued on at his own steady pace. We worked until closing and a little while after that. When the doors were finally shut, I collapsed onto a chair in exhaustion. My busy schedule was catching up to me and I realised something was going to have to give, and soon.

"Gibble, I think I need to get some help for the shop."

"I think that be a good thing, Lady. You be working too hard and leaving Gibble behind – I do not be minding, but I be thinking your customers might be." His eyes didn't lift from the bench he was wiping down.

"What? Gibble, if anyone has given you a hard time, I won't stand for it. You tell me who, and I'll throw them out faster than a hobgoblin can eat a loaf of bread."

"It not be anything, Lady." He shrugged and continued to tidy up.

"Oh come sit down, you big lug. You work yourself to the bone every day and I keep abandoning you. The least I can do is clean up."

He hesitated, then put down the cloth he was using. Everything was done, anyway. He came and sprawled out on a chair across from me.

"Ah, Lady..." His knobbled brow furrowed in consternation. I had a feeling I wouldn't like what was coming next. "Lady, I think you be needing to stop this hunting of bad people."

"Gibble, I promised Olfred. You were there, you *know* I can't back down on that." I perched on a chair across from him, too wound up to relax properly.

"Gibble can do the thing for Lady. Gibble can be owing Olfred a favour in return, and be helping to find the creature. Gibble has many favours to trade, and Olfred... he be old, and somewhat wise. He will be understanding. Lady, I be thinking this be a safe thing to do."

"It's because of Serraceuse, isn't it – you think he's back too?" I asked quietly.

He let out a long, warbling sigh.

"Please Gib, tell me what happened. Tell me about my father and the gaiscedach."

He looked at me in surprise, perhaps wondering where I had heard the term.

"What do Lady be knowing of the champions?" he asked.

"I've heard the rumours, Gib. I thought that's all they were –

until Columbine told me last night. She was one of them, and so was Dad. I *need* to know, Gibble."

After another sigh, he told me the story of Serraceuse. "It be a long time ago Lady, and I not be knowing the all of it. I be telling you what I did see though, so you can be deciding on what you must be doing."

Gibble told me of a time before I was born, when my father was alive. He and some friends were actively fighting for equality, before he moved into taking up the fight on a political level. They'd formed a warrior-band, fashioned on the concept that they were the champions and protectors of those without a voice of their own. They freed wrongly indentured creatures, brokered deals to improve the laws and weren't averse to making threats to get their point across. All was done under cover of pseudonyms and darkness – no one knew who they really were, though many suspected.

Columbine had only told me it was before I was born; however, Gibble knew that my parents had already met and fallen in love after the death of Father's first wife. He hadn't remarried but my mother was already pregnant with me. At that stage it was still secret – there was a concern that my mother would become a target if it were known.

The thought sent goosebumps running over my skin. Father's fight had largely been on the wrong side of the law, but when the kidnapping of several demi-fae had threatened the safety of all the Talented held dear, he and his comrades-in-arms were asked to deal with it quietly. They were given few resources and little promise of protection – they were fighting for a principle.

Somehow, they'd tracked the source of the smuggling ring to Serraceuse. Thinking to take him down unawares, they'd launched an attack on his warehouse, not realising he was already prepared. Gibble said there were rumours that he was tipped off, but admitted it was possible that Serraceuse was just very, very careful.

The attack was moderately successful; enough of the demi-fae escaped to appease the Fae and it was rumoured they had passed on enough information that the Fae had gone back to rescue those still missing. For the gaiscedach however, the nightmare was only beginning.

First, there were messages. Small dead animals left on children's beds and locks of loved ones' hair, taken without their knowledge, posted back to the members of the group. When one of them discovered a loyal pet decapitated in his daughters bed, he'd committed suicide, a note left to say that he hoped it would be enough to keep his family safe. It did, for they weren't targeted after his death.

Dyson's stable had been torched while they were out at a council meeting one night, his horses already killed in their stalls. He hadn't been involved with them at that stage, but was openly courting Columbine.

Another member of the gaiscedach went missing, never to be heard of again. There was a small chance she'd gone into hiding but the common belief was that Serraceuse had gotten to her. Finally there was the attack on my father, leader of the gaiscedach and instigator of the warehouse coup.

An arsonist had gotten inside the house and barred my sisters' doors closed before setting the home alight. The fire was uncontrollable, lit with magic and fed by wards. Ave, my oldest sister, had managed to blast through her warded door and escape, while Gibble freed our other sister with Fathers help. They'd made it out, but only just.

As they fled, a beam collapsed in a stairwell that would have trapped them if they had still been inside. Both girls suffered horrific burns that required weeks of healing by the best Talents Father could afford. Gibble shuddered as he told me and I placed a gentle hand on his arm.

After that? Nothing. Not a peep. A warehouse explosion had occurred three nights later, at a site rumoured to belong to Serraceuse. The kidnapping stopped, as did the terrorising of my family and the others who'd been involved.

"Lady, we did hope it be the Fae who be dealing with the

monster Serraceuse, but Gibble did not be convinced they be making him walk the deathlands. Some did say he be fleeing in fear, others that he be finding a better place to be working. None did be knowing of a certainty, and even Gibble's own asking did not make the Fae tell Gibble the truth of the happening. It did always be a risk that he be returning, and it would be an easy thing for him to find Lady if he did want. If there be any hinting that Lady, the child of the man who did fight him, be the one to go after him now? Gibble will protect Lady with his own life, but that might not be being enough."

He trembled at the last and I put a hand on his arm, my heart breaking at the fear in his face. Fear not of facing this cruel, powerful man, but of losing me, of failing the duty my father had set him. My resolve had never been so sorely tested.

"Will my sisters be safe?" I asked. There was no love lost between us, but I wasn't so heartless as to bring danger to their door without at least warning them.

Gibble nodded. "They be able to take care of their ownselfs. If Serraceuse be here, he not be where they are. They not be listening to old Gibble, but Gibble be sending them a warning through others they be heeding."

Last I'd hear, Ave and Myr were in Europe, but I was glad he would take care of contacting them. Though he said there would be little chance of them listening to him, there was even less of one that they would even give me the time of day.

"Ok Gibble, I'll make you a deal." I reached over to put my hand on his arm. It was thick and bristly and ever so comforting. "I won't go after the ringleader directly, not until we're sure it's not Serraceuse. I'll try to direct Greyson to take down the buyers, and the lower level dealers. Even if Serraceuse is doing this, it's a safe bet he's not doing the dirty work himself, right? If we can disrupt the chain, it'll buy us enough time to go to the Guardians. Surely they'll help?"

"That be a good plan," Gibble said in relief. "The Guardians not be looking lightly on any who be taking their people. If you be having enough knowing of where the dealers be going on this side of the portals, it be enough for them to act, I be thinking."

Hugging him tight, I wondered how much harder this would have been without his support. I'd been treating him poorly lately, and made a promise to myself that once this was over, I'd somehow make it up to him.

Chapter Eleven

After Gibble left for the day, I headed upstairs, locking the door behind me. Deciding on a simple dinner, I heated some instant soup and settled into the couch with a bottle of wine and my bookwork, intending to catch up on some neglected duties while I had time.

Sipping merlot and filling in figures, my mind drifted. I thought of Olfred's love for his creatures and wondered how he fared. Though an Otherworlder, he clearly held a human-like concern for the animals he watched over.

Did he feel the same anxiety and fear that I would if Lenny were missing? Most Otherworld denizens had very little concern with anyone else, let alone those of other races. Olfred was particularly unique in that his care extended towards creatures of the mortal world as well.

More than a passing concern, too. Gibble once told me that Olfred had almost died more than once, trying to channel a quantity of magic that was unsafe in order to heal a suffering animal. If he died, it would be a huge loss to creatures in both worlds. Would there be an afterlife for a once-god turned animal-healer?

"There will be a place for him," a voice said behind me.

I blinked slowly, infused with a warmth and peace that belied the presence of a stranger in my locked house. Lenny growled, whimpered, then ducked his head submissively before lying down with his big head resting watchfully on his paws.

It took all my effort to carefully place my glass on the coffee table, then turn to see the Parlour Guardian behind me, just as I knew I would. Though still in her child-form, she wore a glittering, black dress. A masquerade mask covered half over her face, also black, with crow's feathers jutting out from one corner.

She smiled at me and took my hand, helping me to rise. Despite the myriad questions battering my mind, my mouth felt immobile and full of soggy newspaper.

"Why?" All I could muster was a single word, and she seemed surprised even at that.

"Why am I here? To help, of course. One who stole from us has returned and he has taken one of our children. You *must* find her. This task I give to you, and you alone."

My muddled mind knew there was some spell at work, dulling my mind and stopping me from speaking. The Guardian's magic was as old as life itself and ran deeper than the oceans. Her awesome power made my humanity seem as an ant to a giant. I knew I would have no hope of comprehending her thoughts.

She pulled me towards the door and placed her hand on the doorknob. I'd locked it earlier but she turned it with ease. I had just enough sense left to pull back slightly, resisting the tug on my hand.

"How?" My voice croaked with the effort.

"You have travelled the dream path. You are... open. This is something that must be addressed, but at a later time. Now come, there is something you must see"

Every last bit of free will I had left disappeared. The door swung open and it led not to a narrow staircase leading down to my shop, but to a field of purple grass swaying under a moonlit night. The skeletons of old trees dotted the eerie landscape, and a sparkling silver stream cut through the dead forest. Above, stars filled the sky in a random pattern, while the moon shone with unearthly hues. We were in the Other.

Her arm lifted and my eyes followed her gesture out over the field. The movement of my head seemed to bring us closer to it, swooping in without having taken a single step. A herd of animals grazed, creatures that rolled and played on the edge of a muddy swamp. They had smooth, hunched bodies and two rounded horns protruding from hard skulls. Sharp claws scrabbled at the ground, throwing clumps of sodden dirt into the air while flat tails slapped the ground, shaping mud into divets and mounds, then swiping it aside as they played.

"Watch," came the quiet command, and I watched.

A bright slit pierced the night, widening into a ragged door. The harsh yellow light was blinding but the animals paid it no heed, continuing to play and frolic in the dirt. Three men, no more than silhouettes, appeared and stepped through the portal. The Guardian raised her hand and pointed, a long, silver nail aimed at them like a dagger.

"*Watch.*" The voice was still quiet, but insistent now.

The men split up to search amongst the trees. They would approach each one carefully, keeping an eye on the creatures and waiting so none were near, then would thrust their hands into gaps under the old, lifting roots. The third man approached his second tree, only a few paces away from where the Guardian and I stood. Holding my breath, I waited for him to see us, to sound an alarm. His eyes passed over us without seeming to see us. A moment after kneeling, he stood, holding a soft, squirming lump the size of a basketball.

He headed back to the portal and when there, let out a slow whistle. His companions stood and hastily followed him through. The Guardian turned to me.

"This happened three days before the moon was at its fullest, as the passage of time in your world flows."

I understood what she was showing me now. It was like a Fae security camera recording - a replaying of events that had already happened. We continued to watch as one of the barrow fiends lumbered towards the tree where the man had found the small creature. It plunged its head into the cavity beneath the tree, snuffled about its base. It was looking for something, its movements becoming frantic as it searched. After a few moments, it sat back and let out a piercing, mournful howl. The sound reverberated through me with grief and sadness. My eyes stung with tears and my chest tightened. Then, it vanished.

I looked around but there was no trace of the creature. We waited and I *felt* time pass, though the scene in front of me still moved as normal. The creature reappeared, and howled again. Through the dream, I understood it had gone to my world, that I was watching it pass between here and there - and that as time stood still here, it was flying by on the other side. A day here could be a week in the mortal world, and I was watching the passage of several weeks' time in my own world condensed to a single dream.

Bounding to the other trees, the creature continued to search. Its desperation and grief infected the rest of the herd who moved restlessly, several moving to pull their spawn from under the trees where they were hidden. The herd started to move, slow but steady, away from the site they'd been playing in. The one who'd lost her young remained, head-butting those who were leaving as if to implore them to stay. Her desperation flowed through my veins, an urgent need to find her baby. Then, she vanished again.

The Guardian pulled my hand down to the ground and we sat.

"Do you feel her grief?" she asked.

I nodded. It seeped right through to my bones, making them ache with sadness. Again the barrow fiend returned, and again she vanished after mere moments. We waited, longer this time, until an orange sun started to break over the horizon. Through the shadows stretching across the surreal landscape, we saw the movement of the herd. Some of them were still travelling away, while a smaller group had broken off and were returning. Noticing my curiosity, the Guardian explained.

"They are taking the herd to safety," she said. The herd vanished into a small dip in the ground. "Those who are able will return to help their herd-mate. They would not leave her alone. They will help her seek her infant... if she returns."

However, the grieving barrow fiend did not return. The cluster of fiends milled about, sniffing the ground and awaited her return to no avail. Without warning, they lifted their heads as one and let out a deafening keening. Though I'd felt the grief of a mother before, now I was drowning in the grief of the herd, and I knew that the mother-fiend would not return.

My body trembled, shaking so hard that even sitting, I almost fell to the ground. A slender arm reached up to envelope me, dulling the cascade of grief that washed over me. Glancing to my side I saw a single tear slip down the Guardian's tiny face, though she showed no other sign of emotion. The sun climbed higher as the fiends milled about, knocking heads gently and rubbing against each other to ease their grief, but they showed no sign of leaving. The Guardian made a clicking noise and one shambled over to us. It snuffled her hand like a pet dog and she whispered in its ear.

It slowly approached me and gazed into my eyes. Whirling brown, with flashes of red sank deep into my soul as the weight of grief wrapped around me. A strange sensation filled my chest and made me understand what it wanted - my help. I didn't know how to give it.

A warbling cry broke the still night, a sound of war. A portal split the air nearby. This one was close enough for me to make out details. It looked out onto a river, and a bridge that crossed it. The sight pulled at my memory - I knew the bridge; it was in London. A man stumbled backwards through the portal, almost falling, then caught his balance at the last moment. He looked around, bewildered for a moment as the herd stared at him. A koi fish tattoo on his arm seemed to move as his muscles bunched, his stance dropping into a defensive position. The whites of his eyes displayed his terror even as he readied himself to fight. It wouldn't help him.

Rage filled me, lust for blood and vengeance. As one, the herd rushed him, trampling over his body and leaving it broken in their wake as they hurled themselves through the portal. The beast that had been with us was the last to get there, kicking up sods of dirt as it rushed to join its brethren. Now that its hypnotic gaze was broken, the sensations I felt washed away.

Coming back to myself I watched, horrified as the fiend stopped at the man crumpled on the grass. With a quick duck of its head it picked him up, shook him like a dog with a bone and threw him into the air. As he fell, a swipe of a claw ripped him open. I started forward without thinking, but the Guardian held me in an iron grip.

"You cannot save him. Would you, even if you could?"

The last barrow fiend dashed through the portal a moment before it closed. The Guardian let me approach the man - she was right, he was dead, head twisted at an impossible angle and blood oozing too slowly for a working heart. Sickened, but unable to look away, my eyes settled on another koi fish - this one etched onto his cheek, a tiny version of the one on his arm. It seemed to move in the flickering light of the Other. Finally, I tore my gaze away.

"Would you?" The Fae woman beside me pressed for an answer I couldn't give.

I thought so. I hoped so, even with the pain of a mother's loss still weighing my chest down like concrete.

"I have something that will help you in this quest." My companion held a hand out and I saw a small ring nestled in the palm of her hand. "It holds a portal stone. The barrow fiends-"

"The barrow fiends." I gasped, realising what I'd seen. They'd gone into the mortal world as a herd - there was no telling what damage they'd do. If seen, they'd be hunted and hurt and would fight back. It would be a disaster.

In my fright, I tapped into the power that lay dormant inside me. I shook off the dream-spell and woke in my own home, alone, sprawled across the couch I'd fallen asleep on. It was still dark. Without waiting to catch my breath, I threw on clothes, and traced a spell that would not only unlock my door but open it and the one downstairs, too. Calling for Lenny and fumbling with my phone, I raced downstairs.

Harrod answered the phone on the second ring. "What's wrong?" It was late enough that he knew it wasn't a social call - his voice was alert and ready.

"The bridge," I panted, "You have to get to the bridge."

"I'll leave now. What do I need?"

"There's a herd of barrow fiends coming through a portal - it's underneath, on the east side. I don't know when. Hurry, they might already be there."

"Emma, *which* bridge?" The sound coming through the phone suggested he'd just stumbled, probably trying to get dressed.

"Do you know Masik's bridge? I can't remember what it's called."

"Masik... Oh! Yes, I'll go right away."

It was night-time, so Gibble was gone. I cursed that - I had no idea how to get word to Olfred if he was needed. Lenny bounded along beside me as I ran to the port-gate near my house. It took me two tries to get through, my anxiety choking me so badly I could barely speak the words required to activate it. The gate I used took me across the river, a short distance from the bridge.

Checking only to see that Lenny had gotten through with me, I took off again while gripping my phone and trying to press buttons. In my haste, I dropped it. Cursing, I stopped to retrieve it and waited until I'd dialled before setting off toward the bridge.

"Greyson," came the curt answer.

"It's me," I said panting. "There's a bunch of creatures coming. Under the bridge. East side, the one Masik lives near."

"Ah, hell. I'll be right there. Gimme fifteen. Don't you go in alone Emma; you hear me? Wait for me somewhere safe, I'll be there as soon as I can." A beep signalled that he'd ended the call. A minute later, I reached my destination.

I slowed to a trot and Lenny pulled his pace back to match mine. Creeping up around the corner, I was surprised to see a half dozen hobos settled around a campfire. Watching them, it didn't seem as if anything was amiss. Something made a rustling sound behind me. I jumped, whirling to face the danger, wand out and ready even as my heart flew into my mouth. A familiar voice called out quietly.

"Put your wand down, it's just us." Martin opened his coat for some air and Harrod stood next to him, hands on hips, trying to catch his breath. "What's happening? Harrod just told me to get the car, then we were bolting for the bridge." Lenny sidled up to Martin, who scratched him behind one ear absentmindedly.

"I saw a portal, opening here. A whole herd of fiends came through it into our world."

"Here? That's not likely." Harrod was still struggling to catch his breath as he spoke. "Not here, there aren't any major lines this close to the river. Your source was leading you on a goose chase from the sound of it."

"Source? Harrod, it's here, I *saw* it."

"You *saw* it? How?" He straightened, then looked around again as if to reassure himself there was no herd of wild Others waiting to trample him.

"A dream," I said, distracted. Where was the portal?

"A... dream?" Harrod sounded confused.

"One of the Guardians came to me in a dream. She took me to the Other and showed me what happened. Harrod, I watched the smugglers steal a baby barrow fiend! They brought it to our world, through a portal." I shook my head, trying to assemble my thoughts properly. "Olfred was right. The smugglers are back and they're stealing more than just a few beasts."

"You're not making sense. It can't be a baby, we saw it. The beast that's here is too big, causing too much damage."

"Not the baby, the mother. She's been popping between worlds looking for her offspring. We watched her go back and forth but she didn't return. I think..." I gulped back a sob that threatened to choke me. "I think she'd dead, Harrod. We waited, and a portal popped up in the Other - I saw the bridge, *this* bridge. It was here, dammit."

Seeing no danger, I started down towards the group of people sitting where the portal should have been, Lenny trotting to my side as soon as he saw me move. I stopped short when a large figure blocked my way.

"What you want?"

Lenny pushed in front of me and chuffed at the large being. It was as if he was telling it I belonged to the big dog, and that the troll best tread carefully around me.

"Oh - you're Masik?"

"Me, Masik." The troll pointed to his chest to confirm that that was, indeed, who he was.

"Masik, did you see a portal here earlier? A doorway to the Other?"

"Huh. This bridge. Bridge no have door. Bridge flat, over water. Door? That hole in wall." His big head shook in a condescending manner.

"Did you see any barrow fiends? Anything at all?"

"Barrow fiends Other." Masik waved his big hands emphatically, then pointed at the ground in front of me. "Not here. Here, bridge." Miming a bridge, he looked at me expectantly to see if I understood. I was getting the feeling *he* was the one who though *I* was dumb as bricks.

"I... can I speak to your people, please?" I tried to keep the frustration out of my voice.

Masik was the guardian of this little bridge - at nine feet tall and with a face like a broken pot, he certainly made a good one. Still, he nodded warily and let me pass.

"Um, excuse me," I called to the men and women loitering by an open fire. "Can you tell me - was there a portal here earlier? A hole in the air, leading to a big purple field. Or some creatures, big ones?"

I was met with shaking heads and looks of pity and confusion. Great. They thought I was mad. "Please, this is important."

Masik edged closer as my voice rose, Lenny burring up in response. Along with the bridge, Masik had taken guardianship of those who lived under it. The homeless who slept here were under his protection, and his looming presence reminded me I had best step carefully in his territory.

"It could have been hours ago. A day, even? It was here, I saw it!"

"Masik said no. That means no. He's always here, never leaves."

"Masik would'a seen it if'n it 'appened 'ere."

I turned back to Harrod and Martin. Martin seemed to be on guard for anything that would leap out and attack him. Harrod's focus was all on me. He frowned, hesitating. "You said it was a dream. You're *sure-*"

"Of course I'm bloody sure, do you think I'd have dragged you out here otherwise?" I snapped.

He raised his hands "Ok, it was just a question. After last year, I just thought that perhaps-"

"You shouldn't think, Harrod, you're terrible at it." Martin said to him, then looked at me speculatively.

Greyson picked that moment to pull up in a car with another officer. He jumped out and strode over to me, giving Lenny the same distracted scratch Martin had earlier.

"What's going on?"

"I... oh hell, I don't know. I saw something, saw a portal opening, and it was *here*." I swallowed, trying to ward off tears of frustration. "Except, we're here and the portal's not, nor are the barrow fiends I saw pass through it."

"When?" Greyson asked.

"I saw it from the Other, so I'm not sure. Time passes differently over there; I was watching the fiend that we're chasing, I saw her pass through to this world and back three times. It happened in the space of minutes over there."

"What did you see, exactly?" Greyson asked softly. "No, close your eyes. Picture it in your mind and describe it to me, even the things you don't think are important."

I described what I'd seen - the stump of the bridge, the road beyond, the man falling through. Greyson led me over so I could view the bridge from the same angle I'd seen it through the portal. I pointed to the area I'd seen, Masik and his friends watching on warily.

"You said you saw the graffiti?" Greyson nodded at me as if waiting for me to connect the dots.

"Yeah. It's there, I've seen it before, you just can't see it in the... in the dark." I slapped my head and groaned, realising I'd dragged him out on a wild goose chase.

"It's alright," he said. "It still might be important. It's certainly more than we've got to go on now. What time of day was it, do you think?"

"The sun must have been..." I turned and pointed. "So, mid-morning?"

"Good, good. What else could you see - sky? Grass?"

I squeezed my eyes shut and wracked my brain. There had been a patch of ground just beyond... but here, it was straggling green grass. I hadn't seen grass in my dream, just charred ground. I approached the gathering of mortals now huddled by their fire, talking in low voices.

"Listen, guys, can you do me a really huge favour?" Eyes turned to me warily. "See that bit of grass over there? If it changes - frosts over, dies off, anything like that - as soon as it changes, call me." I found a scrap of paper and borrowed a pen from Greyson to write my number and my shop address onto it. "It could get dangerous here. If there's somewhere else you can go, you should."

There was no response. I imagine living under the watchful eye of a troll makes a bit of grass seem somewhat boring in comparison. Harrod walked over to me and, in a quiet voice, asked if I still needed him here.

"No." My voice was flat and I didn't look at him as I spoke. "Go home. Charlie and I can stay and deal with this."

"Look, I didn't say I don't believe you, I just know you've been under a lot of stress and-"

"Just go, Harrod," I insisted. "It's fine."

"Really?" He darted a glance to Martin, who raised his hands.

"Don't drag me into this, Harrod. You're the one suffering from a permanent case of foot in mouth disease."

Harrod scowled at his brother and turned back to me.

"Really. I'm fine. Go." Lenny whimpered at my tone and butted my hip with his head. I gave it a quick rub as I turned away so Harrod couldn't see my face. Martin waited for Harrod to stomp past, then wandered off behind him after giving me a short wave goodbye.

"Hey, Greyson?" I climbed back up the small embankment to where he was talking to his partner. She looked up and gave me a nod as I approached, as Greyson turned to see what I needed. "Can I trouble you for a lift back to the gate?"

"I'll take you home," he said quickly. "I'm not leaving you to walk the damned streets at this time of night, what do you take me for?"

"Thanks." I didn't have to be asked twice.

Greyson finished his discussion with the other officer, setting a schedule to keep watch over the bridge. "Anything, *anything* that happens or just doesn't feel right, you get them to call it in, right? I'll wait for Miles to get here; he can join you until the next shift starts."

"Sure thing, captain." She flipped her notebook closed, then turned to me again. "I'm Trainor, by the way. The captain told us you've been helping. Gotta say, we appreciate a set of eyes from the other side, so to speak."

Lenny lifted a paw and Trainor looked at him, quizzically. He kept it up and she put her hand out to shake it. Lenny made a snuffling sound, then dipped his head at her before shambling off to jump through a window into Greyson's police car. Trainor gave me a nod then turned to the car. Eyeing Lenny who sat sedately in the back seat watching her, she reached through the front window and pulled out a small bag that she slung over her shoulder.

"How far away is Miles?" she called to Greyson.

"I called him as soon as we got here. Should be any minute." As if on cue another car rolled up. Greyson walked over and had a brief conversation through the window then gave Trainor a quick wave.

"I'm sorry, I really thought something was happening. I didn't mean to pull you away from your people," I said.

"You didn't. I'm headed back to the station; my shift was over an hour ago. My team will keep a watch on the bridge, two officers, twenty-four seven. You think that'll do it?"

"I guess so," I said. I hoped so. Being wrong about what I'd seen would be embarrassing, and a blow to my credibility in Greyson's eyes; being right could turn out to be much, much worse.

Chapter Twelve

When Greyson dropped me off I invited him in for tea, but he declined. He looked tired, the sort of tired that only comes from many late nights and long, hard days. He was clutching at straws trying to close this case – they'd made no progress, but the damage to public property meant the higher ups were breathing down his neck to get it sorted.

Greyson, of course, was more worried about preventing harm to civilians. To make it worse, he'd told me in the car that there'd been a spate of vandalisms, property damage worth thousands. The victims were all half-bloods, and if there had been any doubt the attacks were hate crimes, the awful slurs spray painted at the locations fixed that. It was nothing he couldn't handle – he already had a good idea who was causing the trouble – but it ate into his time and resources.

Once inside, alone with Lenny, I curled up in a chair with a blanket and hot cup of tea.

"Would you like to explain your astounding lack of manners earlier?" I said out loud, looked at my dog with an eyebrow raised.

Lenny made a guttural sound and rolled onto his back, looking up at me wistfully. Sneaking a toe out from under the blanket I rubbed his tummy.

"Seriously, Len, you don't jump in someone's car without permission!"

He whined apologetically.

"Oh, don't pretend. You know everyone is wrapped around your little finger. Well, your paw." I thought back to his interaction with Trainor. "You like Greyson's partner, don't you?"

He snuffed agreement and I smiled. I'd often had late night conversations like this with Lenny. I hadn't realised his recent answers were more than just my imagination and the behaviour of a restless dog. As I moved my foot back into the warmth he curled up on my feet, putting his head down to sleep.

There would be no more rest for me tonight. The apparent ease with which the Guardian had entered my dream disturbed me. She'd meant no harm as far as I could tell, but what would stop it from happening again? She'd completely disregarded my wards, set up months ago but still rock solid.

Begrudgingly, I admitted to myself I hadn't really intended to go to them as I'd let Gibble believe; not directly, at any rate. No, I thought wryly, I was too chicken for that. My plan had been to pass on the whatever information I found to whoever was brave enough to take it, then leave the Guardians to take care of Serraceuse.

Maybe they'd known my intent and circumvented it, just because they could. Maybe they just wanted to meddle. There was no doubt in my mind that 'wanting to help' had no place in their motives. The Fae, and even more so, the Guardians, just didn't work like that. Everything was part of a greater plan and that plan usually worked out to their benefit, or their entertainment.

Glumly, I looked into the bottom of my cup, then tipped the last mouthful of tea into my mouth. Something hard and round caught in my throat, causing a moment's panic as I coughed it up. I spat it out into my hand and a chill ran down my spine. It was the ring, the one that the Guardian had shown me. The dream had ended before she'd had the chance to hand it over.

How the hell did it get in my tea? Damned Fae. Shuddering at the thought of a Guardian wandering around my flat while I'd made the tea, I carefully folded the ring in a tissue and tucked it inside the small satchel I used in place of a handbag. It was almost always with me, and the easiest way to keep the ring close without having to wear the cursed thing. I frowned, hoping it wasn't *actually* cursed.

~

I woke the next morning to the screech of my phone. Shaking off the drowsiness and surprise at having slept at all, I checked the screen. My heart plummeted.

It was the alarm I'd set to remind me of my lesson with Mergime. She hadn't been happy when I'd asked to reschedule and I was sure the early morning catch up was some kind of sadistic revenge. When I double checked and saw it was the *second* alarm and that I'd slept through the first one, I jumped to my feet and started throwing things into a bag. It was a twenty-minute trip and I had half an hour to get there.

Harrod was waiting when I dashed outside twelve minutes later.

"Cutting it a bit fine, aren't you?" was all he said. I ignored him, tapping my fingers nervously as the car pulled out into the traffic.

I did at least have the decency to yell a quick thank you for the lift when I threw myself out of the car a short time later. Barrelling up the door I took a bare second to right myself before knocking.

The door opened. Not to a barrage of attacks thankfully – I wouldn't have been the slightest bit prepared. Instead, Mergime stood there with a scowl on her face. She stomped into the sitting room, leaving me trailing behind. Stopping, she picked something up and threw it at my chest. I flinched, not expecting it. Magic, yes. A newspaper? Totally got me.

Confused, I opened it to see my face splashed across the front page of The Custodian. *High Seat's Secret Weapon* the title read. I went on to read.

Emmeline Beaumarchais, daughter of controversial Freedom

Fighter Lucius Beaumarchais, has been enlisted by the Talent Council as a Mortal Liaison, in an attempt to woo the Talented populace into supporting new changes to the Agreement. The half-blood has been tasked with assisting the police on several high profile cases, and was instrumental in the fatal apprehension of Lord Mikael Opius of the Second Family, earlier this year. In addition, she has been sighted at several locations that suggest she is now involved in a case investigating the alleged escape of a smuggled Barrow Fiend...

I stopped reading. This was awful. Though I hadn't hidden my involvement with the O.C.U., having it make front page news was far more than I'd bargained for. I wanted as few eyes on me as possible, and this guaranteed the opposite would happen. I quickly scanned the rest of the article and... yes, they'd gone on to mention the smuggling connection and even drawn it to Serraceuse and my father's involvement with him. Greyson would be furious.

Mergime let out an irritated cough to get my attention. Hand on hips, her brows were knitted so tight they looked as though they'd joined, lips twisted so sourly they'd put lemons to shame.

"Are you suddenly so competent at wielding the Talent that you are no longer in need of my lessons?"

"What? No! Why would you think that?" I cried.

"I assure you, *I* am under no illusion whatsoever regarding your competency. You, however, seem to be so arrogantly misinformed as to the level of your ability that you've taken on one of the most dangerous criminal organisations known to Talent-kind in the last century."

"Abnett-"

"Would not have requested your assistance if he had not been under the misapprehension that you were qualified for it," Mergime snapped.

"I didn't-"

"Didn't what?" She jabbed her wand at my chest, poking me hard. "Practice? Apply yourself? Dedicate yourself to learning the very basic principles that you struggle so poorly with?"

"*Fine.*" Heat rushed to my cheeks and for once, I wasn't cowed by it.

Anger rose inside me; I was sick of trying to control my loathing for this woman, sick of bowing and scraping to her. Turning, I took a step toward the door.

I stopped. My limbs froze, caught in a web of holding. Damn Talent.

"You will *not* walk away from me, you insolent little half-blood!" Mergime yelled. She hissed out a breath, and when she spoke again, her voice was deadly calm. "I may have dedicated more time to teaching you than you have in learning but that doesn't mean I'm done with you, not by half. You will *not* leave this room until you demonstrate the three basic skills, three times. You will *not* leave this house until you've blocked me twice, *without* letting your petty emotions run rampant and out of control. You will not speak, you will not move and you will *not* trace without my explicit instruction."

The tracing that held me fell away in a blink. Caught off balance, I wobbled and had to grab the wall for support. When I opened my mouth to speak, it was snapped shut by another tracing. I reached out for my gift, vibrant and throbbing in my anger. Mergime saw – she often said I had a set to my face when doing it – and a pitcher of water rose off its tray. Cursing my lack of fortitude, I let go of the rising power.

"At least you have learned *that* lesson. Though, it took more than once to teach you not to use that little Talent of yours without permission."

I tried not to breathe a sigh of relief when the pitcher settled back down. Mergime had doused me over the head with it (yes, twice) for not listening to her, and resisting her with my gift. It might let me block direct attacks, but I couldn't stop her manipulating objects around me.

"Now, the basic skills. Demonstrate!"

I ground my teeth, knowing that what she asked was impossible.

Two of the three basic skills – knowing an objects form, and tracing a spell – were easy. Naming a trace was another matter entirely.

Half-bloods couldn't see the magic worked by another. We were born blind to all magic except our own. This created a double blow, because not only could we not recognise another tracing, we couldn't learn from it either. Half-bloods had to fend for themselves, feeling out the magic by instinct and by trial and error. Luckily, a tracing gone wrong would just fizzle ninety-nine percent of the time. The other one percent... let's just say there was a reason the half-blood life expectancy was a little lower than that of a full Talent.

Mergime held a vase out in front of me. Barely hesitating, I traced its pattern, the thing that made it what it was. She nodded, unimpressed.

"Make it weightless."

Holding my wand out, I sullenly traced over the pattern, embellishing it in just the right places to detach it from the gravitational pull that held it down. It shifted slightly as Mergime let it go to hang in the air.

She pursed her lips and nodded once more. I immediately let the tracing go – affecting something so complex and so pervasive as gravity was difficult. The vase dropped, Mergime snatching out a hand to catch it before it hit the ground.

"Examine my tracing," she said. The vase lifted again.

"I can't see it, you know that," I growled.

"Are you stupid as well as blind?" she asked.

"Well, I know you traced the same spell I did." My shoulders sagged a little, the fight going out of me.

"Reverse it." Her tone brooked no argument.

Reversing a spell meant I'd need to see her tracing, which I couldn't. Instead, I tried to trace a spell that would weigh it down, make gravity latch on to it harder. Another difficult task and one I apparently didn't have the strength for.

My brows knitted as I focused every ounce of concentration I possessed on the tracing. The first part felt smooth, then, as I continued, it was more like trying to write tiny words in dry sand. As I'd expected, the tracing just wouldn't stick – though small portions stood out clearly, others blurred and faded too quickly for them to work.

"Pay attention, you foolish girl," Mergime berated me. "Don't you *see* it?"

"I can't do it!" I said. "You're a Talent, I'm a half-blood. I can't *see* your tracing and I *can't* alter it. What did you expect? I could barely hold the first one you asked me to do."

Mergime pretended I hadn't spoken. "Trace it again – no, not that one, weightless. Girl, if you roll your eyes at me one more time..."

The pitcher in the corner jiggled and I hurriedly tried to cast weightless again on the already-floating vase. Just as my last attempt, it wouldn't get purchase, though this time a large portion of it held clearly. That was strange, it should have been less clear as my capacity for holding the spells diminished with each attempt.

"Oh, for crying out loud, girl. *Tell me what you see.*"

She was pushing awfully hard for a test designed to fail. I thought it though, forcing my aching brain into gear.

"It was easier the second time. Trying to trace over your spell was like writing in ink on wet paper – parts blurred and ran, but small portions stayed crisp, like on dry paper. The second time, it was like the paper was... less wet?"

"The parts that stayed – *why?*" The anger in Mergime's voice had seeped away, leaving a curious urgency.

I rubbed my head. I hadn't gotten enough sleep for this. "I have no idea, Mergime. I really don't."

"Leave."

"What? You said-"

"Come back when you learn to think. I don't have the patience to deal with simpletons today."

Stifling a growl, I did as I'd been told, in part relieved the ordeal was finally over. Still feeling dazed, I plodded down her front steps and into the street outside. The whole session had just been bizarre and I wasn't sure what to think. Wrapping myself in my coat to fend off the drizzle that was just beginning, I set off for home, only realising when a horn beeped behind me that Harrod had come to drive me back. I slid into the car and rested my head on the window.

Harrod eyed me warily.

"What is it?" I asked.

He passed me a copy of the newspaper I'd seen at Mergime's. I tossed it back on the seat.

"Ah. You've seen it then," he said.

"Mergime took it as a personal affront that'd I put myself in harm's way like that. She seems to think I had a choice."

"You could have turned Abnett down – I told you, I can speak to him." To his credit, his voice didn't hold a trace of judgement.

"*Morally*, Harrod. Morally, I didn't have a choice."

"Ah." There was a short silence, then, "I have the map of lines. It took some convincing to let Abnett give me an official copy. I'm heading to see Greyson now if you'd like to join me?"

"I have to open the shop."

He hesitated again.

"Oh, come on Harrod, whatever it is, just say it."

"There's no ley line at the bridge. Or, there is, but it's very weak – water tends to disrupt the patterns. The lines that close to the river aren't even listed on most of the standard maps."

I couldn't help but sigh. "I'm not crazy, Harrod. I know what I saw."

He looked away. Despite my frustration with the conversation, Mergime's words still tugged at my brain.

"Harrod, what happens when you try to trace over another Talent's spells?" I asked.

"Er, what? Depending on who traced it, I usually succeed. I mean, it depends on the spell of course but-"

"What about when it doesn't work, when they're stronger?" I leaned forwards, curiosity overwhelming my sour mood. "What does it feel like, what does it *look* like?"

"I... what are you talking about?" He seemed completely flummoxed by my abrupt change of topic.

"Mergime got me to trace *over* her spell. Twice. The first time was a counter-trace. The second was a re-trace of the spell she had active. It was hard, I mean weight-based spells are really taxing for me at the best of times, but the third time – the re-trace – was easier than the second one."

"You mean it worked, you undid her tracing?"

I winced at the shock in Harrod's voice that my measly ability could outstrip Mergime's. "Of course it didn't work, you lummox. I mean the strain of *trying* to do it was less. The trace – it's so hard to explain. You know when you're trying something outside your ability and the lines just fuzz into nothing? Some of it stayed clear."

"I don't see your point."

"Neither do I..." My voice trailed off as I sank back into thought.

I spent the rest of the drive in silence, so preoccupied with the question Mergime had posed that I almost didn't notice when we reached my destination. Coming out of my reverie, I gave Harrod a quick thank you and a wave before I got out of the car.

Chapter Thirteen

I walked to the door of my shop and coughed politely at the hobgoblin trying to break into my shop. "I have the keys here, Barg. Would you like me to open the door?"

The hobgoblin sheepishly slipped the lock picks back into his pocket.

"Aha, many thanks, Lady. Barg was hoping to speak to the Lenny-dog if he is present and available?"

"You... want to 'speak' to Lenny. The dog."

I received a flourishing bow and a nod in return. Sighing, I unlocked the door and stepped aside as Lenny came bounding out, greeting Barg by slobbering on his small, wrinkled head. I latched open the door and flipped the sign on the door to say 'open'.

"What are you two up to today?"

Barg hesitated, then rushed out a cascade of words that indicated they were simply going for a walk. There was more to this than he was saying, but I didn't push it. He'd never let Lenny come to harm, and in a strange way, I trusted Barg. They left, Barg in his now-usual position astride Lenny's back, and I set to work. Gibble showed up at his usual time, unhappy at Lenny's absence.

"I not be knowing what Lenny-dog be doing with Barg, but Gibble be feeling that it not be good."

"You don't think they're doing anything dangerous, do you?" Worry immediately nagged and I wondered if I should have told Barg not to leave with Lenny.

"Not be danger. Just trouble. Gibble be having to pay debts or make promises, most likely." He sighed, big bristly brows pulling together and wrinkling his face.

"I'm sure it won't be that bad, Gibble. Barg wouldn't let Lenny get into trouble and Lenny wouldn't let Barg do anything *that* stupid."

"Yes, Lady." His demeanour didn't improve and he let out another sigh, softer this time.

"Gib? Something's wrong, isn't it?"

"Something sad be in the air today, Lady. I not be knowing what, but today... it be a sad day."

Refusing to say any more about it, he went about the day's tasks. I joined him, a pit of worry settling deep in my stomach. The last time Gibble had had a feeling like this was three years ago, when a mortal had gone on a shooting spree at the central port-gate, killing everyone in sight. It was a massacre. An event in the Inner City had brought Fae and Otherworlders into the city, via the gate.

So many had died; humans, Talents, Fae and Other, in such a short space of time. The tragedy was still etched in the minds of any who had been in the city that day.

The sense of dread pervaded everyone. The Others who came to shop with me that day were bristly, quiet except for vague mutterings about what was to come. The mortals and half-bloods, though they couldn't feel it, reacted to the others and often left more subdued than when they came in.

After the first couple of sales, I started adding a small packet of heartsease to each order. Ever since I'd learned to enchant my teas, I'd kept a small packet on hand for myself; when I opened the shop I extended that to my customers. There was always a supply reserved for emergencies, and I felt that it may be needed by the day's end.

I was almost relieved when Greyson called me in the afternoon. Gibble answered the phone then handed it to me, ears drooping and a face so sorrowful I thought my heart would break.

"What is it?" I asked him, afraid to take the phone call.

"I not be knowing, Lady, just that the sadness be near." Terrified of what to expect, I put the phone to my ear.

"What's wrong?" I asked, my voice breaking slightly.

"We've found it." Charlie's voice was clipped, urgent. "It trampled a fence, and it's on the grounds of a small estate outside the city. House belongs to a mortal, some tech giant apparently. The place is surrounded and they're about to go in. I'm trying to hold them off until you get here, but you'll have to hurry. I want you on the ground."

"I'll come right away."

Sick with fear, amplified by Gibble's earlier statements, I scribbled down the address. A day of sadness – something was going to go wrong, I could feel it in my bones. I looked at Gibble for a moment, debating. Then, I closed the shop.

"Everyone out. We're closing, sorry. Emergency." Stricken glances met my eyes and I knew my customers felt it too. A quiet snarl from Gibble hurried them up. He held the door open for me and I flicked the lock with my wand as we left.

We headed to the nearest port-gate and jumped outside the city. Greyson had organised a car for me and it was waiting when we got there. The driver, a young policeman with sandy hair and an eager smile, greeted us enthusiastically, even as the car creaked under Gibble's weight when he dubiously sat in it. He didn't take cars often.

"We're only a few minutes away ma'am. The Armed Response

Unit was called in first – the Captain's arguing with them now. I hope we're back before he rips their heads off. He's a sight when he's angry, he is. Well, so long as it's not at one of us, but that doesn't happen often."

I kept half an ear on his chatter as the car slid up a driveway owned by someone with a whole lot of money. The house was monstrous, and dwarfed the dozen marked cars and three black sedans parked in the ample driveway. Greyson stood outside with four of his underlings – I recognised most of them by sight now. Two other officers leaned back against cars talking into radios. One started to approach us, but Greyson beat him to it.

"They're with me," he growled at the other officer.

"She's a civilian." The red faced man continued towards us, jabbing a finger in Gibble's direction. My shoulders tightened and I stood taller, ready to meet the threat. "She can't be here, and *he's* a bloody monster."

"She's a consultant and he's with her." Greyson smirked and added in lower voice, "Paperwork's already been lodged."

"Consultant, pah." The burly, red-faced man looked me up and down disdainfully. "Keep 'em on a short leash, Greyson, or it'll be one more nail in that coffin I'm building for you." He stalked off, after lighting a cigarette, sucking on it, then flicking some ash in Gibble's direction. The boggart just shrugged and turned to Greyson.

"What the hell was that about?" I asked, heart slowing now the beast of a man was no longer in front of me.

"Asshole." Greyson's fists were clenched and I could almost see the steam pouring from his ears. Swallowing down the last of my own rage, I put a hand on his arm to calm him, worried he was about to walk over and throw a punch at the other officer. Shaking me off, Greyson walked back to his car, Trainor inside with a radio in her hand. It crackled to life and someone spoke. Trainor popped her head out.

"Cap', it's a mess in there. Sturk's boys have opened fire and Miles has completely lost control of them."

"Ahh, to hell with it." Greyson reached in the back of the car and hurriedly threw a bullet-proof vest on. "Not letting my people go down for that prick."

"Woah, opened fire? Why can't we hear shots?" I looked from Trainor to Greyson, who slammed the car door shut. "You're not going *in* there, are you?"

Greyson, ignoring me, strode off in the direction of the mansion's front door. Trainor punched the dash of the car.

"Trainor, what the *hell* is going on?" My voice was unsteady as I watched him disappear through the big doors, Gibble's words from earlier bouncing through my skull. *Please, not him.*

"Sturk – yeah, him," she motioned to detective 'asshole' who was speaking into his own radio. "He got here first. Because a mortal called it in as a threat and Sturk has the guns, he figured he had point. Bastard wasn't even going to let us on-site until Greyson threatened to take it to the uppers. Sturk let Miles, one of our boys, and a couple others go in with his team. Miles and their unit leader were supposed to coordinate, but it's been a shit fight the whole way."

"Who are they shooting at?"

"They came across an old barn. Looks like some kind of private zoo, and our fiend has forced its way in. Some of the cages were damaged and a few animals got loose. Between that, the police, and the security on site, it's a mess."

"Why would security be causing problems?" I asked, trying to knit her story together into something I understood.

Trainor snorted. "Not exactly legal to have a zoo full of smuggled animals now, is it?" She jumped when Gibble let out a low growl. "We weren't supposed to find it. A maid called in the incident, they weren't gonna let us in when we got here."

They were shooting at innocent creatures – creatures I'd promised Olfred I would do my best to protect. Steeling myself, I turned to Gibble with fearful eyes. He nodded.

"We have to get in there." I said to Trainor. Her eyes widened but then she looked at me discerningly.

"You taking your friend?" she asked.

"Yes." I waited with bated breath. I didn't want to go against her orders, but I would if I had to. She reached into the back and threw another vest at me.

"Take that. If Greyson asks, I tried to stop you, hear me? Gods, he's gonna have my balls for breakfast when he sees you in there." Quickly explaining the route they'd taken to get into the enclave as I strapped the bulky vest on, she added, "I can't give you a weapon. You're on your own in there."

"Not quite," I said, holding up my wand. My voice was steady, and sounded more confident than I felt, knowing my ability to trace anything would still be painfully difficult from yesterday's efforts. Together, Gibble and I headed in the same direction Greyson had gone moments earlier.

"Oy, stop there," Sturk called. I flicked my wand and the back tyre of his car exploded with a bang. He hit the deck and Gibble and I hurried through the big doors. I prayed he wouldn't follow us in.

The manor was huge but easy to navigate. We quickly found the outer door Trainor had described and headed through. Together we trotted down a short path, then ducked between some bushes that had been trampled. There, hiding behind an overgrown fig, was the barn, one door hanging off a single hinge. Gibble and I stood in eerie silence for a moment, then heard muffled yelling. Gibble held a hand up and pulled the door open. His body blocked the entrance as I heard a gunshot ring out, deafeningly close.

Over the ringing of my ears I heard Greyson yell, "Stand down! Stand down! Goddammit, Faulkes, if you don't put your goddamned gun down, I'll have your goddamned badge!"

I entered to chaos. Next to the door, a man in a white suit splattered with blood curled in a corner, sobbing. A little further along lay the sleek, unmoving body of a barrow fiend. Gibble pulled me back as I tried to go to it. I looked up and realised I'd walked in on a massacre. There were a dozen people here, standing around, some with guns pointed at motionless lumps on the floor. Greyson looked up at my entrance, eyes haunted, face hard. He nodded grimly at me and I noticed the gun in his hand, though not pointed at anyone in particular, was out and just slightly raised. I tightened my grip on my wand and held a spell at the ready.

"Right," Greyson barked. He jerked his chin to gesture at some of the officers. "You, you and you – out, and take them with you. You too, Faulkes." An officer in body armour opened his mouth but was cut off. "Don't you bloody argue with me. You're outranked, and out of your depth. I've got the scene now."

The officers he'd motioned to marched out, each one herding a handcuffed security guard in front of them. Another man stepped closer to Greyson, his mouth in a hard line. He didn't look angry—as he approached the DCI his gaze faltered and he swallowed hard before he opened his mouth to speak.

Greyson didn't let him, cutting him off before the young officer could say anything. "Myles, you here stay with this one." He thrust his chin at the man in the corner.

Myles jerked his head and straightened, said something into his radio and it crackled back at him. "Bus is still fifteen away sir."

"Then you watch him for twenty. He's not hurt, he's a coward. The girl down there gets medical priority. Filthy animals." The last was said in a low voice as if to himself. I didn't think he was talking about the creatures in the room.

The huge space inside the barn had been adapted to resemble a high-tech zoo. The walls were padded with a soft layer to muffle sound and barred rooms ran along the walls, the bareness of the concrete walls broken by plants and greenery. The floors were covered in straw and the stink of animals and blood made my stomach want to heave.

Three cage doors hung open, bent out of shape. I walked carefully through the debris on the floor – broken bits of cement and roof tiles chipped from gunfire, bits of plant matter, water, blood...

Approaching the nearest cage I saw what was inside. When I reached a hand out to the lifeless serpent, Gibble pulled it back, shaking his head. Boggarts didn't have tear ducts. I was glad of that, in this moment, while I tried so hard to keep my own emotions in check.

"Olfred?" I said, looking to Gibble. "Perhaps Deirdre too, if you can find her quickly."

Gibble looked to Greyson. "It be safe for Lady if Gibble be gone?"

Greyson gave him a tired nod. "Any help you can bring... this... this is just bad."

Gibble slipped back out the door.

Further along, one of the locked rooms held a wall of smaller cages, some empty, some not. Three bearded luskes sat quietly in a corner with their plumed heads flared in distress. One opened its mouth at me, stretching it wide to show tiny rows of pointed teeth. It probably knew it couldn't hurt me, but was desperate to ward off any threat in this terrifying place with nowhere to hide. Under the luskes, a reptilian creature lay motionless. There was nothing to suggest it was still alive.

I jiggled the padlock on the door then traced an unlocking on it. A quiet snick, heard in the now silent room, told me it had worked. Carefully stepping inside, I checked over the cages, thankful most were empty. There were some long-eared sorn'ts, and a tiny ball of fur that hissed when I approached. Heartsick, I decided against opening the cages until Olfred could see to them.

A few more steps and I could peer into the next small room. It was empty, the door unlocked and straw roughly swept into a corner. A plastic wading pool in the middle of the room held a murky grey puddle, and grey, congealed grease coated the bottom of the wall as though a muddy soccer ball had been rolled against it. A jolt went through me as I touched the residue. It was too thick to be fresh. It had to be where they'd held the baby fiend, so where was it now?

The rear of the building was built out to create a room a little larger than the others. This one had a proper door, with a clear plastic square fitted as a viewing window. The door sat ajar and I pulled it open.

My knees trembled and my breathing stopped. The cell – for that's what it was – looked almost like a tiny bedroom. A singe bed with a purple coverlet; a tiny side table with a tattered book, a mirror, a hairbrush; a rug on the floor, dirty and faded. And on the bed, curled into the tightest of balls and crushed as close as the wall as she could get, a demi-fae.

The girl looked young – like a thirteen-year-old if she were human. I wasn't great at working it out but that should mean she was in her seventies. For a demi-fae... that was about the equivalent of a young adult human. They'd been keeping her down here to use as... I near y retched on the floor.

A female officer sat in the opposite corner of the cell, eyeing me, as if to warning me not to approach. I didn't. Whatever atrocities she'd been subjected to, a room full of spectators wouldn't be helpful.

Stepping back out, I completed my circuit of the barn, Greyson waiting at the door to give me my space. Thirteen creatures dead, nine injured badly and seven alive and well. I approached the body of the barrow fiend and lay a hand on its back. It twitched slightly. It was alive? I came around to examine its face and one cloudy eye opened. It focused on me and I leaned close to pat its greasy hide, ignoring the sting in my hand where I touched it.

"I'm sorry," I whispered to it, tears dripping down my face. "I'm sorry I couldn't save you."

Icy cold washed through me. The room spun and blackness closed in. A pinprick of light widened and then, I could see a single image. A tiny, dark ball of fur, covered in the slick, protective substance that would keep its skin healthy. Longing and loss pierced me, a feeling of failure; then, a feeling of hope. Understanding rushed through me and I nodded, whispering a promise to the fallen mother. My vision cleared an instant later, and I stood. "The baby fiend is alive."

Walking over to the man huddled in the corner I called out to Greyson.

"Who's he?"

"Him? He's the bastard that put them down here." Greyson spat on the floor, unable to bring himself to look at the cowering man properly.

"Mind if I have a word with him?" I asked in a perfectly reasonable voice. Despite my tone, rage boiled inside me, searing my insides and aching for a way out.

"Oh, go ahead. You're outside the realm of my jurisdiction, you know, so you can do whatever the hell you want." His voice was just as placid as mine, but the man at my feet whimpered and curled tighter into his pathetic little ball.

"Please," he begged, hiccupping as he wiped his nose on his sleeve. "Please, I didn't do anything wrong. I cared for them, gave them a home..."

My foot struck him in the side and he spasmed. Leaning down to get closer to his ear I said in a low voice, "You're keeping a *demi-fae*. Do you *know* what her people will do to you when they find you?"

"The accords! They can't break the accords!" The man's voice rose to a squealing pitch as he spoke. "No, you have to keep them away!"

"Keep them away? I could open a portal for them right now. In fact, the reward for turning you over to them..." My wand traced a pattern in the air as I stood and the man started screaming.

Baring my teeth, I traced a spell of silence on him and the horror on his face increased as he tried harder to make himself heard. After a few moments he gave up, shutting his mouth and squeezing his eyes closed.

"How did you get them?"

He didn't answer, so I kicked him again. My eyes slid over to where Greyson stood, arms crossed and back turned.

"Listen to me," I hissed. "You despicable little man. Your men – whoever they were – took an infant barrow fiend from the Other. *Where is it?*"

I waited until he looked ready to speak and lifted the spell.

"-my men, they weren't my men! I just bought the animals off them, I didn't take them, I'd never do a thing like that"

Holding my wand up was enough to get him to stop talking again. "See that?" I pointed to the barrow fiend. "You had one of those, a baby. Where. Is. That. Baby."

"I'll make you a deal, I'll tell you, I'll tell you everything if you promise to keep them from me."

"No deal. You tell me everything now and I won't open a portal at my feet. After that, you're on your own." I lifted my wand expectantly.

"Fine, fine!" Tears streamed down his face. "I sold it, I sold the thing. I couldn't afford to keep feeding it, Carter didn't tell me how much it needed and I couldn't keep up. I sold it back, at a loss, I lost twenty grand on it, oh no, oh god please don't-" I silenced him again, then traced a bubble around Greyson and I so he couldn't hear us.

"I think he's ready to tell you anything you need," I said.

"Thanks. Sorry. Sorry you had to see all this. And deal with him." His face was worn and gaunt, and I had to resist the urge to pull his head down to my shoulder. There would be time for that later.

The door to the barn opened just as I dispelled the privacy spell. Olfred thumped through, then stopped, aghast. He'd have known it would be bad, but I don't think anything could have prepared him for this. A low keening sound started in the back of his throat as he walked through the room, placing a hand on each of the dead creatures he passed. He ventured into the cages, his presence soothing the frightened animals as mine had roused them to hysterics. His low voice spoke a language I couldn't comprehend as he treated each one with care and tenderness, never ceasing the low cry for his fallen friends. He passed the cell at the end and I called out to him.

"Olfred please, see to her. She needs your help."

"I dinna treat Fae or Human, ye know that lass. Hers will come. They not be waiting long." He proceeded over to a cage where the fallen serpent lay and placed a hand over its face. A sound at the door made me jump, and I turned to see Deirdre storming through, Gibble close behind. She faltered for only a moment when she saw the carnage in the room. Giving Olfred a low bow, she made the hand sign for peace and respect. Olfred, though he'd clashed with her in the past, seemed to accept this.

"Ye be needed in th' back, lassie."

Deirdre looked at me for confirmation and I nodded, pointing to the cell where the demi-fae was still cloistered.

Watching her gently approach the door, I leaned into Gibble for a moment of comfort amongst the heartache. Greyson's voice murmured in the background as he spoke to the white-suited man and jotted notes down – I hoped the scumbag knew enough to lead us straight to the barrow fiend's pup.

Leaving Gibble, I went back to the small cell. The demi-fae hadn't moved and neither had the officer. Deirdre leaned over the bed, looking worn about the eyes, suggesting it had taken a good deal of magic to heal the girl. Remembering the ring the guardian had given me, I dug it out of my bag.

"Here," I said carefully and reached out to place it on her bed. "Someone gave this to me, but I think maybe it was meant for you. Do you know how to use it?"

Strikingly blue eyes widened. The child was pretty, like a finely sculptured porcelain doll. It tore at me to see her ebony hair lank and dirty, her dark skin swollen and bruised.

"The old ones – they sent you to rescue me?" she asked in a tiny voice.

"Well... I guess so. I'm sorry – I didn't do a very good job." I had to clench my teeth to stop my lip trembling.

"Your spirit-pet, she came and found us." The demi-fae lifted wide eyes to me. "No one else could. The man in white, he paid for wards that would keep my people's eyes away. Your spirit pet, she found us anyway. She saved us."

"She was very brave," I said, forming a tiny smile. The girl moved to take the ring.

"The good man – he is your knight?" she asked.

"Which man?"

She pointed at Greyson. "The other men, they came in with weapons and they killed. Your knight stopped them. He protected us, he and his people. They are good people." She paused, her face darkening. "Why did the others who came try to hurt us?"

"I… think they were afraid," I said, hedging my bets. I'd be speaking to Greyson about that later. "They didn't understand what was happening here, that you were being held against your will. They saw the creatures and thought they were dangerous. I'm sorry. I'm so sorry."

"I must go," she said. "I must tell of the Knight and the Spirit. If I do not, my people will have anger towards yours. I must tell them you saved me." The demi-fae slid the ring on her finger and slipped into a sliver of light that vanished as soon as it was formed. The officer in the room with us reached out instinctively to stop her, but she was gone.

Gibble came over and I realised he'd been watching.

"It be good that she did go. Hope that she be speaking to Guardians. They be angry if they be thinking the humans be doing this and none did stop them."

"Oh, Gib." I buried my face in his side as he wrapped leathery arms around me. "How could this happen?"

Chapter Fourteen

The sharp rap on my door late that evening wasn't unexpected. Greyson waited patiently until I let him in, then stalked inside to pace the room with an irritated stride.

"Sturk's always had it in for the O.C.U. He got the call and he knew... he *knew* it was my jurisdiction. He ignored every damned code and took point anyway. His men are as bad as he is. Close-minded, trigger-happy, misogynistic bunch of assholes. My boys said they should never have let a round off, but I'm *still* not surprised the damn thing turned into a gun show." Clasping him arm and guiding him upstairs to sit while I made tea, I asked what had gone so wrong.

"Myles led the team in, they were supposed to answer to him. When they got to the barn, a few creatures were loose. The big one, our fiend, had one of the hired security bailed up against a wall. It hadn't done anything to him, the man was fine. Myles said they were all just frightened animals looking for a way out of the building, none of them were a risk."

Greyson's head dropped. "He tried to get the team to move aside, let the creatures run. One of the on-site security tried to stop them. 'Valuable merchandise' I believe was the term used. Sturk's men panicked opened fire on the animals. It was a slaughter; poor beasts didn't stand a chance."

His eyes were dull and his voice flat. I'd ever seen him like this before. I placed a hand on his shoulder and he leaned into my waist, face hidden. He started to soften as I rubbed the knot of tension from his neck.

"I'm going after them, Em," he said in a quiet voice. A heavy weight settled in my gut, a feeling of dread and certainty. I opened my mouth but it took two tries for the words to come out.

"So am I."

I didn't open the shop the next day, or the day after. Melanie called, but I didn't answer my phone. It felt like too much to try to explain. I stayed locked up inside, grieving for the lives that had been lost and the deaths I should have been able to prevent.

It was only Lenny and Gibble that gave me any solace, Lenny nuzzling my face when I cried, Gibble sitting with a book and an endless supply of tea. Neither expected me to speak, work, or doing anything of consequence. Together, we mourned for those who had no one to mourn them.

Martin phoned on the second day. The discovery of the underground zoo had finally made the news that morning, and he'd wanted to check on me.

"Emma, we saw what happened. Are you alright?"

"Yeah, Martin. I just need a few days to myself, that's all."

"Understood. Well, *I* understand; Harrod's probably barrelling over right now to check on you." He sighed. "I probably should have thought to stop him. Sorry."

"It's fine. He wouldn't have listened." Cringing at the thought of Harrod turning up while I was in this state, I resolved to tidy up as soon as I put the phone down.

"Well, you're right about that. The man's an expert at ignoring the sage advice of his younger brother. Anyway, you take care and promise you'll let me know if you need anything, whether it's a cup of tea or somewhere to hide a body." I winced at his choice of words, but told him thank you. Just as I said goodbye, Harrod knocked on the door. *Typical.* Letting him in, I wrapped my shawl around me to hide a coffee stain on my shirt, then collapsed back into the chair I'd been hibernating in. Gibble didn't look up.

"Was it bad?" Harrod asked.

"It was terrible. I keep seeing it when I close my eyes. All the blood. The bodies. That girl, Harrod. The pain in her eyes, and what she'd endured... demi-fae are so beautiful, so graceful. To see one beaten down like that is just awful."

"It's over now." Harrod perched on the couch next to me, giving Gibble a timid glance as he did. "You've done your part and fulfilled your promises. You can start moving on, put it behind you."

I looked at him, confused. "Harrod, what do you mean? They haven't found the smugglers, just one buyer. I need to track them down, I need to find them and get the pup back to its herd."

Harrod sighed. "You have to stop. They're smuggling demi-fae, Emma, these people are dangerous. You're going to get yourself killed if you keep sticking your nose in this"

"Sticking my - Harrod, I'm trying to help stop monsters." For the first time in days, andrenalin surged through me. "They *took* a *demi-fae.* You know how serious that is, what it means. The Fae could go to war over it if they think we're not doing enough. The mortals don't know, they don't understand what war with them would mean. You can't seriously think I'm going to sit back and let that happen?"

"Why do you need to be the one to do it?" Harrod's voice rose and out of the corner of my eye, I noticed Gibble's ear flick. Harrod kept talking, oblivious. "Leave it to Greyson and his department, and to the Council. It's their job, not yours. You're not an officer, not a Lord, you're just..."

"The tea lady." I snapped the words out with more venom than I'd ever spoken. "Oh I get it, Harrod. You think I should stay here in my little shop and let the *important* people fix it, the clever Lords with their incredible Talent. I've got news for you - *they're not.*

They're not doing a damn thing to stop this from happening. Have you even *spoken* to Abnett to see what his solution was? He offered to increase my retainer. He's not devoting a single resource to this other than *me*."

When Harrod tried to speak, I slammed my fist into the table, cutting him off. "The police are doing more harm than good with bigots like Sturk getting involved, and Greyson's hands are basically tied dealing with him. Who does that leave, Harrod? Not the special people, not the mighty Talent Lords, people like me. People who run tea shops. Old gods. Boggarts. Even Martin's offering to help and all you can do is tell me to keep out of it?"

Taken aback by my outburst he tried to backpedal but I wasn't in the mood to hear it. I told him to leave and when he refused, I glanced at Gibble. When the boggart stood and took a few threatening steps towards him, Harrod finally understood I was serious.

He gave a bewildered glance to the creature he'd thought of as friendly, the one who'd once sworn to protect him... and who was now threatening to grab him by his perfectly stiff, white collar and throw him into the muddy gutter outside.

Harrod left, and I went back to sitting in my chair, wishing the pain would go away.

An hour later, I cursed as someone else rang my doorbell. Peeking through the window I cursed again when I saw Bee standing out front. I'd forgotten she was coming, though she must have arrived early. We'd scheduled for four o'clock and it was only... ah, hell, it was five past. Had I really lost the entire day?

I opened the door and called down for her to come up to my living quarters, then threw a few coffee cups into the sink and some clothes into the laundry basket. To say my flat looked 'lived in' was an understatement, but I couldn't muster up the energy to care.

Bee entered the room, looked around and gave a polite snort.

"Oh, Emmeline. I know you've been through a lot in the past days, but really…"

I glared at her through narrowed eyes, entirely prepared to give her the same treatment Harrod had received not long before.

"Don't look at me like a sullen child," Bee said briskly. "You have work to do."

"Work?" I asked.

Bee seemed surprised at my question. "Of course. You don't think this debacle is over, do you? The mortal police force that killed the poor souls in that place have set something off far bigger than they realise. Half the Other is ready to go to war over it."

My head dropped to my hands. "Bee, what can I do? I utterly failed at protecting even the barrow fiend. I got there too late and only because Greyson called me there. *He's* the hero, I'm just the useless bystander."

"You *care*, Emmeline. That might be just enough to save us, but not if you give up now. You returned the child, now save the pup. When it matters, you will make a difference. You *will* save them. For now, though, your tasks are somewhat simpler." She eyed me up and down, then shook her head disparagingly. "Get dressed. Brush your hair and wash your face. I can't work when you're in this state."

I did as requested. When I returned to the living room she had a dress of sombre charcoal and lace, adorned with small stones that looked like glittering tears. It fitted my mood perfectly. Bee fussed around, making minor adjustments.

"Is that buffoon of a Talent Lord behaving himself?" I rolled my eyes and she sighed. "Why is it that the more power a man has, the less wisely he uses it?"

"I don't know, Bee. I swear, he thinks I'm completely *incompetent*." She tactfully didn't mention I'd been feeling the same way. "I'm sick of him trying to wrap me in cotton wool and I want to slap him for his self-righteousness. At least Greyson can accept my choices."

Bee smirked. "And how is our esteemed Captain?"

"Oh, Bee." Pain welled in my chest as I remembered his visit. "You should have seen him the other night. He looked so... broken."

"The other night?" she asked, her smile deepening.

"Yes, he - oh, stop." Bee raised a delicate eyebrow. "It wasn't like *that*."

"And Harrod?" she asked.

"What about him?"

"Is he taking this well?"

"Bee, there's nothing to take! Harrod and I are just friends, though right now I'm hesitant to even call him that. The man needs to look around and realise he's not the only person in the room with half a brain, and start treating people like equals instead of misbehaving children."

"Well yes, there is that. The two of you need to work out your differences before the Gala." She caugfht my gaze, drilling her words into me. "You'll need to show a united front, no matter what's going on between the two of you."

The conversation lapsed and she continued to work, lifting my hair then letting it fall, pulling it over my face then pushing it back and holding up various pieces to see how they looked.

"Bee, why did you have to come today? You've never fitted a dress for me before, you just make them."

She was silent for a moment. "I wanted to check on you. You saw terrible things, Emmeline. You mustn't lose heart though; good things will come. Chin up, child. We're relying on you."

It wasn't until after she'd left that I realised she had booked the fitting weeks before. How had she known I'd need her that day?

CHAPTER FIFTEEN

Greyson stayed in touch over the course of the next few days. He'd made some progress on the information given to him by Markson, the rich socialite who'd been buying Otherworld beings on the black market.

Two more properties had been raided by Greyson's team, both belonging to socialites with too much money and not enough morals. Over a dozen creatures at each had been rescued and set free, shepherded back to the Other by Olfred with no casualties at either site.

There were few leads on the dealers though - word must have gotten back to them, as the abandoned factory Markson named as the meeting place burnt down the night he was taken into custody. The slimy little creep was now out on bail thanks to his deep pockets, but Greyson had someone keeping tabs on him.

Sunday morning I decided I needed a change of scenery and mind-set. I had to patch things up with Harrod, or at least give him the chance to set things right, so I sent him a message asking if he and Martin would like to join me for lunch. He responded almost immediately, leaving me rifling through nearly empty cupboards and wondering what I was going to serve. I picked up Lenny's lead and gave it a jiggle, causing the giant canine to jump in excitement and nearly topple a chair.

"Alright, alright. Settle down, we'll go in a second. I *suppose* we can pick you up a treat while we're out."

Lenny sat up properly and gave a happy whuff at the mention of a treat. We walked briskly - well, Lenny did and I trailed along as fast as I could manage. We wandered the market, picking up some cold meat, fresh bread, olives, cheese and other bits and pieces that took my fancy. Just as I was getting ready to leave for home, Lenny whined and gave a gentle tug at his lead. I looked over to see a rope of enormous sausages hanging in the window of a nearby butchers. Laughing, I headed inside.

"Can I have two pounds-" Lenny butted my leg. "Oh, fine, three pounds of the sausages please?" I asked the surly man.

He weighed them out and only just had enough to cover my request. Gruffly he asked for my money, then called out the back. "Oi, Ronson, you got more snags coming or what? You said they'd be out half an hour ago."

"Oh 'old up, they're comin'." A second man - Ronson, I assumed - backed through the swinging doors balancing a wide tray loaded with fat sausages. Lenny stood and I glanced down at him, surprised to see his hackles raised. He was growling, low enough that I almost couldn't hear it, but his chest vibrated on the side of my leg. Startled, I looked at the tray of meat, wondering what on earth could have upset Lenny. A muscled arm moved back and forth loading sausages into the refrigerated display case, a koi fish tattoo rippling across it as he worked. A quick glance at his face made my heart stop.

"Get that mutt outta here. Dog's ain't welcome in this shop, 'less you want 'im ending up in the window, if ya know wha' I mean." The tattooed man's voice was high and mean, and sent shivers down my spine.

"Sorry," I stammered. "He's just hungry. C'mon Len, we have to go."

Stumbling outside and around a corner I whipped out my phone to call Greyson. Words stumbling over each other, I told him what I'd seen.

"Emma, I want you to listen to me. Start walking, now. Don't rush, and don't look back. If they see you hanging around, they'll get suspicious. Go home, make sure no one follows you. I'll meet you there."

"Greyson, I can't just *leave*!" I exclaimed, then quickly darted a glance around and lowered my voice to a whisper. "He's involved, I know he is. What if he isn't here when you get back?"

"Safety first. Go, now. I'll send a car over to watch the place as soon as I'm off the phone."

Cursing at the thought of my target slipping away, I went to leave. Catching sight of a pastry shop across the road, a thought occurred. It wouldn't look at all out of the ordinary if I were to stop there first. I dallied, browsing the window for some time while I watched the butcher's in the reflective glass. Nothing.

I went inside, ordered some croissants, and made light, distracted conversation with the girl at the counter, who fussed over Lenny. Every few moments, my eyes darted towards the doorway, towards the butchers. Still nothing. Finally, feeling awkward, I stepped outside, just as the butcher's shop door opened. The tattooed man stood at the door. His eyes met mine, and narrowed. Losing my nerve at his glance, I looked away and strode down the street toward home.

I took a roundabout route, once doubling back on my path to see if anyone was behind me. Unable to settle my worry, despite the empty street, I finally got back to my shop and warded the door behind me, then shook my head at myself when a knock sent me running back down before Harrod set it off. Dammit, I'd forgotten all about lunch.

Harrod and Martin came inside, Martin stopping to kiss me on the cheek on his way past. He handed me a bottle of wine.

"A token of appreciation for putting up with my idiot brother," he said. Harrod raised an eyebrow at him. "And for lunch," he added.

"Yes, well, I suppose I do owe you somewhat of an apology for-" Harrod's cheeks were pink, making me wonder what Martin had said to him.

He was cut off by a honk as Greyson pulled up outside.

"I, er… didn't realise we'd have company." Harrod looked disappointed at the notion of Greyson joining us.

"Look, guys, I'm really sorry. Something happened while I was at the market. I saw - wait, I'll explain when Charlie gets in."

Martin cocked an eyebrow at my use of the detective's first name as I held the door open for Greyson to pass through, shaking off a smattering of rain that had caught him on his way inside. "Have you eaten today?" I asked.

Greyson shook his head at my question, then looked at Harrod. "I'll get something later. Don't want to put out your plans."

"They're out already," I assured him. "Come up, I can throw all this onto plates while I talk. Upstairs?" Trumping upstairs behind them, I gave my wand a quick flick to re-ward the door. Today was not a day for taking chances.

Upstairs, Gibble was sitting on my couch with a book. He stood when we entered. As I stacked five plates on the table and opened the paper packages I'd bought for lunch, I explained what I'd seen at the butcher shop.

Greyson helped himself to my kitchen, finding butter, knives and the last of a few beers I'd bought for him weeks ago when I'd asked him over for dinner He passed one to Martin, then held one out to Harrod, who shook his head. Before I sat, I passed a plate to Gibble, who had gone back to his book. He'd eat on the couch - my dining chairs were too small for him.

As he took the food from me, he gave me a piercing glance. The look was clear. 'Be careful'. My eyes dropped, aware that waiting after Greyson had told me to leave was a stupid move. As easy as it was to convince myself I was being clever at the time, my logic couldn't hold up to those eyes.

"This visit from the Guardian," Greyson said. "The one that showed you this guy. Not exactly the standard sort of Talent magic, that. Any chance there's something else to go on?"

I looked at him confused. "What do you mean? I can't prove what happened, not with physical evidence but I *saw* him. I saw his tattoos. I didn't imagine it."

"He means something admissible in court." Harrod didn't look up as he slathered butter on a roll. "It's not that he doubts you. Neither do I - I'm sorry if I gave you the impression I did. He can't get a warrant based on trust, though. The mortal courts have allowances for Talent based evidence but only if it fits specific criteria, and this... well, it's out of the ordinary even for us."

Greyson nodded, confirming what Harrod said. "We'll have to get at them somehow."

"I could go back," I offered. "Ask questions, pretend I want to buy something they'd trade in."

"Too dangerous. These people operate deep in the black market. A stranger off the street asking questions would ring too many alarm bells."

Lenny woofed and tipped his head. Gibble grunted and Lenny woofed again. Gibble sighed.

"Lenny-dog does offer to be going to the smugglers," he said. I froze. "He be the kind of thing they be wanting, with some help."

"What do you mean?" I asked in a hoarse voice.

"They be wanting Otherfolk, yes? Lenny be not of the this-world now, not all of him. The dressing-fae, Bee, she be able to make him look more Other. If you be willing, they be taking him and you be following."

Lenny whuffed again and wagged his tail.

"No." Were they joking? There was no way I'd risk Lenny, especially after almost losing him once already.

"We *could* do it. He wouldn't have to be in danger." Greyson said in a careful tone.

"*No.*"

"I'd help." Of course, the one time I needed Harrod to extoll what a stupid idea something was, he'd be on the wrong side. "Emma, I don't think they'd hurt him. He'd be valuable to them."

I turned on Harrod. "He's a *dog*. He doesn't understand any of this, I won't put him in danger."

"Lady, Lenny-dog..." Gibble shrugged, his wrinkled forehead bunching up as he tried to turn his thoughts into human words. "He not be the same now. He be understanding, it just be in a different way. He be knowing the danger and wanting to help the Other. He be knowing they did save him, and he be wanting to make things right. Lenny-dog does know we be keeping him safe."

"You know this?" I demanded. "You're certain?"

Gibble nodded. "Lenny be speaking in the way of the Others. Gibble be hearing him and he be wanting to be brave. He be wanting to be like you, Lady."

Be like me. Brave? No, stupid and headstrong and mad as hell at anyone who got in my way. Damn dog. He still sat there, wagging his tail at me with eagerness in his eyes. The promise I'd made to Olfred was because of Lenny, how could I risk his life to keep it? *Because his reason for offering is exactly the same as mine,* I thought. Ah, hell.

"How would it work?" I asked, still unsure.

"Tracking device," Greyson said. "We can wire him up so we know where he is at all times. We'd follow close behind. As soon as they take him, we've got grounds for an arrest, but ideally we'd wait to see if they lead us to their warehouse or a hand-off point. If we can let them - *safely* let them - give themselves enough rope, they'll hang the whole damn organisation. We might be able to shut them down completely and recover any livestock they still have."

"But you could pull him out early if you had to?" My stomach twisted at the thought of agreeing to this ridiculous idea, knowing the alternative meant leaving the barrow fiend, and countless other creatures, at the mercy of monsters.

"Of course." Greyson reached over the table to squeeze my hand. "We wouldn't risk him just on the off chance they lead us to something."

I looked at Lenny, who stared up at me with the same hopeful eyes that usually just wanted me to share my sandwich. What Gibble said was true - he wasn't a normal dog any more, I'd known that for a while. Barg was certainly able to speak to him, and he understood my words to an uncanny extent. Harrod reached across the table and put a hand on my arm.

"Emma... whether you do this or not, you've got my full support. I'll help in any way I can. I really do want to make it up to you."

At Harrod's words I closed my eyes. "Is there another way?" There was silence. "Alright. Only if I'm there with you every step of the way. I want to know what you do, every second."

Greyson nodded and Lenny trotted over to nuzzle his hand. Greyson smiled and gave him a rough pat, then slipped a bit of ham under the table for him.

"And none of that," I said, throat tight. "You'll teach him bad habits."

Greyson left us to continue our lunch while we waited for his call. It came a few hours later. The sting was set up for the following afternoon. Lenny would hang around the butcher shop for a while before closing, hopefully catching the attention of the smuggler I'd identified. He would appear to be alone, and made up so that they wouldn't pick him for the dog they'd seen the day before.

With luck, they would take the opportunity presented by a stray Otherworlder, and a quiet street at dusk, to snatch him up and take him to wherever they kept their unsold animals. So much depended on luck, and I shuddered, thinking of what could happened if it turned sour.

$\sim$

The next day Greyson, Trainor, Martin and Harrod all arrived at my place at lunch time. Trainor immediately remarked on the wonderful job Bee had done that morning to make Lenny look like an Otherworlder.

She'd smoothed the hair along his back but roughed it up near his head, giving the appearance of a shaggy mane. Dark marks provided contours to give his already long body a supine appearance, and his normally brown eyes were now an unearthly shade of green. The changes weren't extreme - they were subtle enough that he could run the streets without frightening people, but anyone who looked closely would be easily convinced he was Other. Trainor ran a finger along his coat then examined it.

"Bee said it won't rub off," I explained. "It'll fade after a day or so though. Will that be long enough?" I asked, part of me wishing someone would say no, Bee's work would entirely unsuitable and the whole plan would need to be cancelled.

"Sure, we won't leave him in too long. He'll be fine, Emma, we'll make sure of it." Trainor gave me a reassuring smile, and I tried to convince myself she was right.

After a quick bite - or on my part, a slow shuffling of some food on my plate that ended up going to Lenny - we started talking logistics. Trainor explained how the tracking device would work. It was a small box with an aerial protruding from it, attached to a bright red collar.

It looked garish and obvious, but when I pointed that out, Trainor smiled and snapped the clasp shut. As soon as she did that, my eyes slid off the tracker. Even though I knew it was there, I couldn't make myself look at it. Even touching it, my fingers ran over the woven nylon collar, but dodged over the box. To someone who didn't know its little trick, they'd never notice it.

"Who traced the spell for you?" I asked, but Trainor just placed a finger on her nose, grinned, and shook her head. "Not even a hint?"

"If I told you I'd have to kill you," she said in a serious voice.

She explained that, though they could track it from a few miles away, the accuracy was far better over short distances. That, added to the need to be close enough to snatch Lenny back if something went wrong, meant they'd have officers undercover watching as long as possible. We would trail them from a few blocks away. She took the collar back off and set it next to the computer they would sync it to.

"Emma, maybe it would be best if you stayed behind. They know what you look like." Greyson's face didn't hold much hope that I'd agree, and my raised eyebrows met with a defeated sigh. "Oh, fine. But you need to stay out of sight, and you *have* to do what I say. You'll need to trust me, Emma. Can you do that?"

"Of course," I said. "I know you've done this before. If I didn't trust you, I wouldn't have let Lenny help. I need to be there though; I need to know he's safe. I promise I'll keep out of the way." *As long as Lenny is safe,* I silently added.

We met the rest of the team an hour before the operation commenced, crowding into a coffee shop that looked so much smaller with a large boggart perched on a chair in the corner. Harrod and Martin were both already there, tucked into a tiny table and generally looking like they didn't belong. Despite feeling like a goose, I took Lenny aside and had a chat with him.

"Are you absolutely sure you want this, Len?"

"Wuff." He wagged his tail.

"I'll be close by, ok? Anything goes wrong you get the hell out of there, I don't care *who* you have to bite to do it."

"Wuff." A wet tongue made for my face and I ducked, laughing. Wrapping my arms around his lithe, wiry body, I prayed nothing would go wrong. I stood to go back to the others and nearly fell over when something cannonballed into the back of my legs.

"Apologies, Lady! Barg did not see you, Lady!" He rolled over to Lenny and jumped on his back.

"Barg, what are you doing here?"

"Barg is Lenny-dog's protector, Lady! Barg will join the humans in their quest for most glorious victory! Barg understands the chief headquarters will be at this place of warm beverage consumption, Lady! Barg will be most pleased with offerings of chip-chocolates for his involvement in this proceeding." Barg grinned at me, then added a belated, "Lady!" He saluted from Lenny's back, then nudged his bony knees into Lenny's sides. Lenny rolled his eyes back then trotted over to Greyson and his team to be fitted with his collar.

"I take it you weren't expecting Barg?" Harrod asked, startling me. I hadn't seen him come over.

"No. How did he even know we were here?"

Harrod grimaced. "I have no idea. Gibble didn't-" he stopped when I shook my head. "Oh. Well, I just hope he had the sense not to tell anyone else."

"I might have a chat with him, see if he'll tell me how he found out we'd be here. Not good if news about a covert op is being passed around the Other."

Greyson, finished with Lenny, ambled over. "Where are the undercover people?" I asked, cringing at the nervousness in my voice.

"They're undercover. You won't see them, but they're there. I trust my team; they do good work. We won't let anything happen to him, you hear?"

Nodding, I clasped my hands behind my back to stop from fidgeting.

"Right. Trainor, you're my right hand. If I go in, you're running things from here." Trainor nodded, all trace of her earlier easy demeanour gone. Her shoulders were set and her eyes bright, eager for the responsibility she now had. "Steenson, I want you monitoring the GPS and radio, filtering the information from our plants and keeping me informed."

Steenson, a wiry, grizzled man, nodded from where he sat by several coffee tables shoved together and laden with equipment and screens. Much to Barg's delight, I dug in my bag for some coins and bought him a chocolate chip muffin. I set him up under Gibble's watchful eye and hoped he could manage to stay out of trouble. Barg had the best of intentions, but I didn't want him getting in the way of the experts.

Lenny turned his face up to me, waiting for permission to go. Giving him one last pat, I set him loose. He bounded out of the small shop and rounded the corner, out of my sight. A few minutes later, Greyson beckoned me over to where he and Steenson were sitting. Crowding in to look over his shoulder, I could see three small screens - one was the GPS tracker, one had a jumble of text information and the third showed a TV screen. On it was a jittery picture of the butcher's. Greyson nodded to it.

"This camera's on one of our plants. She'll keep a visual as long as possible. It's the only one we could get for the department, but it comes in handy."

The image moved, swaying up then down as the officer with the hidden camera moved slightly. Then, I saw Lenny. He wandered down the street in a random fashion, sniffing at the ground and shying away from passers-by. His movements were smooth and graceful, almost feline.

I wondered how he'd managed that. Perhaps Bee had given him some kind of enchantment without telling me. As he passed the butchers he sniffed at the meat hanging in the window. He lingered just long enough to catch their eye, then retreated. He strolled down the street, sniffing the air, then went back, repeating the move several times. Each pass looked entirely random and authentic, like a stray animal attracted by the smell of fresh meat but wary enough to stay away from the people around it.

We waited, and watched. Minutes crept on into hours, and the few officers left inside the cafe wandered about, restless. Martin stretched out across a bench seat, while Harrod frowned at his indecorum. On the small screen in front of me, Lenny eventually settled into a lazy ball by the door.

Twice, he was disturbed by customers stepping over him to get into the shop. Once, a man in a dirty white apron came to shoo him away. Upon getting a closer look at Lenny, however, he paused. The man ducked inside, then came out with a bone and threw it to him. Lenny darted into the air to catch it, then sat chewing it by the front window of the shop.

Finally, dusk started to creep over the city. Lenny had moved his position to across the road from the shop. He wasn't visible on the small surveillance screen, but the camera had turned twice to give us a brief glimpse of him rolling on the pavement and snapping at flies. I hoped he didn't ruin Bee's work.

The butcher's door opened. A low, female voice said, "Target moving." Lenny strolled past, giving no sign of being rushed as he wandered into the middle of the street. He turned his head to look at the officer. The setting sun glinted off his eyes, making them glow a fiery green. His hackles were up, tail switching in a very lionesque sort of way.

A man appeared in the doorway of the butchers, standing very still. Lenny didn't move any closer, but yawned and stretched. Then, padding over to the window again, he sat looking up at the last bit of meat still hanging there. I heard a whistle. The man stepped forward and turned his head to Lenny, showing the small tattoo on his cheek. *Ronson*. Lenny perked his head up at the man watching him and Ronson held a hand out, dangling a bit of steak.

Lenny twitched his head in interest. His eyes followed the meat that was swinging from Ronson's hand. Lenny stood, edged closer, then shied back. He played at this for a few minutes. Then, he lunged to catch the piece of steak that was thrown at him. Ronson stood back and watched him eat.

"Why is he just watching? I thought he'd be trying to get closer." I glanced over to Greyson when he didn't answer.

His brow was creased and the corners of his mouth down-turned. A terrible thought occurred to me and my eyes darted back to the screen. I watched as Lenny, meat gone, took a few wobbly steps towards Ronson, then went sideways. He turned, dragging his feet and pulling himself away with an effort. Then, he fell to the ground.

"Lenny?" My voice was panicked. I stood, but Greyson grabbed my wrist.

"Wait. They won't hurt him, he's worth more alive. Just wait."

Ronson called out, words too indistinct to make out. A second, unfamiliar man emerged from the shop carrying a large sack. Together, he and Ronson laid it flat on the ground, rolled Lenny onto it, then lifted it like a stretcher. They disappeared back inside. A minute later the second man came outside and looked directly into the TV screen. I shuddered and my breathing quickened. He walked over to the undercover officer with quick strides.

Dropping bag in front of the lens he said, "Ya didn't see nuthin', roight?" He leaned forward as he spoke, the side of his face moving close, obscuring our vision. It took me a minute to figure out what he was doing and when I did, I nearly retched.

"Nuthin' ter see. Oi, what am I s'posed ter do with a bag o' sausages?" The woman's voice was hoarse and a little slurred.

"Take 'em ta the shelter off Church. They'll let ya cook 'em there."

"Stingy bastard."

The man disappeared back inside.

"I swear to God, Greyson, you fucking owe me for that," a muffled voice said quietly through the speakers next to me. It made me jump, for it sounded nothing like the voice from a moment ago.

"You good, Sallaway?" Greyson said, after clicking a button on the mic in front of him.

"I'll live. You still owe me." She sounded unimpressed.

"If we take him down, I'll kick him in the balls for you."

"If you bring him into custody I'll do it myself."

Greyson barked a laugh. "You're a lady, remember."

"Fuck you, Greyson."

The last was said with a quiet chuckle. Greyson glanced over as if remembering I was there, and blushed.

"Oh. Ah, Sorry 'bout the language. Comes with the job."

One corner of my mouth lifted in response and he smiled back, then ducked his head back to the video screen. It wobbled sickeningly, turning to one side then righting itself. Sallaway was lurching down the street. Then, she stopped.

"What is it?" I asked, as Steenson made the same query over the radio. Harrod glanced up from across the room at the alarm in my voice, but didn't intrude.

"They're going by car." Sallaway explained, just as the camera turned to show an old Volvo chugging down the street away from the shop. I closed my eyes and took a steadying breath. Greyson twisted his head up to look at me.

"It'll be fine. We accounted for this. They won't be moving too far, operations like this tend to keep things close. We've got people stationed in each direction, they can move in quicker than Sallaway can catch up. If they see her again they'll think it's strange, so someone else will take point now. Steenson, where're they headed?"

"Toward the river, Boss." The radio crackled and went silent as Steenson clicked off.

"Myles?" Greyson asked.

"No," Steenson said. "Beefcake's closer."

Hurried words passed over the radios, passing directions to several officers including Beefcake. Then, Steenson said, "Looks like they've stopped. Hang on, let me check the location. Trainor, you ready?" He rattled off an address as Trainor clicked at a small computer in front of her.

"It's a warehouse, Captain. Belongs to a C. M. Smith. Er... dog food, it says here."

Well *that* was reassuring. Backing away from the monitors, I took a seat, clasping my hands in my lap and reminding myself to stay out of their way. My instincts screamed at me to run for the warehouse, ploughing through anyone who stood in my way. Instead, I sat quietly, body as tense as a violin string.

"Ok, they're stationary now. No eyes on the target, Captain."

The next fifteen minutes were fraught with tension. The tracker was stationary, and the officers watching outside saw no movement in or out of the building. As the weight in my stomach grew, I turned to Gibble.

"Gib, if something happened to Lenny... would you know?"

He shook his head worriedly, then turned to Barg.

"Little friend, you do be knowing the Lenny-dog. You be telling the truth, for this be of great import."

Barg shuffled his feet, looked at the floor and twisted his hands. Gibble made a low rumbling sound and Barg winced, bony arms covering his head defensively.

"Barg be so sorry, Lady! Barg be taking the Lenny-dog to the racing and we did be winning so many, but then we did be put against another and his rider, they did be joined and there were so many chips against us, Lady! Barg has never been seeing so many chips! None did expect us to be joining, and... we did make *so many chips*!"

Dismayed at the angst in his voice and completely lost by his explanation, I turned back to Gibble for an explanation. Barg couldn't lie but I'd found he was *very* good at dodging the truth. Gibble sighed.

"The racing do be a thing of the Others, Lady. A rider and his steed be set against another pair, and who wins does be getting a cut of the winnings. Barg do be bad at the wagering - when he did stop coming to ask Gibble to be saving his wrinkly skin, Gibble did be wondering."

"What did he mean by joined?" My words were tight, angry. Barg whimpered and edged under a table.

"It be a thing of the racing. A rider may join his steed, or it may be the steed who joins the rider if it be choosing so. It do be making them run faster, but it be a thing that, once done, be done for all-time."

I turned to Barg and he cowered. "*All time?* You did something to Lenny and you can't undo it *for all time?*" My voice made the hobgoblin squeal in fright.

"Lady," Gibble's voice held a tone of moderation in it. "The thing Barg has done, does not be harming Lenny-dog and could not be done without his consenting. Perhaps, Lady, it do be a boon in this-time. The bonding be joining their souls, a tiny part of each be put in the other one. They be knowing if their bond-mate be hurting, or be in danger. It be a good thing on this day."

"Harrod?" I snapped. "Do you know about this... joining?"

Harrod, who'd been watching the exchange while Martin snoozed beside him, shook his head. "Sorry. I know *of* the process, but hardly anything about it. It seems to be fairly common though. I don't imagine it would be if it was harmful."

"Lenny-dog is safe, Lady," Barg was quick to say. He'd manoeuvred himself so he was standing a little behind Gibble. "Lenny-dog, he did want the bonding, he did tell me himself before Barg even did suggest it Lady! Barg swears! Lenny-dog is Barg's mostest of friendships and Barg would *never* be doing hurt to him!"

Being Other, he couldn't lie. I believed him... Mostly. "Is he safe? What can you tell me?"

"Lenny-dog is safe, Lady!" Barg saluted. "Barg would know if Lenny-dog hurts, or fears, or finds a life-mate."

I pulled a face at that. "But you don't know anything else? If he's unconscious he might be in danger, but not afraid."

Barg cowered. "Lady, Barg is sure Barg would be knowing if Lenny-friend would be in the danger, even if Lenny-friend did not know himself. Barg would never let Lenny-friend be hurt, Lady." His pointed ears drooped and he looked at me with big, mournful eyes.

Letting out a growl of frustration, I turned back to Greyson.

"So what do we do now?"

The cafe door banged open, making me jump. A shabby figure with a small, overloaded shopping cart pushed through, grumbling obscenities under her breath. No one else in the room reacted. Parking the trolley in a corner, she proceeded to remove her large, grime encrusted coat and pull off her oversized trousers to reveal a pair of black tights and a singlet top underneath. Both were thankfully clean. Greyson tossed her a small duffel and she opened it, pulling out a woollen dress, hairbrush and some other toiletries.

"Next time you want someone to dress like a hobo, you might consider doing it yourself Captain. I think I've got fleas. You gonna foot the bill for the spa treatment I'll need to get this shit out of my hair?" The woman's voice was prim, but I recognised it from the radio conversation.

"Oh come on Sallaway, you know you love a chance to get dirty," Greyson said.

"I'm a lady. Ladies don't like dirt. Asshole."

Sallaway walked over to the table and slapped something down. She looked at me.

"That's a smart pooch you've got there, and one hell of an actor. I found these after they left." On the table before her sat two slimy pink pills, one with a tendon of meat hanging off it.

"That's what they spiked the meat with?"

"Pretty sure." She used a wipe to scrub at her face and ears. "I saw him flick them away when our perp turned away for a moment, so I checked on my way past. He's not out - smart ass dog winked at me as they carried him inside." She stopped talking for a moment, as she pulled the dress over her head. "Since when do dogs wink? Anyway, I thought you'd feel better knowing."

"I do. Thanks." I let out a small, relieved breath. Knowing of Barg's bond with Lenny - something that had offered some reassurance despite making me entirely furious - and finding out he'd duped the dog-napper made me feel a lot safer.

Now that Sallaway was dressed and clean, she looked... *wow*. Neat hair in a bun over a sedate grey dress, stockings, small heels made her look like an upper-crust lady. She clasped a striong of pearls around her neck to complete the look. The woman oozed class and elegance in a way that was completely at odds with her language.

"Cap, they're still not moving. You think we should make a move?" Trainor piped up from across the room.

"Too risky without eyes in the building," Greyson replied. "Tell Myles to hurry up with that. They might be waiting for another contact to move him somewhere else. Did we get any more on the premises?"

"HQ sent through blueprints, but they're at least thirty years old. They could have refitted the interior, there's room in there for sure. Latest we have is three levels inside, mostly open areas. Used to be a textile workshop, owner went bust a decade ago. Now owned by..." She checked the notepad in front of her. "Extension Applications Incorporated. The dog food company is one of their smaller arms. Can't find a scrap of useful info on any of them."

"We need a visual, dammit. How many do we have in the vicinity now?"

"Nine, sir." Trainor said. "Straud and Banksy on the way now. Will I send them in?"

"No." Greyson shook his head. "We need to keep a few men out in case they move again. What's the holdup?"

"Beefcake said there's a ward up."

Harrod perked up. "Who's Beefcake?"

"One of our half-bloods," Trainor explained. "Hardly any actual power, but he can sense the presence of a ward from about twenty feet. Can't tell what they do, but it's saved our skin more than once."

"Esteemed Captain! Barg can go, Barg is *very* good at sneaking!"

Greyson shot me a glance over his head. He looked dubious.

"Barg, do you have hiding powder?" Greyson asked.

"Pah! Barg can't afford that, hiding powder is forty-seven chips for a squinch! Barg can be careful though, jumping on roof with quiet feet and peeksing in a window from up high. Humans, they don't look up high. They do forget about us sneaking ones."

Greyson looked at me, and I shrugged. Barg was fast - *really* fast. I'd seen him dodge the grasp of many a creature faster than humans. He seemed to attract that sort of attention a lot, and over the years had become adept at avoiding it too. I told Greyson what I knew of Barg's ability and added that though he ran riot on his own, he was good at following instructions.

"You're on point, Trainor. What do you say?" Greyson asked.

"Well, we're still on sketchy ground for a warrant. If we wire him up with a mic and camera, that could get us enough to go in clean." She looked at me. "You're sure he can get out in a hurry if he needs to? If something goes wrong, we're responsible."

"I'm sure." I shrugged. "And look, if we're honest? Your higher ups aren't going to give a damn if something happens to him, or to me."

Trainor looked at me. "Just so happens *my* superior *does* give a damn. I don't give a toss what the rest of the department thinks - I work for Greyson, not them, and I care as much as he does. I won't send him in unless you tell me it's safe."

I met her eyes. They shone with honesty and I nodded, satisfied Barg would be taken care of. Within a few minutes he was wired up and looking as though he'd just won an award. I hoped he could reign in his excitement enough to get the job done safely.

One of the screens flickered to life and we could see through his eyes, or at least through the pin on his shoulder. A mic was attached as well, though Steenson didn't manage to get the earpiece to stay on. Barg instead draped the cord around his neck and promised to hold it to his ear every few minutes to check for instructions.

Off he went. The camera sped through the street, bounding off walls and scurrying around corners. Once in sight of the building, he stopped. A shadow passed at a window, then he shot up the side, an occasional hand coming into view, digging gnarled fingers into impossible handholds.

Trainor looked worried.

"Captain? Looks like we've got a mic problem, I'm not getting audio."

"It was working when he left. He didn't turn it off?" Greyson frowned.

"Says it's transmitting."

"Maybe there's just nothing to hear," I suggested.

"It's highly sensitive," Trainor said, shaking her head with worry. "We should be hearing his steps, movement, breathing. I've got the sound at max and there's nothing."

"I think you're underestimating him. He can be pretty damn quiet," Harrod said. He'd joined me, peering over my shoulder at the video feed.

Trainor looked unconvinced until a deafening voice boomed through the speaker. She and Steenson both lunged forwards and fumbled the volume down to a bearable level.

"...the back. You know, the blue thing? Give it a poke and see if it's still kicking."

The voice was muffled then trailed off as Barg climbed to the roof. Once secure, he stopped and a hand fumbled around in front of the camera.

"Officer Lady, Cappy-tahn, are you hearing Barg? Over?"

His voice was a raspy whisper.

"We hear you Barg. We can see you're on the roof. What's your plan?" Trainor asked.

"Officer Lady, Barg is feeling the Lenny-dog most closely at the bottom-most of the building, in the rear-end corner. Barg is very near to being on top of him. Over."

"Barg, see if you can get a look inside," Trainor said. "All we need is proof they're holding Others in the warehouse and we can go in. And Barg? You don't have to say over."

"Yes, Lady! Over and quiet!"

The video screen waved around as Barg plucked it off his shirt and held it out so we could see him salute. I shook my head in exasperation while Trainor snorted softly.

Another wobble of the camera and he was off across the rooftop. There was barely a scrape as he shimmied down a pipe, jumped to a windowsill, dropped to the ground and peered inside.

"Psst. Lenny-dog? Barg has come for rescuing you!"

"Barg, you're only there to look. Don't go off half cocked, you'll jeopardise the operation. Just show us what we need and come back, ok?" Greyson had a note of worry in his voice.

"Yes, Boss-arini! Barg will follow the illustrious leader and all his demands!" Barg's voice was a loud whisper and I cringed, wondering if he'd be heard. "Lenny-dog, Barg has a serious mission to be completing, yes? You be waiting for his triumphant returns."

Creeping back from the window, Barg scuttled along a ledge to the next window. It was dark inside and nothing moved when he softly called.

"Ah, Officer Lady? Barg is feeling something in this room. When the cavalry does descend, please bring ones who can help this one. It does not heed Barg's calls."

Trainor glanced back at Greyson, eyes worried. Gibble signalled me, then quietly left the cafe. Greyson looked at me, surprised.

"He's gone to get Olfred," I said quietly. That the old god was needed again was a sad, sad thing. Harrod put a hand on my shoulder and squeezed.

The image on the screen was suddenly filled with light. Barg looked to be peering through a window, bars crossing in front of the camera lens and obscuring the visual for a moment. It was a small room, bare and dirty with a tree branch propped against one wall.

Sitting on that branch, tail wrapped around to hold it steady, was a miniature albino dragon. Its wings were held tightly against its body, making it sit awkwardly. Black eyes swung to the window, directly at the screen as a serpentine mouth opened, tongue flicking out to taste the air.

"Gods," said Harrod, face white.

"Got it," said Greyson, smiling in satisfaction. "There's no way that's legal – you can't even get a permit for a dragon. Right boys. We ready to go take these bastards down?"

We waited by the radio with Trainor as the task force entered the warehouse grounds. Barg, perched atop the roof again, watched black-clad officers run silently around the corner in single file, then peel off to surround the building. Our eyes were up front, where Greyson would take the main entrance with four of the team. Trainor explained that each officer held a small, warded stone designed to disrupt any nearby wards. They would be kept safe from any traps laid, but if a warded alarm was set the person who created it would know it was down.

We watched the small screen as they stopped as one, waiting for the signal to move in. We watched as Greyson held up a hand, then let it drop. We watched a dozen armed officers advanced toward a building full of dangerous smugglers. Together we watched as, in a single motion, every one of those officers dropped to the ground, unconscious.

CHAPTER SIXTEEN

"Oh, God." Trainor's eyes were wide, her face white. "Greyson? Captain? Miles, Beefcake, *anyone*?"

Harrod and I glanced at each other for a heartbeat, then moved as one for the door. I grabbed the last transmitter off the table and dropped it in my pocket as I passed.

"Wait, you can't—" Trainor swallowed. "You don't know what happened to them."

"The wardstones failed, they're in danger." Harrod's voice rose as we fled into the street outside. Martin, woken by the noise, bolted upright and looked around, bewildered.

"Get backup," I called. "We'll let you know where to send them."

We arrived at the warehouse in moments. Stopping abruptly, we crouched behind the small brick wall and peeked around the corner to see four men, moving about in the shadows cast by the stark street lights. They approached the fallen officers one by one, crouching down to tie their hands and feet.

"Can you see anything?" If it was a ward, Harrod should be able to see it affecting the fallen officers.

"They've got guns," he said. "I think they're tying the officers up."

"I mean the *ward*, Harrod."

"Oh, right." He squinted and his eyes focused on something in the distance. "It's... different. It's not a trace I've seen before. I... don't think I can disable it from here." His voice lowered in shock as he spoke With a power as strong as his, it would be rare to come across something he couldn't fight.

"Then what do we do?"

"We wait for backup." Harrod sat back panting, eyes wide.

"Harrod, we *are* the backup. No one else is coming; I'll have to go in myself."

"What?" he yelped. "How are you going to get past the ward?"

"I can block it. Whatever this is I'm sure I've fended off worse. Where's the ward? If I can get to it, I can take it out. They'll wake up, won't they?"

"Emma, you can't even *use* your block!" He grabbed my arm, hard.

"That's Lenny in there," I spat. "And Greyson is lying on the ground outside, trussed up like a roast dinner. You think I'm not terrified? Pissed off at the monsters who did this?" I bared my teeth, unable to restrain my fury. "Harrod I've got a firmer grip on my power now than I've *ever* had before."

He looked at me for a long moment, lips pressed together. I expected him to tell me to stay, half expected him to try to force me. Instead, he let out a frustrated breath and said, "Barg."

"What?"

"Barg. Tell him you're coming; he might be able to help."

I put the ear piece in and clipped the tiny mic to my shirt. I turned it on and immediately heard a voice.

"...answer me, dammit. Harrod? Emma?"

"Yeah, it's me, Trainor. There's a ward, it took everyone out. Harrod can't dispel it but I think I can get past. I'm going in to see if I can shut it off."

"Is that safe?" she asked.

"If I don't, you've got an entire team of officers lying helpless on the ground for god knows how long. It's the safest option we've got."

Trainor didn't miss a beat. "Right. What do you need from me? Barg's still up top, scene looks about the same as when you've left. No movement."

"Tell Barg I'm going in."

A light click sounded in my ear, then, "Barg I've got you patched into Emma. She's coming in."

"Ah, Lady is very brave! Very sensible Lady. Little-man is staying behind?"

"Yes." Trainor snorted and I had to stifle a nervous giggled. I had no idea why the Others in my life insisted on referring to Harrod as 'little-man,' but the name had stuck. I was glad he couldn't hear my conversation.

"Ah, that is most sensible of him. Lady may pass the sleeping ward but little-man would be like a snoring snootle if he did try."

"A snoo-? Never mind. Barg, can you scoot down and see if that window on the ground floor... the smaller building, the side facing us. I think I can get through there. Can you check it out without being seen?" I could get to that with little effort, and the window locked easy enough to climb through if it was unlocked. A smaller window on a higher level was directly above. I'd have to be quick, and hope for the best.

I heard no response, but peeking out from behind the wall I saw a small dark figure slipping down the side of the building. A moment later, he waved, and I headed forwards, ducking down and staying in the shadows so I wouldn't be seen. Power coursed through me, my gift in easy grasp while my adrenaline was peaked.

A few metres closer to the building and a prickling sensation washed over me, like wiggling ants being held against my skin. Shuddering but relieved I'd successfully blocked the ward, I continued forward. One of Greyson's men lay sprawled on the ground. Putting my hand to his cheek, I funnelled enough power into him that the blocking ward faltered. He stirred, and I moved away quickly, leaving him to drop back into slumber before he made a noise.

"He's alive," I whispered into the mic. "They should wake up once the ward is down."

"Thank God," Trainor replied, her voice thick.

A shadow passed on the ground where a patch of light shone down from the window. Heart beating so loud I was sure they'd hear, I froze, flattening myself to the ground and staying as still as I could. It passed and I waited five breaths before scuttling over to the wall. *Safety*. I let out the breath I didn't realise I'd been holding.

Barg waited for me at the now open window. He waved at it with a flourish then hopped through. I climbed in behind, tripping as I landed with a light thud. Wincing, I looked around. Small noises came from a distance, but no cries of alarm. That was a good sign. We were in what looked like an office reception, though it smelled like a poorly kept zoo. A quick shuffle of paper and a peek in some drawers revealed nothing of interest, and I was anxious to move on.

"Which way?" I whispered.

Barg pointed at a door leading to the rear of the building. Muffled noises came from that direction, sounds of banging and mumbled talking. Pressing an ear to the door, I figured the noises weren't coming from the adjacent room. Holding a trace in my mind and my wand at the ready, I gently pushed the door open.

It led to a short hallway, narrow and dim, lit by a single naked bulb hanging loosely from the ceiling. There was a door at the end, and one leading off to each side.

Letting out a breath I crept forward, Barg darting around my legs to point to the door on the right. A quick listen revealed silence. The door was locked, but I shook my head when Barg pulled a small pouch from his belt. I traced it open without much difficulty, cracked the door open, and slipped into the room.

The door snicked shut behind me and I jumped. Reaching a hand out to try the knob, a cold fear settled in my stomach as the handle didn't turn - it had locked again. *Breathe* I thought to myself, knowing I could unlock it with the same spell I'd used to get in.

I used my wand to trace a small globe ball of light and looked around the room. There was a door across from me, a table in the centre, and something hanging on the wall next to me. Bile rose in the back of my throat. Muzzles and restraints dangled from the pegs, along with several barbed choke chains and an assortment of leather harnesses. The noises I'd started to become accustomed to were clearer here, and I could make out scraping and banging and the low rumble of a parked truck.

"Come on, they won't stay down forever." The muffled voice sent my heart into my throat. "The boss would have a fit if we gotta leave any behind. Nah, nah, load the dog crate first. It'll fit better."

My chest constricted in fright. The voices were right on the other side of the door and from what they'd said, I only had a short time. Something clinked behind me and I spun around, ready to unleash a force spell. Barg was at the rack, holding one of the harnesses.

"Not nice, not nice," he whispered. "That would be fitting across a winged nulkin, Lady. Ooooh, Barg would like very much to use it on one of these humans."

His voice vibrated with emotion and his eyes flashed. For a bare moment he was not the funny looking little person that rode my dog like a jockey. No, he was a vicious demon, ready to unleash his fury on those who had hunted these innocent creatures.

He twisted the harness in his hands, snarling as if ready to strangle someone with it. Far from being disturbed, I felt the same urge. Anyone who'd treat a living being like this deserved to be strung up the same way.

"Barg, the ward?" That was my first priority. If we were caught before I could disable it, we were done for. Barg looked at me quizzically.

"Barg does sense it, Lady. So close."

I searched, looking at the floor, the table, the walls. It was while I was on the floor, looking to see if it had been drawn under the table, that I saw it. There it was, etched beneath the wooden floorboards of the upper level. Magic wouldn't interrupt it; my gift worked on me and anything I touched, but I couldn't use it from a distance. Hell, even full contact with it would probably only disable it until I took my hand off of it.

Cursing, I wished I'd thought to bring something with me to disable the ward, not relishing the thought of using one of the torturous devices on the wall. Barg, sensing my need, emptied his pockets, turning out a small stone knife. Thanking whatever power was granting me luck tonight, I nudged the table so it was directly under the ward and stood on it. I could just reach - all I had to do was change the ward enough to shift its meaning and the spell would be broken. I stood on the chair and reached up, steadying myself with one hand on the ceiling above.

The second door to the room slammed open.

"Where's the- HEY! It's the bitch with the dog!" Light from the open doorway flooded the dim room and blinded me. I threw my wand out and traced a spell, slamming the door closed. Instead of a lock, I made the handle seize. Maybe that would confuse them, just for the smallest moment. As he banged on the door and screamed at the others in the warehouse to get inside the room, I gouged at the hardened wood with the knife.

Barg jumped off the table and jammed a chair under the handle of the door we'd come through. I hadn't thought of that. Working furiously, I scratched as hard as I could. The crawling sensation on my skin vanished. Now, I just had to find Lenny, stop the smugglers, and get out alive. *Piece of cake.*

～

So far, there'd been no tell-tale noises at the first door. As I jumped down, Barg kicked at the chair he'd used to jam the door to dislodge it. We dashed out into the hallway, turning right to go deeper into the complex.

A door ahead slammed open and I reeled around to flee the other way. We fled back into the first room and through a side door. That led to another dark, empty room. A staircase ran off it, and I sprinted up the stairs

I raced across the wooden floor then stumbled to a halt. It ended in a platform, surrounded by a rail that looked out over the warehouse. If I'd kept going, I'd have ploughed straight through the flimsy railing and plummeted two stories onto solid concrete. A clattering on the stairs heralded my followers and I pushed a trace of power, aiming for the forehead of the first one up the stairs. My aim was good.

He tipped backwards, arms flailing, and fell back on his companion. Another judiciously aimed trace sent him tumbling a second time, though I staggered with the effort. He dodged the third spell, whipping his gun towards me and firing off a round as he ducked back into the stairwell.

Trainor's voice sounded in my ear but I ignored it. I backed up to the edge of the platform as the two started to close in, guns out. Barg darted towards him and he let off a shot as the hobgoblin slipped past and shot down the stairs. My head pounded and my stomach wanted to empty - my spells were getting wobbly and wouldn't have much power left in them.

"I think she's spent, mate," one of the men leered, then spat through the gap in his teeth.

I cast a shield, but it slipped away. Desperate, I tried again, shaking my head to clear the mind fog that was closing in. Gap-tooth feinted towards me and I let out a shriek, skittering backwards into the rail.

The second man gave a nasal laughed and walked forward, pointing his gun directly at my face as I stood trembling. "Be a shame to mess up this pretty thing. Wonder if we got a collar downstairs that'll fit her?"

A high-pitched war cry pierced the air as a large, dark object flew through over the railing. A ferocious beast with a very angry rider hit him in the chest, pinning him to the ground, jaws snapping at his face. The creature, with its supine body and ferocious mane of bristled hair, looked up at Gap-tooth and bunched its muscles, preparing to lunge.

Terrified, the smuggler backed up, tripped, and fell down the stairs. The one under the slavering dog had been knocked out by the fall. Lenny turned to me and I threw myself at him as Barg flipped off his back and gave a bow.

"Lenny! I was so worried about you." My words were muffled in his thick fur, my face buried in his shoulder as I heaved, trying to catch my breath. A wet nose snorted in my ear, then a growl rumbled from his chest. I looked up as he stood, then stated wagging his tail. Harrod burst through the doorway onto the platform, wand out and ready. Panting, he looked around.

"Oh. Everything ok? I heard you scream, I thought you'd been shot."

"Yeah. Lenny got here just in time." Harrod helped me to my feet and I sagged against him. He looked down at me in concern.

"I'm fine," I said. "Just overdid it. What's happening?"

"They're all awake - a bit confused, but they recovered quickly. Greyson's downstairs leading the raid." The sound of yelling corroborated that. It sounded like it was under control, but I waited until I heard his voice over the radio.

"Emma? Are you there?"

"I'm fine. Is it safe to come down?"

"It's safe. You're going to want to see this."

∼

Harrod held my arm as I went down the stairs, Lenny close behind. Barg simply vaulted over the side of the platform into the room below. Greyson met us at the bottom and led us back through the warded room and out the other side. It opened into a large area, the space filled with two removal vans and piles of crates, leashes and cages. An oversized side door was being opened by Greyson's men. Greyson himself beckoned me over to a cage that had been busted, iron bars twisted and bent. "What do you think did this?"

Lenny yipped, wagged his tail and sat on his haunches looking inordinately proud of himself. Greyson and I looked at each other. I said nothing. It couldn't have been... could it?

One of the officers called Greyson over to another door.

"Boss? You need to take a look at this." The young officer's brows were pulled together pensively.

The door led to a hallway lined with padlocked doors, small grated openings in each one. I peered through the first to see the tiny dragon curled up in the corner, wings tied back with a leather strap and pearlescent scales dulled by its confinement. Seeing the creature this close made my heart ache.

"It's ok, buddy. You'll be out of here soon." I pressed my hand against the grate but Greyson snatched it away as the creature darted for me.

Shaking him off, I put my hand back for the serpent to sniff. A forked tongue tested my scent, then tickled my palm. Through the touch, I could feel its thanks like a warm trickle alongside a searing desire for vengeance. I tried to open the padlock, but my tracing slipped off and sent zinging pain through my head. Harrod would have to deal with these if good old bolt cutters didn't work.

The next cage was standing open, as was the third. The fourth contained a feline, a large tiger-like creature with golden eyes that shone in the dim light. It regarded me seriously and flicked its tail as I passed.

The rest of the cages were empty. Two had straw and feeding bowls - Lenny growled at one of these - and two were pristine. Not being used? Harrod popped his head in down the end to tell us Gibble had returned with Olfred.

"Hey, can you open this for me?" I asked Harrod, gesturing to one of the padlocks.

"Yeah, sure I-" He stepped back in shock. "Er, there's a dragon in there."

I raised an eyebrow at him and he winced.

"If it burns the place down?" he asked.

"It won't. It's seen me."

"What do you mean, *seen* you? Is this thing dangerous?" Greyson asked, looking between us.

"'Seeing' is a term specific to the dragon species. If they see you, it means they've... well, they've sort of seen into your soul, and judged it. If you pass, they'll communicate with you, in a manner of speaking." Harrod interrupted his own explanation and looked at me. "You're sure?" I nodded, and he opened the cage, standing well back.

It didn't move. I approached the cage gently, holding my hand out again. The dragon dipped its head and I carefully reached back to undo the leather strap holding her wings down. I guessed it was female - the striking colour was rare in males.

"May I call you Pearl?" I asked as I removed the harness.

She dipped her head again in acquiescence. Stretching her wings, she gave them a solid flap but stayed on the ground. Even for a miniature, she was small, but I couldn't tell if that was her age or malnourishment. A high-pitched growl emanated from her throat. She sounded like a disgruntled kitten.

Darting her head forward, she latched onto my shirt with her teeth, tearing the fabric. Once attached, she used her grip to climb her way up my arm, the claws on her two feet digging in painfully until she was settled on my shoulder like an oversized bird. *Right, then.*

Greyson looked on in awe as she turned to examine him, leaned her little head in and cocking it to one side. A moment later, I heard a sudden intake of breath. For a moment, it looked like a tear was glistening in the corner of the detective's eye. He took a sudden breath, blinked, then shook his head as the dragon turned to nibble a strand of my hair. Hiding a small smile, I asked, "You ok there, Detective?"

"Fine, fine. That was..." Greyson shook his head again and laughed self-consciously. I didn't press him.

"I suppose you want me to free the giant predator beast down the end, too?" Harrod asked, peering down the short corridor.

"Please."

Lenny was already sitting by the cage door, waiting. He'd probably been playing chess with the thing, or doing calculus. Damned dog kept pulling out new tricks by the day lately.

Harrod sighed and went to the cage. Once unlocked, he pulled the door back and let the beast leave. It padded gently past us, giving Greyson a stare on the way through.

"Mind the cat, boys!" Greyson called out the doorway as one of his men started at the sight of a giant animal calmly padding through the warehouse. I moved to the doorway in time to see it walk directly over to Olfred, gently head-butt him, then walk outside. A leap and he was gone, hopefully to find his way back to the Other without running into any humans.

Catching sight of me, Olfred beckoned me over.

"Aye, it's good ter see ye, ye beautiful thing!" He reached forwards to scratch Pearl under the chin. She crooned in delight. "Ach, the bastards dinna take care of ye at all! No matter, we'll 'ave ye right in no time. Och no, ye canna sit wi' me, I've got work te do, ye silly creature."

He shooed her away as she tried to climb onto him and overbalanced, piercing my shoulder with her claws. Wincing, I tried not to move lest I make it worse, and she quickly settled back.

Olfred dug around in his magic bag and pulled out a length of cloth.

"Stop that, ye'll make her bleed," he chided the reptile. "Come on now - or ye can feed yerself next time ye shedding." She obediently climbed off. Olfred beckoned me down to his level and I kneeled. He bound the cloth over my shoulder and across my chest to pad my shoulder and make a secure perch for the dragonette.

As he worked, he told me she was one of his regular visitors, swooping in every few months for oiling and a meal. He'd noted her absence but had assumed she'd just not needed his tending. Once done, he lifted her back up to her perch. She wriggled, kneading the cloth with her claws.

"So, what's the verdict?" I asked Olfred.

He shook his head sadly. "They've no' been treated awfully, but they should'na be away from th Other like tha'. They're no' well, and they need to return. I can take them, and I can tend them, bu' if this dinna stop..."

Olfred heaved a sigh. Uneasy at the prospect of this continuing, I looked up to find Greyson and Harrod watching our exchange. Seeing my glance, they headed over to us.

"We lost a couple of the smugglers," Greyson explained. "One was the guy from the butchers, he grabbed a bundle and bolted. Two of my guys tried to chase him down but they lost him. The others aren't talking much, but it seems they're working for someone else, someone not very nice. They're scared, but we'll see what we can get out of them."

My blood ran cold. Harrod looked at me, concerned. "What is it?"

"He saw me." I didn't speak loudly, but both men reacted with worried looks. Setting his face, Greyson shrugged.

"Doesn't matter," he said. "We take care of our own. You'll have a full detail on you until we get this wrapped up. We *will* get them, Emma, I promise."

Harrod just put an arm around me and hugged, tight. "Look,

you've got the gala tomorrow night. We can talk to Abnett if you want, see if he can offer any protection. Mergime wouldn't let anything happen to you either - she's desperate to show you off as her student, and couldn't take the blow to her reputation if she let something happen to you." He spoke lightly, but his voice was tight and there was worry in his eyes.

Taking a deep breath, I tried to shrug it off. "I've got Lenny to look after me, and Gibble during the day. Do you really think anyone could get close with those two around?" I asked.

Gibble grunted behind me and I jumped. He must have come through the back way without me seeing. "Gibble be staying for the all-time, Lady. Gibble not be leaving for Other at moon-rise. Lady be right, Gibble and Lenny-dog will be keeping her safe." His mouth twisted into a comforting smile and I left Harrod's side to wrap my arms around the boggart.

Gibble had gone away at night for as long as I could remember. He'd never spoken about where he went or why, but I was sure it had something to do with whatever forces bound him to my family. They were present during the day, meaning he had to stay in our world and close to someone he was bonded to or to their home, but at night he was free to do as he wished. He took full advantage of that, usually disappearing into the Other as soon as dusk fell. The thought of making him give that up sat sourly with me.

It took some time for the operation to wrap up. Those who had been caught were charged and hauled off to the station. They would be transported to a special precinct that had been warded by the Talent Lords long ago, to make sure there were no attempts to break them out. While I waited for Greyson to give us leave to go, I sat curled in a corner with Gibble, Lenny, and the tiny dragon, who'd snuggled into my lap and gone to sleep as soon as we sat.

There had been more Otherworld creatures in the truck. It seemed that once the ward had been activated, the smugglers had tried to jump ship, taking as many of the animals as they could. Harrod explained that the cages of the dragon and the cat had been warded, strongly. Both animals had Talent of their own and would have been able to escape a normal cage. Whoever ran this operation had Talent themselves, but the men left behind had been left with no means of getting them out.

There was no indication of where the truck was headed, but Greyson was optimistic that at least one of the men they'd arrested would give up enough information to bring down the organisation.

"I'll have to get more help on this one," he said. "There's a few units I can pull in, ones I trust. They don't have the experience with Otherworlders that we do, but they know how to deal with organised crime. They'll help," he promised. I wondered if he was saying it for my benefit, or his own.

Eventually, Greyson gave us the all clear. By that time I was so exhausted I could barely stand. The effects of the Talent I'd overused was really taking its toll. Gibble helped me out to the car Greyson had organised to take us home. He settled me inside, waited until Lenny, Harrod and Barg had joined me, then said he'd meet us back home. Too tired to argue, I rested my head against the cold window and dozed, rousing briefly as we stopped to collect from the cafe Martin.

Gibble beat us home. Forcing myself to at least shower before bed - the dragon had drawn enough blood from my shoulder to ruin my shirt - I emerged to find Harrod fast asleep in my living room, stretched out on the couch.

"Little-man be keeping Lady safe," Gibble said, looking down on him fondly. "Gibble be staying, but am being glad he be watching when Gibble cannot." Then, he retired to the next room, small leather book in hand. I brought a blanket out for Harrod and draped it over him. Though I'd cursed the man often enough in recent weeks, tonight, I was simply glad of his friendship.

Chapter Seventeen

Nervously I ran my hands down the front of my gown, smoothing the fabric for the umpteenth time since I'd put it on. Bee tsked at me and fluttered around, readjusting the delicate belt chain I'd messed up yet again.

"Emmeline, calm your nerves, you've done this before. I swear, anyone would think it's your first time."

"My first what?" Distracted by my own thoughts, I barely paid heed to what she said.

"Your first Gala! Come, child, this isn't like you. What is it?"

Bringing myself back to the present, I heaved a sigh. "Sorry Bee. I've just got a lot on my mind right now."

"You *must* focus, Emma. Abnett wants to show you off as his poster child for the success of the new relationship between mortal and Talent. He's looking at some kind of official recognition, but for now it's vital that he make it known you work for him, for the Council. The Fae and the Guardians have yet to decide whether the taking of the child is the work of individuals, or a symptom of a greater problem. They will have watchers at the gala, to gauge the sentiment of the people. *You* will need to be on your toes."

"What do you mean, Bee, and what does it have to do with me?"

"You saved the child," she said casually, fiddling with my hair. "Did you do it for political gain, or because it was right?"

Whipping my head around to argue with her, I stopped when I saw her face. She knew why I'd done it. Trouble was, my self-imposed exile from the Talented community meant not many people knew my feelings on any of this. Some saw me as Abnett's pawn, others as a manipulative political player, trying to get my own people a foothold in the agreements that defined the rank and responsibilities between Talented, mortal and Fae.

"So, is Lord Harrod the cause of our distraction tonight?" Bee asked, her tone dropping.

"What? No, Bee. It's this damned smuggling case. It's getting dangerous."

"If you move your head like that again, you'll be wearing this gemstone up your nose. You knew the risks when you agreed to help. What has changed?"

"I didn't expect to run up against anyone this... it's bigger than I thought, Bee. They had a ward that even Harrod couldn't break."

Bee twisted another lock of hair and pinned it back. "And yet, *you* got past it with barely a thought."

"Yes, with a gift that's unreliable, uncontrollable and really not much use against big, scary men with guns." I winced as a pin jabbed me in the ear.

"You have a mortal dog charged with Otherworld magic and an overprotective boggart for housemates. A feisty little hobgoblin too, if I heard the story correctly?"

How *had* she heard the story? I wondered. "Bee, I appreciate what you're doing. I just think this is too much for me. Harrod was right, I'm not equipped to deal with something this dangerous. I don't have the Talent or the experience."

"And now we get to the crux of it. Emma, you are more than capable of taking this on, despite what your darling egotist boyfriend thinks. I know he hasn't a bit of faith in anyone but himself, but that doesn't mean he's right."

I sighed. I had to open my big mouth, didn't I?

"Bee, he thinks I'm useless. And he's *not* my boyfriend."

"Rubbish." Bee yanked at my hair again and I wondered what had gotten her in such a bad mood. "He thinks the world of you, and he is terrified of losing you. Of course, he's showing you that in the absolute worst way possible. Stupid human. Shall I talk to him for you?"

"Don't you dare!" I chided. The last thing I needed was someone else sticking their nose into an already complicated situation.

"I was only offering." Bee pulled away and nodded. "There. It's as perfect as it will be with you fidgeting like that."

I turned to look in the mirror. Rather than the charcoal gown she'd shown me earlier, this dress was a deep red. Plates of hammered silver formed the bodice, and the skirt was slit to the hips at either side to show glimpses of soft leather leggings as I moved. My hair was braided at the side like a Norse goddess, hanging loose at the back in long curls, dotted with tiny glittering gems. The stones ran onto my face, set on my skin to form a mask. It made my features look almost serpent-like. In all, it felt more like I was heading into battle than into a civilised gathering of nobles.

"He hasn't been too bad lately," I offered.

"That's exactly the problem. When he's saying silly things, you fight back, defend yourself. As soon as he starts to realise he's being ridiculous, you soften up and start thinking he was right all along." She turned me to face her. "You're stronger than you think. And smarter. You don't need Talent to be powerful Emmeline, you've always known that. Don't start forgetting it just because he's in the room with you."

After a moment deep in thought, I nodded. She was right - it was much easier to disagree with Harrod when I was mad at him, which to be fair, was a lot of the time.

Once she finished, she led me downstairs. Martin was attending the Gala tonight, courtesy of an invitation from one of the Fae. They really had been passing him around like a delicious treat, but he seemed none the worse for it.

Once his date arrived - Lavender, a Fae who, like most of them, dressed to her chosen name in cool amethyst - we drove to the Inner City and the Gala.

Taking a deep breath and gripping Harrod's arm tightly, I stepped through the ornate doors of the residence We followed the uniformed faske through to the ballroom and, once introduced, entered. Lord Stuckley had put on an incredible showing. Iridescent hummingbirds flitting through the dancers and ribbons of light twisted forth out of the instruments played by the orchestra. Dipping in a low curtsy to my partner, I began to dance.

"Your dancing has improved since our first gala," Harrod murmured in my ear.

"I aim to impress," I said lightly, trying to hide how hard I was concentrating.

Without warning, Harrod dipped me almost to the floor and I gasped. I slapped his shoulder as we came back up, almost losing my balance as he smoothly continued across the dance floor. He chuckled.

"Don't do that!" I chided. "I've improved, but only to the point where I'm not tripping over my own feet. Don't try anything fancy or I'll end up falling on my face."

"You need to give yourself more credit," he said. "You're doing wonderfully."

We continued, and I allowed myself to enjoy the music. This part of the gala was always my favourite. Free from the politics that usually came with the later part of the evening, the dancing was all about the spectacle.

Music, beautiful dresses, and the opulent surroundings dissolved my anxiety and brought a smile to my lips. Here, I was another person, in another world. Losing myself in the enchanted music, I let myself pretend I was only here to dance. That fantasy was rudely interrupted by someone tapping me on the shoulder and clearing his throat. At the same time, a loud *crack!* rang through the ballroom.

Bee stood facing a Talent Lord, who was now sporting a bright red handprint across his face. She spat in his face then stormed off, raising a flat hand at the faske who tried to offer her a glass on her way past him. Harrod and I watched as she disappeared, leaving her stunned target looking around for support. When he found none, his eyes dropped to the floor and he shuffled off through a side door.

"Oh, dear," Abnett murmured from behind me, breaking the silence.

I started, then turned to him, stammering. "I'm sorry, High Seat, I didn't-"

"It's quite alright, my dear. Didn't mean to startle you, I just came for a dance." He held out his hand for mine. Harrod resisted for the barest of moments, before giving a small formal bow. He stepped back, letting Abnett take his place.

"Who was that man?" I asked, then blushed at my rudeness. Abnett didn't seem to mind the informal address.

"The Lord is a tailor, quite a good one, in fact. He doesn't quite have our Lady Bee's flair, but the two seem to have struck up a bit of a rivalry." He looked down on me, making the loose skin of his neck form an extra chin. "Ah, dear girl. I'd hoped to have seen you before now. I trust everything you are working on is under control?"

Though Abnett danced well, he didn't have Harrod's skill at leading an inexperienced partner. Stepping quickly to keep from kicking his ankles, I dropped my eyes to concentrate.

"For the most part, my lord. We've shut down a portion of the smuggling operation, but the barrow fiend's mother died. We haven't found the baby." Abnett's steps were growing faster, out of time to the music.

"You're still looking? That case should be closed. The animal that was terrorising your people is gone, is it not?"

"It wasn't her fault; they took her baby. She was only trying to protect her young."

Abnett took a sharp breath at my words, pressing his lips together. "Still, that would make the case complete, yes? Your task was to stop the monster, *not* to faddle around with these so-called smugglers." His feet tripped over mine and I gripped his shoulder to keep from falling. He frowned at me as though it were my fault.

"With all respect, High Seat, these men are using unsanctioned portals into the Other, kidnapping the creatures there and selling them on the black market. I'm pretty sure that qualifies them as smugglers."

"Still," he said. "Not our business - or yours. Your official involvement in the investigation is over, I need you for more important things now."

"More impor-"

"*Please*, Emmeline." He spoke hoarsely and I looked up, seeing him properly for the first time that evening. He was exhausted, worn down to the point of breaking. Unease settled in my bones. "Please, for your sake and mine."

"No." My heart leapt at my audacity, but I couldn't back down. Abnett looked around frantically for a moment, then firmly took my arm and led me away from the ballroom. He took me through a side entrance and into a small room, the sound of the music now muffled and the light dim.

"Lord Abnett, I don't think you know what's at risk. The Fae—"

Abnett shook my arm and cut me off. "*Risk*? Child, you have no understanding of the word. Emmeline, they know who you are. You're in terrible danger, you simply must stop at once. Please..."

His face shone with a layer of perspiration and his eyes were too wide. Backing away, I glanced at the door. Abnett drew his wand. He traced a spell and a shimmering, transparent box appeared between us. Alarmed, I looked at him but he just nodded towards it. As I watched, a disembodied hand reached towards the box and lifted the lid.

Inside lay a pixie. She was dead. A scrap of paper fluttered out and the spell focused on it, swooping in until I could read the words.

There was a young girl and a boggart
Who thought they could step on my feet
They tried and they missed
They're next on the list
Along with the Lord on his Seat

I was saved from replying by the cessation of the music, and a small bell to signal the next phase of the evening. Sick to my stomach, I looked up at the noise just as Harrod appeared at the door, looking concerned. Upon seeing me with Abnett, his expression faded to relief, then worry as he saw my face. As I opened my mouth to speak, Abnett put a finger to his mouth. Snapping my jaw shut, I set my shoulders and walked out of the room, taking Harrod by the arm.

It took some time for everyone to finish mingling and find their seats. Dismayed to find dinner would be served in a formal dining room, everyone seated at the same long table, I said nothing to Harrod about what Abnett had shown me.

Martin and Lavender joined us at the last moment, just before another bell chimed to signal the beginning of the first course. The food was already set on the table, covered by large silver covers that were whisked away by piskes, replaced by others who flew around serving the diners.

The idea was good in concept but didn't work so well at a gathering this large. The piskes were rushed, trying to keep up with the demands of the guests and avoiding each other mid-flight.

"Wow. Stuckley clearly didn't think this one through," Martin muttered to me under his breath.

I shot him an admonishing look, then sighed. Regardless of what I'd just seen, life would continue as it had, for now.

"So when will the esteemed Lord Umbers host his own gala?" I asked, desperate for something safe to talk about. "You're well and truly back in society now, people will start to wonder if you don't host your own every now and then."

"Oh, I hardly think so." Harrod reddened. "Besides, it's a lot of bother, not to mention the expense."

"Oh?" Martin said. "This coming from the man who claimed he could out-do any other High Lord's attempt this year. You can't say something like that and not back it up, my dear brother. Besides, I'd love the chance to plan one these shindigs and I certainly can't host my own."

"Oh Lord Umbers, what a truly wonderful idea," Lavender gushed. "Of course Bee will insist on dressing the ballroom, and the dining hall of course. You'll have it at the golden manor, won't you? It's *just* the place for a party." Her purple eyes lit up and she sat back, lost in her imaginary party.

"Er, no. No, I really couldn't." Harrod picked up his napkin and waved it at Martin threateningly. "Don't you try and meddle in this Martin, you know I don't like this sort of thing. I don't even like attending the damn things. If I'm hosting it, I can't even leave early!"

He seemed positively flustered at the idea he may have to host his own gala, but I had a feeling Abnett would be pushing him into it before long. The thought of Lord Abnett made my stomach clench immediately. Harrod touched my hand briefly, and shot me a questioning look. There was nothing I could do except reply with a tight smile to indicate all was well.

Abnett gave a short, customary thanks to the attendees, and raised his glass after absentmindedly patting the perspiration from his face. We all returned the toast and he sat, the guests immediately tucking into the delicacies provided.

"Abnett looks nervous tonight," Martin commented.

"Mm. He smells it too." We all looked at Lavender, who shrugged and took another bite of her dinner, a vegan dish provided for the Fae attendees and those humans who preferred it.

"I saw you dancing with him Emma; did he say anything?" Martin asked to my dismay.

"No." My voice shook just the smallest bit. "I'm sure he's fine. He has a demanding position, it's sure to affect him to a degree."

Martin gave me an odd look, but didn't say anymore. Lavender whispered something in his ear and he frowned. The rest of the meal passed with little conversation and no one remarked on my untouched plates.

～

After we ate, we retired back to the ballroom. In our absence the room had been completely changed, set with soft furnishings and decoratively stacked books. I appreciated the low key end to the night - some gala hosts preferred to end with a show, or with more dancing and wine. The length of the events was enough that by the end, anything that required effort became exhausting and tedious.

We chose a spot by a large window and sat, talking lightly and watching the other guests. I drank my wine, wishing it was coffee to get me through the final hours, while I kept my eyes on Abnett.

He was heading towards me but had been waylaid twice now, by people wanting to speak to him. He disengaged and made a beeline for our little group. Setting my shoulders and ignoring the gnawing in my gut, I stood to greet him.

"Lord Umbers, I'm afraid I'm here to steal Emmeline away from you yet again. Martin, Lavender, I trust you're enjoying yourselves."

He leaned in to kiss my cheek. "The choice is yours, my dear," he whispered as his face grazed mine. My thoughts hadn't been far from the words left on the note since he'd showed me, but for a brief moment, the image of the dead pixie flashed into my mind. Her bloodless face and head that twisted in just the wrong way. Somewhere, deep within my fear, a spark of anger flared.

My mouth set and nerves steadied. It was as though having finally acknowledged and accepted the very real chance I'd have to give my life for this, my fear became irrelevant. It was still there; it just didn't matter. Abnett took my arm, then looked at me with sad eyes.

"I see. Then, lest I do not have the chance later, I'd like to thank you for your service to the Council, my dear. I think we made a good team."

He gave me a small smile, as together, we marched off to meet the masses. What followed was an evening of talking, of tedious politics interspersed by moments of fear, pride and anger.

We travelled the room, telling each group of guests the story of the raids, the smugglers, and announcing our vows to end them by whatever means necessary. Our words stirred hearts and many glasses were raised in our names, many voices clamoured to join our cause. Harrod had been right about Abnett - he had a charm, a way of speaking that roused people's spirits and made them want to be the centre of his world.

After speaking to the fourth group of nobles, I turned away to stifle a yawn. Lavender appeared beside me and took my arm, drawing me away from Abnett.

"Your High Seat made it known that he'd received a nasty little message about all this," she said in a gentle voice. "He *did* tell you, didn't he?"

When I nodded, she hugged me. "You are very brave, Emmeline Beaumarchais. Your father would be proud." She flitted off without a backwards glance, leaving me behind blushing to the roots of my hair. My father, the man who I'd looked up to more than anyone in the whole world, would be proud.

I watched Lavender greet Martin by a nearby door. He tipped his head at me and smiled as she took his arm. They wandered off into the gardens, heads close together.

"Shall we continue?" Abnett asked and I sighed.

"I suppose. I know these people are all supportive of us, High Seat, I just wish they'd offer something more than platitudes. Could you imagine how quickly we could take out the whole operation with an army of Talents hunting them down?"

"Small steps, Emmeline, small steps. One day, perhaps, we might even make a difference. *If* we live through this, of course."

The older man gave me a brave smile, then took my arm again. Off we went, trying to change the world one word at a time.

Finally, the night ended. Once Harrod, Martin and I had piled into the car, Martin's date conspicuously absent, Harrod turned to me.

"What did Abnett say to you in there? You've spent the whole evening looking like you just found a monster under your bed."

Leaning my head back on the seat and closing my eyes, I told Harrod and Martin what I'd seen. Harrod dropped his head into his hands, while Martin turned a little pale. His eyes flashed with approval when I added what Lavender had said.

"Where is she now, Martin?" I asked.

"She left earlier," came his cautious reply. "Said she had some business to attend to, something important. Do you think she's off telling the Fae about tonight's events?"

"Most likely." Harrod lifted his head, eyes red rimmed and creased with fatigue. "Emma... I know you don't like being told what to do, and I'm not... just, if you'd feel safer staying with us, you're more than welcome."

A smile touched my lips, the first real one in what seemed like hours. My heart went out to him, knowing he was trying so, so hard to be a good friend, rather than an overbearing Lord.

"Thank you, Harrod. For offering, and for not flipping out. I think we'll be fine. Gibble is staying with me nights and Lenny is... well, I think he's probably a bit tougher than I realised." The memory of his two-story leap up to the platform in the warehouse crossed my mind and I wondered what else the dog was now capable of.

"Alright." Harrod seemed unconvinced. "Either way, you'll need to let Detective Greyson know we may lose the support of the Council."

"You don't think Abnett will continue to help?"

He sighed. "No, he's not that brave. You know I'll do anything I can to help. I won't let you go it alone, but you really do have to take care. If they've gotten to Abnett, it means they can get to anyone; things are unsteady at the moment, so we've made sure he's under secure guard. If Serraceuse or Ronson got past that, who knows what else they're capable of."

"I didn't see anyone watching him." I frowned, sure that I would have noticed.

"Some of the guests were also bodyguards, you wouldn't have noticed them. They're circulating, taking turns at being close to him. It's the only way we could pull it off for an event this exclusive."

The politics of the Inner City baffled me at times. "I don't understand, what was special about tonight?"

"Tonight was all about being seen." Harrod sat back as the car purred along, explaining Abnett's latest strategy. "Tonight's gala was the first of several elite events - if you were lucky enough to get an invitation, you're one of special few, not just one of the rest. Did you notice everyone there was a supporter? Abnett's using the galas, and even the Fae merchants to cement the idea that supporting him isn't just right, it's fashionable and sought after. The Fae want him to succeed, so they've agreed to show favour to his people. Nothing too blatant, just shorter wait times, advance notice of new products, that sort of thing."

"The merchants - you mean Bee? That's how she keeps dropping information she shouldn't know," I said.

"Perhaps. I'm not privy to all the mechanics, but I know he's working with some excellent advisers on that front."

I settled back into my seat and for the rest of the drive, mulled over the evening's events.

Harrod insisted on taking me home first. The car idled outside while I unlocked. I waved farewell, shut the door, and only then did I hear the car pull away. Aching with tiredness, I put my hand on the door to the tiny stairwell, then froze at the sound of scraping over my head. There was someone upstairs, in my locked house. Where was Lenny? He should have greeted me at the door.

That thought sent my heart into my throat. If someone had broken in he'd have attacked them, no question. As carefully and quietly as I could, I crept up the stairs, wincing when one of the treads creaked underfoot. I reached the top and cracked the door open to hear a low voice on the other side.

"Lenny-dog, it be most difficult to be reading while you be sitting there."

A rush of relief washed over me and I opened the door, bones weak with relief.

"Lady, please be telling the Lenny-dog he be sitting not in a seat, but on the lap of a very angry boggart?"

I shooed Lenny off Gibble's lap and collapsed into the sofa. "Dammit, Gibble, I'm not used to you being here at night. I thought you were an assassin."

"Lady knows Gibble will not be leaving until it is safe."

"Lady forgot. Lenny seems to have adjusted to you being here though." The dog was trying to scramble into Gibble's lap again, much to the 'angry boggart's' amusement.

Gibble declined my offer of blankets and pillows, instead leaning back on the sofa with his book while Lenny, finally giving up on finding a comfortable place to settle, bounded off into my bedroom. Great, now I'd have to fight him for the bed. Shaking my head with another small smile, I kissed Gibble on the forehead and went off to battle for the space to lie down.

Chapter Eighteen

Fibres tickled my nose and I opened my eyes. Blinking and pushing myself up on to my hands, I found myself lying on a thick, plush carpet, the strands of which had been responsible for interrupting my sleep. Pulling myself up onto the daybed next to me, I looked around. I was in a small sitting room, and the walls were green. Unfinished needlework sat discarded on a stool beside me. A tapestry of a large, angry boggart terrorising a sandy-haired man hanging on the wall drew my eye. As I watched the painting, it almost moved - grasses swayed in an imaginary breeze and if I squinted just right, the boggart seemed to close in on his frightened victim. One edge of the tapestry started to lift and curl, smouldering away with a thin wisp of smoke.

"A vague premonition, or perhaps a memory. One that could go both ways, though I suggest you heed it regardless." I jumped, and the woman behind me laughed at my surprise. "I am most pleased you have returned. I did so want a chance to thank you for freeing our children. Of course, there is still more work to be done once you wake."

The Guardian reached up into her dark, meticulously curled hair and pulled free a silver pin, dislodging her coiffure. Tight ringlets tumbled over her shoulder. I watched, mesmerised by the flowing locks.

"Emmeline - oh dear child, time really is of the essence, isn't it?

Such a pity, I'd so hoped we could chat." She sighed, then adjusted the collar of my nightdress. "You need to return, my sweet. Return to the world of the living before you no longer belong there."

What did that mean? I couldn't form the words to ask, my open mouth moving senselessly.

"Focus." Her voice was urgent now, eyes snapping brightly at me. Those fathomless eyes, pools of ancient knowledge. "Emmeline! Your gift - you must embrace it. You must wake!"

She drew out the pin she had taken from her hair earlier. With impossible speed she whipped it in front of my face and scratched my cheek. Jerking my head back upset my balance and I fell to the floor, landing sprawled on the rich carpet. Her cold, expressionless face looked down on me from above. My heart beat faster and pain lanced my chest with every breath. I coughed, choked. Trembling, I tried to suck in more air but the carpet was over my face, stifling me. Heaving, I lashed out with my fists, then my feet, trying to hit or kick or grab at whatever held me down.

"Until next time, Emmeline." The voice was distant now, but it seared into my mind.

Power flooded into me, a raging torrent of release. The world popped.

I sat up in bed and drew in a ragged breath, choking on acrid smoke. Dazed, I coughed and rolled off my bed. I hit the floor with a thump. The boards beneath me felt hot on my bare skin, but the smoke wasn't as thick down here. It was dark and a roaring noise filled my ears, confusing me more.

"Lenny? Gibble, where are you?" My voice was hoarse and my efforts sent wracking coughs through my aching lungs.

Reaching around I found my bearings - the side table in front of me, my wand atop it. I clutched at it, cast a light globe. The little bobbing light was unable to penetrate far into the haze filling the room.

Pulling my shirt over my nose I tried to filter out some of the smoke, managing to get enough breath to call for Lenny. There was no answer He'd gone to sleep on my bed- I reached up and ran my hands over the rumpled blankets and found a soft mound. I shook him then, when he didn't respond, ripped off the covers and grabbed him.

The power inside me overflowed into him, pushed by an effort I didn't quite understand. He jolted upright, frantically scrabbling back out of my reach. A soft thudding onto the bed told me what I needed to know. This time, when I woke him I held him tight, coaxing him over to me.

"I have to keep a hold of you Len, got it? Where's Gibble?" My voice croaked the words out but Lenny guided me, one hand wrapped around his collar and touching his neck, over to the rug in front of the fire that served as Gibble's bed. It took only a moment to know it was empty.

"Gibble!"

The crackling roar that surrounded us drowned my words, but I didn't stop calling for him. Lenny led me to the door. There was no choice but to trust him. The dim light from my globe was near useless, though I left it there for the small bit of reassurance it gave.

The door to the stairwell was already open. Down we went, crouching as the smoke billowed over my head, seeking the most vertical path it could find. The shop below was lit with an eerie orange light, dancing and throwing shadows all around.

Lenny shied away and I had to drag him along with me. A whooshing noise sent a rush of heat towards us and the glowing heat intensified in a corner of the shop. As I stepped into the room a column of flames in the corner, shot up to the ceiling, then across it, towards me. Tendrils of fire snaked through the room, one climbing up a curtain on the other side of the shop. My skin burned as the temperature climbed; We had to hurry.

Yanking at Lenny's collar to try and guide him to the door, I nearly fell over him when he pulled back. He whined, scrabbling the floor with his claws. Tugging him behind me, I reached the door, flicking my wand out to trace a spell. The lock snicked open, but when I turned the handle, the door wouldn't move. Choking on a sob I pressed my hand against the pane of glass, feeling its ice cold surface on my scorching skin. I kicked at it, with no more effect than a mouse trying to beat down a brick wall. Lenny pulled again, trying to go back into the room, towards the flames that now ran across the wall and up the stairs. Tears streamed down my face, blurring my vision but I could just make out what he was doing.

Between us and the wall of fire, a huge lump lay on the floor. Lenny guided me to it, while I ducked my head to shield my face from the raging heat. Unable to see, I stumbled, landing on Gibble's tough hide. The moment we made contact I pushed my power into him and he reared up, then cowered down from the fiery ceiling.

Careful not to lose my grip, I followed him back to the door, trying to shout to him, tell him it was warded shut. My throat stung and my lungs screamed; no sound came out. Gibble pushed at the door, muscles straining. Nothing. He let out a visceral bellow, then stood tall and thrust his arms out, knocking me back and dislodging my hand from his arm.

He didn't fall, he *grew.* I'd seen this once before, in the Other. Bony spikes sprouted from his arms and down his back and his arms. His legs widened, muscles bulging. The flames shrank back from his terrifying roar, skittering away and drawing the thick smoke with them.

Ramming his body forward in a single motion he plunged at the door, breaking it clean out of its frame and exploding glass in a rain on the pavement outside. I fell through after him, hauling Lenny behind me and collapsing after a couple of steps.

Gibble reached down, wrapped an arm around my waist and lifted me, carrying me away from the flames that now reached out of the hole he had left in the wall behind us.

A shot rang out, then a flurry of others. Chips of plaster exploded from the wall as bullets screamed past. Gibble dropped me back to the ground and shielded me with his monstrous body until it stopped. Turning bleary eyes towards the street, I saw a man walking towards us, reloading a handgun. Lenny growled and looked to me for permission.

Barely breathing let alone able to speak, I pushed myself up, raised my arm and pointed to the man. He paused, fumbling with his gun for a moment before raising it again, aimed directly at me. Lenny bounded towards him as Gibble stomped onto the road.

The shooter dropped his gun and fled.

He never had a chance. I heard his shriek as Lenny caught him, and an unearthly growl as the raging boggart caught up. The screaming intensified, then cut off, leaving my ears ringing against the roar of the fire behind me. I sank back to the ground and watched everything I owned crumble before my burning eyes.

Chapter Nineteen

Cool hands touched my face and I heard a dramatic sigh. I cracked an eye open to find a blurry mess of golden curls obscuring my vision.

"I told you, she's my *patient*. The paperwork is all in order and as soon as she wakes I can-"

Something tugged on the skin at the back of my hand as Deirdre spoke and I gasped. The intake of breath to speak sparked a bout of painful coughing. Someone ran hands over my back, gently rubbing it in soothing motions as a tracing slipped off me, making me shiver.

"Emma, can you hear me?"

I nodded, wheezing loudly, eyes closed against the bright, burning lights.

"You need to let go of your block, sweetheart. I can heal you, if you let me."

Surprised, I reached inside to let go of my gift, not realising I'd been holding it in the first place.

"The drip, please?" Deirdre's voice was soft.

A moment later I felt a sharp pain in my hand, like a large splinter being ripped out. I grunted in pain. Then, another tracing touched me. This one pierced deep, healing my torn lungs and blistered skin. When I opened my eyes I could see clearly. The pain washed away and a deep breath filled my lungs with sweet, cool air.

Deirdre stood in front of me looking satisfied with her work while a nurse wheeled away a bag of IV fluids. To one side, my wand sat on a white hospital table, beside a plastic water jug and a box of tissues. Examining my hand I found a smudge of sticky residue, the only sign left from the cannula I assumed had been there moments ago.

"She's healed?" Greyson's rough voice startled me and I turned to see him hovering by my shoulder, eyes rimmed with red and his face creased with worry.

"Yeah," I answered before Deirdre could. "I feel fine."

Greyson helped me sit - I was well, but weary after the healing. "What happened? Where are Lenny and Gibble, what about my house?" The words tumbled out as memories of what had happened overcame my initial disorientation.

"Woah, slow down," Greyson exchanged a quick look with Deirdre. "You got burned pretty badly, you need to rest up."

"Charlie, I'm fine but I need to go." My eyes darted past Greyson, past Deirdre standing behind him, to the door of the hospital room.

"You've got no clothes."

His bland statement had me reaching for a rebuttal before I stopped and realised he was right - embarrassingly so. I'd escaped in my nightdress and was now wearing a hospital gown. Pulling the blanket back up that I'd started to thrust aside, I sat back in the bed, disjointed thoughts racing through my head.

"Where's my bag? Why don't I have a bag? Is there a faske around? Why wasn't it sent for a hospital bag, I thought that was standard procedure on admittance now?"

He looked at me, mouth downturned and brows furrowed. I took a breath, then another one.

"There's..." I swallowed, took another breath and tried again. "There's nothing left, is there?"

I tried to keep my voice steady, to stay calm and controlled in front of Greyson's stoic form. I tried to be brave, to keep a clear head in front of Deirdre who had seen people go through so much worse. I failed.

Deep breaths turned into shuddering gasps and I started trembling violently. Deirdre darted to my side as Greyson wrapped a strong arm around my shoulders.

"It's alright. Just breathe, that's it, keep breathing... that's right. You're ok." Greyson's voice murmured soothingly in my ear while Deirdre sat holding my hand.

"Lenny and Gibble?" I managed to ask.

"Lenny is fine, Harrod's taken him back to his place for now. Not a scratch on him."

"Gibble?" Why hadn't he said anything about Gibble?

"We... think he's ok. He disappeared after-" he coughed. "After *apprehending* the suspect."

Oh gods, they'd taken down the gunman. Would Lenny and Gibble be in trouble? Greyson saw the panic on my face start to return and quickly added, "He's fine, by the way. The suspect, I mean. He was found on the road outside your home, prints all over a gun that more than likely matches the bullets we pulled from the scene. Someone scared the pi- the pants off him, but they left him in one piece - more or less. He might have tripped over in the street after they left, knocked a few teeth out, but who's to say. He's in lock up now."

Last time Gibble had tapped into the power of the Other and changed like that, he'd disappeared for days. Forcing my breath to slow, I reminded myself that was likely why he couldn't be found.

His Otherworld magic would have protected him from the bullets, he wouldn't be lying somewhere - banishing that thought, I pressed my fingers against my eyes, held my breath for a moment and exhaled slowly. Inhale, exhale.

When I opened my eyes again, Harrod was standing in front of me. He dropped the small parcel he was holding and strode to the bed, leaning down to give me a hug. Greyson moved back over to the corner of the room.

"Emma... You're ok?"

"All healed up," I said nodding at Deirdre. "Thanks to Deirdre."

Harrod looked to her and she smiled. "She's fine, Harrod. In fact, my dear," she ran her eyes over me and nodded. "I'd say it's safe to let you go. I'll go find a doctor to discharge you." Deirdre left the room just as Martin wheeled Melanie in. She nodded briskly at the two, then disappeared down the corridor.

"Oh Emma, what have you gotten yourself into this time?" Melanie asked as she came over to the bed. I leaned down to give her a hug, and she handed me a shopping bag with some clothes in it. I thanked her, relieved my clothing issue had been resolved for now. Reminded of what I'd lost, I had to bite my lip to keep the tears away.

"Harrod, is Lenny alright?" I asked.

"He's fine, he's resting at my place. I took the liberty of setting up a room for you, too, if you want it. You're more than welcome, for as long as you need. Gibble and Lenny too, of course."

"Oh. Right." I examined the crisp white sheets on the bed, trying to keep breathing.

"If you'd rather somewhere else, I'd understand..."

"Oh, it's not that. I just... I hadn't even considered it. I was too worried about Lenny and Gib and... wow." Another breath. Then, another. "I don't have a home any more. Nothing was saved?"

"We drove past, hon." Melanie put a hand on mine. "It doesn't look like it. There's not much left of the building. The place was still smoking and there was a fire engine out front, so we didn't stop."

"Oh." My voice was small as I looked down at my hands, wishing I could wake up from this nightmare. "What about my neighbours? No one was hurt, were they?"

Greyson pulled a face. "It was a targeted attack, the only building damaged was yours. The fire chief said wards were found on some of the shattered glass and on the door. Our guy thinks they were to contain the fire to your premises." Looking at Harrod, he added, "I've made sure they won't destroy anything. You mind taking a look later?"

Harrod nodded and the two men exchanged a look - the kind two guys give each other when they're helping a damsel in distress. I shook my head and turned to Melanie.

"Thank you for the clothes," I said.

"Harrod had another parcel - oh, it's here." She nudged her chair back so she could reach it. "There's toiletries in there and Martin made a quick stop on the way so I could pick you up some things. The rest is in his car. Oh, *gods*, Em! I was so worried when I found out!"

"How *did* you find out?" I asked.

"Martin came over while Harrod was getting Lenny settled. He knew I'd want to know, and wanted help to grab you some clothes. You're lucky he did - the man has taste but no eye for sizing." She grinned. "You just got a new wardrobe, courtesy of Lord Harrod."

I closed my eyes and groaned - I'd have to figure out a way to pay him back later, if I could even get him to take it. Still a bit unsteady, though more from shock than any physical reason, I stood up and grabbed the bag of clothes. Excusing myself I headed into the tiny hospital bathroom to change, one hand gripping the hospital attire tightly closed.

Luckily Mel had guessed my size right and I shortly emerged feeling somewhat more human in a three-quarter shirt, skirt and tights. Greyson met me at the door, a little away from the others.

"How are you feeling?" he asked quietly.

"I'm fine. Deirdre doesn't do things by halves, I don't have a scratch on me." I knew my smile shook but it was the best I could do.

"That's not what I meant." He glanced down. "Emma, you nearly died. You lost your home and everything in it because someone tried to kill you. How are you *feeling*?"

I tilted my face up to him, looking him straight in the eye. "I'm angry," I said, surprised to find it was true. "I'm terrified, confused, devastated, and exhausted but most of all, I'm angry. The people who did this think they're above the law and immune from the treaties. They prey on innocent creatures and kill anyone who gets in their way. I'm angry, Charlie, and I want to make them pay." My voice was low but that didn't keep the heat from it.

"We've got the guy who did it," he said. "It's just a matter of time before we get their leader."

I shook my head emphatically. "The gunman didn't do this. It was Serraceuse. I know it." Stories of the fire that had almost taken my family echoed in my head. "You'll lose men if you go after them without Talents on your side. They've got magic and we still don't know how much. Don't you *dare* leave me out of this Greyson, not after this."

He nodded reluctantly. "We can talk tactics later. You need to get some rest. Will you stay with Harrod and Martin?"

"I don't have much choice."

He cleared his throat and looked away. "You could-"

"It's fine, really." Dammit, this was all too much. Stopping to take a breath, I tried to explain. "They've got the space. Not everyone can say their house is big enough for a boggart. I'll be fine at Harrod's, and you have more important things to worry about."

Greyson raised a sceptical eyebrow at that. I tried to give him a reassuring smile and on a whim, reached up to touch his cheek. He gathered me up in a bear hug, holding me tight enough that my feet nearly left the floor. Then he put me down with a chagrined smile, and headed for the door. "I'll drop by later to talk, if that's ok?"

"Of course. You know where I liv—where I'll be." I forced a smile and waved goodbye.

Harrod made sure we stopped at my house on the way to his. I sat in the car, watching tendrils of smoke rise from the rubble that was once my house. The vacant gap was juxtaposed between two perfectly clean and intact buildings.

The car was permeated by the smell of smoke and for a moment I was transported back to the burning building, surrounded by smoke and flames. My breath came in short gasps and I started shaking. Harrod reached over and squeezed my hand.

Two officers stood by the roped off area, next to a melted awning. Seeing the car, the taller one headed over. It was Sallaway. Davoss slid the window down and Sallaway leaned her head in.

"How you doing? Cap said you almost didn't make it out."

"I'm fine. Can I... can I go have a look?" As awful as I felt, I had to do it.

"Sure." Sallaway jerked the door handle and swung it open for me. "Just stay 'round the edges, it's still a bit toasty in there. The fire-guy dug through it a while ago, got what he could find for evidence. Said it was like nothing he'd seen - magic?"

"Yeah."

Harrod waited in the car while I picked my way over to a spot where most of the wall had come down. I could see enough to know that nothing would be saved, except maybe a warded chest I'd kept stashed under my bed. I asked Sallaway if they'd seen it.

"Not yet. We'll drop it by if we do. Captain knows where you're staying I bet." That was said with an exaggerated wink. "Oh here, before I forget..." Sallaway jogged over to the police cruiser and returned juggling a wide cardboard box. "People keep leaving stuff here."

"What do you mean?" I asked.

"People. Well, Others, mostly. And *stuff*, like the sorts of things you'd give to someone who just lost everything, I guess."

She handed me the box and I looked inside. There were swathes of fabric, some bottles, soft leather. It was a little unwieldy, so I didn't unpack it to see the rest of its contents. Sallaway helped me put it in the trunk and said goodbye. As the car pulled away and the sight of my broken house slid past, I was filled with unbelievable sadness.

The perfect cure for that awaited me at Harrod's house. I was slow getting out of the car - by the time I headed up the path to the front door, Harrod already had it open. A large brown shape flew past him and barrelled into me, jumping to put his paws on my shoulders and cover me with slobbery dog kisses.

In that moment I knew without a doubt that what people said was true. No matter what you lost, your house, your things, all of it - none of that mattered, as long as you still had the ones you loved. The few scattered tears that fell were of relief and joy at seeing him safe.

Laughing, I put my arms around him and hugged. He lifted his big feet to my shoulders and licked my face. Standing on his hind legs he was taller than me - he was still growing after Olfred's healing.

Harrod showed me to the room he'd made up for me and set the parcels from Melanie on the bed, hesitated, then awkwardly excused himself once he was satisfied I was ok on my own.

The room was huge, with its own small ensuite. The four poster bed was enormous. I hoped no one minded Lenny sharing the bed, there'd be no keeping him off it. A silverwood dresser sat against a wall, empty except for some blankets in the bottom drawer. A matching wardrobe had dozens of empty hangers inside.

I closed the door and smoothed the blanket on the bed, then sat carefully on the edge. This was my room now. For the foreseeable future, this was home.

CHAPTER TWENTY

Later that day, Harrod joined me for tea in the parlour. We'd just gotten settled when Harrod hushed me. The silence was broken a moment later by a metallic scratching coming from the door.

"Barg," Harrod called out. "Can you *please* just knock? You don't need to pick my locks every time you visit, I'm happy to let you in."

The lock snicked and the door creaked open. Feet pattered down the hallway and a chagrined-looking Barg popped his head into the room.

"Barg was not wanting to be disturbing the Lordly resident of the domain, Sir. It is no bother to open the door my ownself, although it would be a small bit easier if Barg did not have to also be sneaking through the wards, litt- ah, Sir."

Harrod's eyes narrowed and I stifled a snort. I decided against asking how Harrod had managed to convince Barg to stop calling him 'little-man', and instead asked Barg if he was here to see Lenny.

"Lady! Sir! Barg has many important businesses to discuss. Shall we adjourn to the kitchen-room?"

"Barg, if you need something to eat, just ask. I don't mind feeding you, you know," Harrod said, and did his best to keep a straight face as the overjoyed hobgoblin requested several jam sandwiches. Once Harrod passed the request to Cym, his faske servant, Barg threw himself up on a chair and wriggled about until he was comfortable.

"What's up, Barg?" I asked.

"Foremost and first, Barg is bearing a message from Gibble. Gibble is currently residing in the Other, and will be on his return in an exact approximation of three days." He held up four fingers, looked at them and frowned. He folded down two and brandished them happily.

A band around my chest that I hadn't known was there suddenly loosened. "Oh, that's such a relief. He wasn't hurt, was he?"

"No, Lady!" I let out a quick sob of relief and Harrod grinned, seemingly as happy as I was at the news. "Gibble is taking the time to be the Gibble of the this-world once more. Now, the foremost and second point of being, is... wait..." Barg screwed up his face and scratched his wrinkly scalp, then jerked in remembrance. "Ah! It is the box of things. Did the officer-lady procure it for you?"

"She did, but I haven't had a chance to open it yet. She said they were gifts?"

"Yes, Lady. Some of your most regular tea-buyers from the Other were most worried about your predicament. They said 'Barg, where can we take things for the tea-lady, so that she can be dressed in clothes and drinking of the teas that she makes so kindly for us'. Except, they mostly grunted, but Barg knew the words they did mean to say, and told them to give the gifts to the officer-lady with the nicest of shoes."

Summoning Cym back, I asked him to retrieve the box from my room. We put it down and I sat on the floor to unpack it.

Barg dived right in, taking out the items one by one to exclaim over the craftsmanship of the piece, or expound on the kindness of the giver. He was right - the box had several dresses and shawls made from the finest of fabrics and coloured or painted in the most beautiful way. Barg explained the small pouch of beads were seeds from an Elder tree, a gift that was highly thought of by Otherworlders. Harrod noted that three feathers on a chain were from a saff bird's nest. Two leather strips came out and Barg showed me how to wrap my feet in them, creating shoes that fit perfectly and felt like heaven.

There were several boxes of my own tea, returned to me by their buyers. They were enchanted with sleep, comfort, heartsease and fortitude - things I'd need over the coming days. There was a set of clay bowls, simple yet striking, and a four place setting of the most finely crafted silverware I'd ever seen. A comb made from redwood and a matching mirror came out after a set of jewelled hair clasps.

When I pulled out a swathe of rolled up blue silk and stood to shake it out, Barg tugged it gently out of my hands.

"Apologies, Lady! Barg did commission this piece for his ownself. It was to be delivered to the tea-shop in the case of Barg not having a place to be receiving such goods."

He shook it out to reveal an embroidered wall hanging that depicted him riding astride Lenny. Both wore armour in the medieval style, and Barg carried a pennant raised in a victorious salute. The two of them had been spending so much time together it was understandable they'd grown close; I just hadn't realised how devoted Barg had become to Lenny. I smiled as a wave of emotion hit, closing up my throat and wetting my eyes.

"Of course... If Lady does request the ownership of the item... considering the circumstances Lady is in, Barg would of course relinquish it immediately." He held his breath, waiting for my answer. He could put any puppy to shame with those eyes.

"Barg, I'm so grateful for the friendship you've shown Lenny. The hanging is beautiful, but it's yours. I wouldn't dream of taking it away from you."

He toed the floor bashfully for a moment, then threw himself at me, hugging my legs like a small child. Staggering to keep my balance,

I patted him on the back until he dislodged himself, blushing furiously.

After he left I went upstairs to put my treasures away. They might just be the most valuable things I'd ever owned - not for their beauty and worth, but because of who they'd come from. Strangers, who had no reason to know me except for a few boxes of tea. So many of them had become friends.

The gifts had no names attached, typical of Otherworld customs. They would want no thanks or recognition of their gifts - to do so would be considered rude. It was enough that their gifts would be used.

The clothes were a long way from filling the wardrobe but they eased a little of the loss that kept rising up to suffocate me. I put the bowls and silverware in the bottom drawer of the dresser; the brush, combs and clasps on top.

Satisfied that everything was neat and orderly, I headed downstairs. There were phone calls to make, services to cancel, paperwork to sort. The practice of denying insurance to those with Talented blood had never hit me so hard.

Rather than get to work, I made tea. Heartsease and fortitude together made a wonderful mix in times of crisis. Harrod was still in the sitting room and I joined him with the steaming cup.

"Feeling ok?" he asked.

"I guess so," I said. "I don't think it's sunk in yet. There's so much I have to do, and I don't know where to start." My voice trailed off as, once again, the overwhelming task of rebuilding my life hit home.

"If you need anything at all, just ask. Do you need to go shopping? I can call the car around."

"I do." I sighed. Shopping was my absolute least favourite

pastime. "Three hours until everything starts to close. How much do you think I can get done?"

"Would you like me to come? I'll carry the bags for you."

As Harrod drained his cup, there was a knock at the door. A faske had come with a delivery and needed help bringing it inside. It was a good-sized trunk, lined with copper detailing and a garden scene carved on the top. It was addressed to me.

Hoisting it into the sitting room, I opened it to find it stuffed full of clothes. A note from Bee sat on top. She'd made me an entire wardrobe full of outfits. I pulled out pants, dresses, tops and - much to Harrod's embarrassment - underwear. With a cough, I quickly closed the lid. Gratitude and relief filled me and I had to blink away tears yet again. Confident that those needs were taken care off, I crossed clothes shopping off my list of things to do.

By that evening, I had a new phone, a small laptop and everything I needed for at least the next couple of weeks. On Harrod's advice, I didn't buy anything I'd need when I got my own place again as he assured me there were things he'd been meaning to take to a charity store that I could have. On the way back to his house - my house now, for the time being at least - we drove back past my old building.

It was almost dusk, and in the falling light I could see people working at the site. As we drew closer I was shocked to see who it was. I recognised most as Otherworlders who frequented the shop.

There were kobolds and gnomes, two half-giants, and brownies, piskes and faskes, all working together to clear the rubble. And clear it they did. Much of the rubble had already been removed.

The larger beings hoisted the heavier rocks and beams while smaller ones ferried bags of rubbish all over to a large, trembling machine near the centre that groaned and squawked as it digested the piles of debris fed into it. A murmured question to Harrod revealed it was likely a gnomish contraption used in the mines to remove dirt from the shafts.

In the middle of it all, calling out vague orders and rousing the workers with the occasional cheer, was Barg.

He spotted us and waved but didn't approach, busy directing the workers. When we left, my cheeks were wet and my heart swollen with gratitude. I thought back to the first time I'd seen the small flat. It was tiny but cheap, and set up so that I could sell my tea downstairs and live on the upper floor. It was the fifth one I'd seen, but I somehow knew it was the one. In the five years I'd lived there, I'd come to know all the little traits of the building, like which floorboards squeaked and how to thump the wall to stop the pipes rattling.

It was a place I'd called home, not just for the walls around me, but for the community I'd found while there. My little shop had thrived and the customers, many regularly dropping by and sharing gossip and personal stories over the years, were now friends. Those friends were out there in the falling light, helping me to build back a little of what I'd lost.

Greyson visited the next evening, looking more worn than ever. He handed me a box, a tiny chest packed with my most valuable possessions. It was fitted with the most protective wards available, a heavy investment that had apparently paid off beautifully. The box was pristine, untouched by fire or soot and still locked shut. My throat tightened as I took it from him.

"Sallaway said you were looking for this," Greyson said, thrusting his hands in his pockets. "Forensics took it thinking it might have been related to the cause of the fire, but they cleared it an hour ago."

Thanking him, I asked how the case was going.

He sighed. "Well, we didn't get much out of the shooter apart from his name, which is Arnold, in case you were wondering. He seems alright in normal conversation, but when you ask him about his boss? Bloody bastard starts shaking and gasping like he can't breathe. Lasts for ninety seconds. Exactly ninety, every damn time."

He shook his head in amazement and I wondered how many times he'd 'tested' that theory. I squashed that thought. Charlie could be full of righteous fury, but he'd only bend the rules so far. He was a good man, a better person than I could ever be. Oh, how I longed to get Arnold in a room and hurt him like he'd tried to hurt me.

A shiver went through me at the anger I felt. It wasn't like me; it wasn't how I'd been before the fire. Serraceuse and his men had made me into something I wasn't, and all that did was stoke my rage.

It was a feeling I hated, but if I didn't embrace it, use it to prop me up and keep me going, I'd fall apart. The ache of what I'd lost gnawed at me, alongside fear of the people so callous that they could lock someone in a house and burn it down with no remorse. If I let go of the anger, those other emotions would worm their way in and crumble my resolve. I couldn't afford that, not until this was all over.

"Hey." Greyson noticed the goosebumps prickling my skin, and touched my arm. "You want to sit down?"

Deep in my reverie I'd almost forgotten he was here. I'd lost track of our conversation and looked up at him, knowing my confusion was written on my face.

"Sorry, Charlie. I'm ok, just tired. What were you saying?"

"We've got someone coming in from the other side of the wall. We're hoping they can help break the curse on our perp."

"You got nothing at all out of him?"

"Oh, I wouldn't say that - he was eager enough to rat out three more buyers. I've passed those details up the chain and a task force will handle that as a simultaneous raid on all three properties. There'll be animal handlers on site and your friend, the veterinarian that looks like a tree? We've kept in touch with him; he'll be on the task force as well." His face darkened for the barest of moments. "Don't want a repeat of last time."

"You said 'they' - your team won't be involved with the raids?"

"Nah, we're off to fry the big fish. My crew's only focus is to shut this thing down from the top, but I've made sure the guys running the raids are people I trust."

He told me Ronson hadn't been seen since the raid, which made my heart skip a beat. He was still out there, along with Serraceuse. Greyson's team was good, I knew that - I just had to trust they'd bring them down before I got caught in the crossfire.

Greyson made small talk after that, but fell quiet after a short while. The inaction stifled me, making me want to run, act, escape from this strange house and the way people looked at me with pity in their eyes. Ever-perceptive, Greyson flitted me a look through narrowed eyes.

"Bloody hell," he said, eyes widening. I looked at him quizzically, unsure what he was talking about. "You're itching to go, aren't you? I know that look, I see it on my officers when we've been beaten down by a case but we know we're close. You're dying to get out there and take them down." He ruefully ran a hand through his hair.

Emotions warred inside me, but he was right. "Yes," I said. "Greyson, I'm tired of being scared and I'm sick of being one step behind them all the time. We got to Markson's too late, and they got away from the warehouse. I want to find them, rescue the baby fiend and then... I want to make them pay." Anger burned deep within me, alongside a loathing for those who'd done this. Fear of being made to sit out, give up. Eagerness to get moving and break the stasis of the last few days.

By the time Greyson left I felt like a nest of ants was crawling under my skin. I retreated to my room and sat on the bed for a short time, then used my wand on the small box in front of me. It had three wards - one for heat, another for moisture and a third to keep it securely locked. Inside were some old photos, various papers... and a ring.

Frowning, I pulled it out. It looked like the ring the Guardian had given me in my dream, but I'd given that to the demi-fae child. It had been months since I'd last opened the box, so how had in gotten in there? *Damned Fae.*

It slipped over my finger and fit comfortably. I'd know it would - Fae jewellery had a habit of doing that.

Later that night I dreamed of normal things - like road trips and movie scenes and deadly fire climbing towards me, intent on eating me alive.

Chapter Twenty-One

By the time I woke the next morning, head pounding from broken sleep and bad dreams, Harrod had left. Cym gave me a note that said he'd gone to attend a meeting with Abnett. I didn't expect him back for some time if that were the case; Abnett was notoriously long-winded and perpetually running late to appointments.

The note insisted that if I needed anything, to 'charge it to the household account'. It sounded like Harrod-speak for 'let me buy you stuff'. The credit card Cym handed me was given straight back. I had a small amount saved for emergencies and I was pretty sure this qualified.

As I dismissed the faske, Martin stumbled into the kitchen. He was puffy eyed, hair squashed down on one side of his head and spiked up on the other. I raised an eyebrow at him. He squinted at me, grunted, and poured himself a glass of juice.

"You look like you had a rough night," I said wryly.

"Not as rough as you've had recently."

"Are you sure about that?" I asked, unable to stifle a laugh. He really did look awful.

"Well, I wouldn't say it was a *bad* night. It certainly was rough, but I'm not one to complain about that." He mustered up a cheeky grin, then decided to go back to bed after draining his glass. I'd never put stock in the bachelor stereotype, but with his string of Fae liaisons he was certainly living up to it.

With the day to myself, I decided to head out to the garden. I took my new laptop and sat at a small table in the sun to set it up to work on my business concerns. Orders would have to be shut down for a time, though I should probably start building up my supplies again. Harrod had the space for casting and for storing my teas, there was no question of that.

My eyes kept drifting from the work in front of me. There were a few plants from the Other scattered between the local varieties, and they attracted sprites and nymphs. The tiny creatures flitted to and fro, glassy wings catching the sunlight and throwing pinpoints of light across the ground.

A shadow crossed over them and a silver serpent flapped down noisily into the flowers. She wasn't as graceful as the sprites, but she was stunning. The sun hit her ivory scales, sending rainbow reflections darting around the garden. Big dark eyes sparkled with glee as she romped with her tiny companions.

"Pearl?" I called.

The dragonette swooped up and spun around, showing off her delicate wings, then fluttered over to perch on the back of a chair. Her foot slipped, claws glancing off the metal bar and her wings flicked out to help her balance. I carefully put a hand out and she leaned forwards to let me stroke the back of her neck, stretching it out and crooning as I scratched it.

"What are you doing here?" I mused, more to myself than the dragon. She stayed for a few minutes more, then opened her wings to flap away, leaving her new friends to gallivant in the sunlight without her.

Tearing my eyes away from the garden, I tried to focus back on my work. Clicking through to my emails, I set about answering the few that were urgent. As I scrolled through the list, one from the O.C.U. caught my eye.

I'd already opened it - it contained the details I needed to log in to their system - but I clicked it anyway. Clicking again, I opened the link to the database, typed in my username and password, and checked for any updates to the files I had access to. I veered away from the reports added in the last few days, the ones that covered the attack on my home and my own near-death. There would be time for that later. Instead, I opened the maps that Greyson had shown me, hoping for some kind of lightning bolt idea that would give me the breakthrough I needed.

As my eyes ran over a map littered with little pins and notes they snagged on something. Greyson had marked the bridge I'd called him to. Nothing had happened there yet and in all the excitement, I'd forgotten all about it. Highlighting the pin dropped there, I noted the warehouse location and the building that Markson, the tech giant with the zoo in his back yard, had tipped as one of the meeting places. The bridge wasn't far from either. Desperate to go out and do something useful, I made a quick decision, then called Lenny for a walk.

It took about twenty minutes to get to the bridge through the nearest port-gate. When I arrived, Masik was standing at the gate with a large box.

"Hi, Masik," I said, momentarily unsure if the troll had somehow known I was coming.

"Greeting, huma-" His surly frown fell away as recognition spread across his face. "Wait! Masik know this one. This door lady! Did you find door, Lady?" His eyebrows were raised in eagerness for my answer, and he looked downcast when I ruefully shook my head.

"No, I'm still looking for it. Are your people keeping an eye out for me?"

He shrugged, the motion of his big shoulders moving his entire body.

"They look, but no door on bridge. It *bridge*, not door. Poh-leese are gone now." He said 'police' like he was speaking around a potato, rolling the unfamiliar word over his tongue. "My people not liking the poh-leese watching us bridge."

So, Greyson had given up on my information, too. With all that was going on he'd probably just run out of people to spare, though I wished he'd told me. Sighing, I accompanied Masik back to the bridge.

When we arrived he greeted the gathering of homeless and dropped the large box on the ground. They clustered around it, pulling out coats and boots and blankets, exclaiming over them and arguing over who got what. They sounded good-natured and I assumed Masik had brought enough to go around. The troll turned to me with a large, crooked grin, contentment shining in his eyes.

"It be winter soon. Humans not like cold. Masik, he go get warm-makers for humans."

"That's very kind of you Masik. Where did the clothes come from?"

Another shrug. "Masik find." He'd probably stolen them. Trolls don't exactly respect the concept of ownership.

Poking around under Masik's watchful eye, I examined the campsite while Lenny rolled on the ground, begging for tummy scratches from anyone who walked by. I stayed until the sun had climbed higher than it had been in my vision dream, yet there were no burnt patches of ground and nothing had happened.

Defeated, I returned home, arriving only to feel the need to leave again. Frustrated, I paced around, wishing there were something I could do.

"Are you trying to wear a hole in the floor?" Martin's voice made me jump.

"Oh, I'm so sorry, Martin. I woke you, didn't I?"

"If you've ever tried to sleep through a hangover from Fae wine, you know damned well I wasn't sleeping." Looking him over, I could see he really was hurting, though I couldn't dig up much sympathy. Only an idiot would let a Fae get them drunk. "You didn't disturb me, but I heard you come in and I thought... well, I wondered if you could do something for me?"

My eyes narrowed. "You want me to enchant you a tea for your hangover, don't you?"

A hint of colour touched his cheeks. Even with his dark skin, he looked pallid and sickly, enough that I felt sorry for him. "You're lucky. I just so happen to have the best hangover cure known to man or Fae. But you know the best cure is prevention, don't you?"

He grinned, then winced and put a hand to his head. "I knew you'd do it for me. You wouldn't let anyone suffer like this. You're too nice."

Rolling my eyes, I set off to rummage through Harrod's kitchen to see if he had any fresh tea. His comment about letting people suffer pricked at my conscious. Was I a nice person? I wouldn't let my friend suffer from a self-induced headache, but I'd gladly string up Serraceuse, Ronson and the rest of their crew, regardless of the consequences.

The rest of the afternoon was spent holed up in the room set aside for spell tracing. I could easily have done it in my bedroom, but the quiet, warded space allowed me to concentrate uninterrupted and the lack of windows meant the faint aroma of tea soon permeated the whole room.

With my eyes closed it almost felt like home, and the familiar task let my mind finally rest while concentrating on each trace. I worked for as long as I could stand, giving up only when my hands started to shake. Whatever I worked loose in that room, absorbed in the spells and concentrating on nothing but familiar techniques, left me feeling lighter than I had since the gala.

That night as I lay in bed, staring at a ceiling that wasn't mine, I made a plan. Oh, it wasn't much of one, and it probably wouldn't lead to anything, but it wasn't like I had anything better to do. Losing my shop meant my normal daily rituals were gone. With nothing to soak up the hours, I was left to dwell on what I'd lost, what I faced and all sorts of other horrible things. Staying busy was the only way I could stave off the boredom and restlessness. Sensing my mood as he always did, Lenny wriggled up to nuzzle my face.

"Tomorrow, Len. Tomorrow, we begin again."

The next morning I visited Melanie. I'd called before I left, so she knew to expect me. As always, I was met with a warm greeting and a hot coffee.

"Here it is," she said, pointing to her printer. "I can't believe Harrod doesn't have a computer. How does he function? The man must use carrier pigeon to send messages." She showed me how to access her network and within a few minutes I'd run off a few copies of Greyson's primary map. I'd zoomed it in to the area I wanted to cover.

"You sure you don't want to stay for coffee, Em?" Melanie asked. The concern in her voice made me wince, but I shook my head.

"No. I need to be outside, doing something."

"Come on. I know you're up to something, at least tell me what so I know where to send search and rescue?"

A smile pulled at my lips. Yes, Mel would support me even as I ran headfirst into danger with my eyes closed. Hoping that wasn't what I was doing, I told her my plan. It didn't get any simpler, really; I intended to walk the streets between the bridge and the warehouses until I stumbled on something useful. Together, over coffee, we marked out the section of London I wanted to focus on.

"You can scratch out this area." Melanie used a pencil to section off part of the area we'd marked. "It's all government buildings. They wouldn't be brazen enough to set up there, would they?"

"Probably not. What's this area?" I pointed to a section that was shaded grey.

"A ghost town. Old area, all listed buildings with tight restrictions. No one wants to take on anything so derelict, with so many strings attached. I went to look at property there once, but even if the buildings were worth saving, living in a place like that with no one around?" She shuddered. It seemed as good a place as any to begin my search.

"Emma, are you sure about this? I mean, you should at least take Gibble or Harrod with you."

"Gibble is... away. Harrod is busy. Lenny will be with me and besides, I'm just looking. There's a good chance I won't even find anything, but if I see the slightest thing out of the ordinary, I'll be straight on the phone to Greyson." I wasn't lying—I just wasn't entirely sure if I was telling the truth.

"You promise? Absolutely, for sure, no hesitation?" Melanie put her cup down to look at me, eyes piercing.

"I swear, Mel. Even if I was willing to risk myself - which I'm not - I can't take them on, and I definitely can't risk them getting away again; we could lose their trail forever. As soon as I know *anything*, I'll call anyone and everyone who'll listen, and we'll take the bastards own together." My words even convinced me. I didn't have a death wish, I just wanted—*needed*—to do something.

Satisfied, she reached across the table to squeeze my hand. "You will, Emma, I don't doubt it for a second."

After I left Melanie's I went straight to the bridge. After briefly greeting Masik again, I set off walking the streets. With each turn I took, I marked off my path on the map. I had no idea what I was looking for or where to find it, but I had faith that I would. If one of the Guardians had made the effort to return the ring, then I would need it.

Twisting the ring as I strolled along a bustling street, I wondered why they'd gotten involved. Were they seriously considering going to war with the humans? I couldn't begin to imagine how bad that would be. Our kind - both Talented and Mortal - had done some really awful things to the Otherworlders over the centuries. Slavery, abuse, now poaching, which wasn't at all a new thing. Not knowing what the Guardians wanted with me now made me awfully uncomfortable.

For the next three days, my routine was the same. I'd get up, eat breakfast with Harrod and Martin, then make some excuse and leave for the morning. The thought of telling either of them where I was headed never even crossed my mind; I knew Harrod far too well to try and explain why I needed to do this. He wouldn't understand and it would only lead to an argument.

The walks took me out of the house, away from the awkward feeling that I was living in a hotel, and away from my growing concern that Gibble hadn't returned as expected. As hard as I tried not to worry about him, it was just one more thing piled on top of all the others, weighing on my mind and adding to the vague sense of urgency I felt.

Then, on the third day, I opened the door to find Barg standing on the other side brandishing a lock pick.

"Barg?"

He flourished a deep bow, then saluted me. "Lady! Barg does wish the company of the Lenny-friend if he may be spared, Lady!"

"Are you racing him?" I asked warily.

"Yes, Lady! Lenny-friend is most quick, and Barg is of the spending way at this very moment, Lady! Barg might be persuadable to share the proceedings of the Lenny-friend's racing, if Lady wishes?"

It seemed like a genuine offer, but I shook my head. Though I trusted Gibble's reassurance that what they were doing was safe, I didn't want to be involved. "It's ok, Barg. You and Lenny go have fun." Lenny whined and pushed his head against me. Barg frowned at Lenny, then looked at me.

"Lady, Barg has had a... a changing of the plans. Perhaps a nice sleep will be the ordering of today."

"What did he say to you?" Great, now even my dog was playing protector.

"Say, Lady?" Barg sidled back towards the footpath. "What would make you be asking a thing like that? Lenny-friend, he is often talking and he does say many things, why, yesterday he told me-"

"Barg! What did Lenny say to you *just now*?"

"Oh." Barg's face fell and Lenny made a grumbling sound. "Lenny-friend did say Lady be... ah, doing something that may require his assistance." At my glare, he added, "Lenny-friend... well, the wording of the words are coming from himself, Lady, not Barg, Barg would *never* say Lady is doing the stupid thing!" He clapped his hand over his mouth as if horrified at what he'd let slip.

I cocked an eyebrow at Lenny who sat back on his haunches, whumped his tail once and gave the canine expression that was equivalent to a shrug.

"Stupid? Well unless you have a better suggestion, it's all I've got. *You* don't have to come." Lenny immediately stood and pushed against my legs. "That's what I thought."

"Barg will be departing now, Lady." The little hobgoblin, once realising I wouldn't blame him for what Lenny had apparently said, walked back up to us and gave Lenny a vigorous scratch under the chin. Lenny's leg twitched with enjoyment.

"Wait, Barg. Do you know where Gibble is? It's been more than three days and I'm getting- "

"Barg! Did you not be telling Lady Gibble does be returning?" Gibble's voice preceded him up the drive and I flew out to greet him, Lenny racing ahead. The big dog galloped around Gibble's feet like a puppy while I gave Gibble a hug. The relief that ran through me was so strong that my nose prickled and I had to blink away tears.

Barg blushed. "Ah, sorry, Lady. Master Gibble does be returning. Ahh... today."

"Gibble! I've been so worried, when you didn't come back on time, I thought-"

"Oh Lady, that be Gibble's fault. Gibble did be forgetting that Barg does not be thinking of the time in the Other and the time in the this-world, and of there being a difference. Gibble does be most sorry, Lady, for causing worry."

Leading Gibble inside by the hand, I took him through the house to the sitting room. Cym popped his head in to check if we needed anything and gave Gibble a respectful nod when he requested a book to read.

"Thank you, little-helper, any book will be being the right one."

Cym scampered off while Barg made his apologies for depriving us of his wonderful company, waved goodbye to Lenny then darted off to goodness knows where. Shaking my head as he left, I wondered where he was going. I explained to Gibble what had happened over the days he'd missed.

"Yes, Lady, Gibble do be knowing of the house, and of those who be going to build Lady a new one." At my look of surprise - I'd known they were clearing the site but had thought that would be the end of it - he said the Others were planning the rebuild of my house and shop. He smiled at my shock. "They do be caring for you, Lady. After many years now of seeing you, and your helping of them for little things, they do be wishing to help you now. We all do be very sad for what did happen, and Gibble does offer most sincere apologies for being gone for many days since."

"It's fine, Gib. I had Lenny, and Harrod and Martin to take care of me."

"Yes, little-man does be looking after Lady well, Gibble thinks. But why did Lady be going without him? Lenny-dog did be saying that Lady be hunting. That do not be safe, not after the fire and the killing-one." His name for the man who'd tried to shoot us chilled me, but I wouldn't let it sway me from my course.

"Gib, I'm not putting myself in danger, I swear." Grateful as I was at Gibble's safe return, I tried not to let irritation prick at me. "I can't drag Harrod out on a wild goose chase, I'm just walking around the city, that's all. If I find anything, and it's a big if, I'll call Greyson straight away, and Harrod, and I'll send Lenny for you."

"Lady, Gibble do think it be better if we did go together."

"Well *Lady* do think that a boggart crashing around might just tip off the people we're looking for." Despite my frustrations, guilt nagged at me for snapping at him. "Gib, I love that you care so much. And I do rely on you to keep me safe. This is just something you can't help me with. Not like that, anyway. If anything goes wrong, Lenny will come for you." Gibble's forehead knotted and his big mouth screwed up in distress. "Please, Gibble? I need to do this."

Finally he nodded. I briefed him on what I was doing and where I was looking, so that if anything did happen, he'd know where to look for me. Trying not to let his unease get to me, I beckoned to Lenny. Together, we set off to walk the streets once again in search of a killer.

Chapter Twenty-Two

Lenny sat beside me and looked up benignly as I cursed. After three hours traipsing the streets I was tired, sore, and completely empty-handed. Berating myself for what now seemed like a ridiculous plan based on hope and fairy dust, I veered back towards the port-gate.

After all my faith I'd turned up nothing and I was debating whether I even wanted to do this again the next morning. Feet aching, I shuffled along the footpath, then slowed at the corner to check for the car I heard approaching from behind me. As I turned my head, fear engulfed me. My heart raced, my skin prickled with cold and my knees shook.

A feeling of desperate loneliness warred with pure terror and I twisted my head back to hide it from the approaching vehicle. As it trundled by, the sensation intensified and darkness closed in. Stumbling against a wall like a drunk, I slid down it to wrap my arms around my body, shaking violently. Lenny whimpered at my distress as I panted in short breaths, willing my heart not to explode in my chest.

The van passed. The feeling subsided.

Sucking air through my nose as my heart slowed, I tried to focus.

What just happened, a panic attack? No, it had gone too quickly. It seemed to go when the van... *The van*. I stood to look and just saw the tail end disappearing into a driveway, right down the end of the street. Tugging on Lenny's lead I ran, hurtling up the footpath until I was a few houses down from where I'd seen it stop.

The property looked abandoned. Bushes, grass and weeds were unkempt, almost choking the long driveway lined by an enormous, straggling hedge. The brick fence was crumbling and the old gate rusted, though a shining new padlock hung around a chain that dangled loose off one side. Were they only making a short stop, or were they expecting someone else? I scanned the street. No one.

Afraid of being spotted, I approached cautiously. I placed a hand on the gate. A tentative nudge made it whine loudly, so I used the decorative ironwork between the bars as a foothold and climbed over. Lenny paced along the gate, then bunched up his hind legs.

"No!" I said in a loud whisper. "Lenny, I need you to wait outside. If I don't come out in an hour, get Gibble. Hell, get *everyone*. Can you do that?"

Whump. His tail hit the ground and he ducked his head, panting. Hoping that meant yes, I watched as he turned, and trotted off into someone's garden across the street. A bush rustled and a brown face popped out, then withdrew. *Good boy*, I thought.

I checked again to make sure no one was coming, then crept in behind the hedge, following the driveway up past the vacant old manor. As I closed in on the rear of the property, the feeling of terror threatened to envelop me again. I knew the shared sensations were to do with my trip to the Other, that it had to do with my acceptance to the pack. With it, came some understanding of how to use it. Acknowledging the emotional cry for help, I pushed the feeling away and it dwindled to a manageable level.

A white van, similar to the one left behind at the warehouse, idled at the end of the path. Two men opened the door at the rear of the van, then lifted a blanket off a large cage inside. As the cover came off, an ice cold shudder ran through my body as I saw what was inside.

The creature was no bigger than a soccer ball. Compared to its brethren, it was tiny. Beady, red eyes blinked in the sunlight and it wiggled back, pressing itself into a corner of the cage. The small barrow fiend still had the purplish skin and patches of fuzz that preceded the growth of sleek fur and its mewling cry was far from the deep harrumph of the herd I'd seen in the Other. The cries he emitted penetrated my psyche, and I could feel his terror and loneliness.

He didn't know where he was and he missed his pack, and the companionship and protection they provided. Somehow, seeing the fiend and knowing that's where the emotions stemmed from kept them separate from my own. I couldn't stop my heart reaching out to him.

Somehow, he sensed it. He quietened in the cage and swung his head back and forth, looking for one of his kind. Finally he settled back, cowed, but not asleep.

The men complained constantly as they stood on guard - they were bored, they didn't like the presumptuous attitude of the buyer they were due to meet and their 'boss' had been on edge. When a third man walked up to the truck, they fell silent. The man was short and wiry, with a mean looking face and a crooked nose. A scar hooked around his jaw, adding to the impression he was not a man to cross. Lady Columbine had mentioned a scar like that; Serraceuse. My stomach turned and I pressed one hand to my mouth to hold back a cry.

The thin branch my hand rested on wavered; I was gripping it unconsciously. Easing my hand off, I crouched lower as the men passed in front of the thick hedge I hid behind. A vehicle rumbled at the house of the house. The men paused, listening as it came to an abrupt stop and a car door slammed.

"Someone's out front. Jones, go check." Serraceuse thrust his chin at one of the men, who promptly jogged off down the long driveway.

Jones returned a moment later, calling out from some distance away. "Yeah, it's him."

"You saw him?"

Jones hesitated. "Nah, but it's his car."

"How many people were in the car? Was he alone?" Serraceuse snapped.

"Look, he always comes alone. We been dealing with this one for ages, why'd he start bringing people with him now?"

Shaking his head and muttering about the incompetence of his employees, Serraceuse pulled a gun and set off down the drive, beckoning the last man to follow. This was likely to be my only chance - if they returned with the buyer and I lost track of them, the poor fiend could be gone forever.

Keeping an eye out for movement, I pushed through the branches of the hedge, ignoring the scratches and scrapes. A quick glance down the empty drive and I dashed over to the truck. The cage sat in the open tray, baby fiend inside. The lock came open easily. I was surprised the simple tracing worked, but perhaps they didn't feel the need for such high security here.

The fiend jiggled and wobbled in joy, then started to scurry around in circles in the cage. I reached in to grab him and he looked up at me. He shrank back in the cage, out of my reach.

"C'mon, over here." I whispered desperately.

Using the tow bar as a step, I lifted myself up so I teetered at the edge of the cage. Uncertain, the small creature backed up further, terrified. Putting my wand next to the cage, I braced myself with one hand and leaned in, stretching as far as I could.

Something shoved me from behind, hard, pushing me forwards into the cage. Pain lanced through my shin as I struck it and my face connected with the bars hard enough to make me cry out. Hands grabbed at my kicking feet and forced them up. Then, to my horror, the door slammed shut. Trying not to crush the fiend underneath me, I twisted around in the small confines of the cage to see Serraceuse standing there, baring his teeth in an evil grin. He dangled my wand just out of reach and gave a vicious laugh.

"I'm sure we can get a fair price for you, whoever you are." The nasal voice held a note of scorn for the girl who dared come after his merchandise.

"Let me out," I gasped, knowing the words were useless but unable to stop them falling out of my mouth.

"Sure, I'll let you out. 'Course you might not be *alive* by that point... unless there's a profit involved, of course." Serraceuse's cold chuckle sent a shiver down my spine.

"Serraceuse, what's going on? Where is my product?" a husky voice called out from behind. Serraceuse spun around.

"Hold your horses. The beast's in there, just had a minor mishap is all."

Serraceuse stepped to the side to reveal an older man, well dressed with a pair of silver glasses perched on his nose.

A Talent Lord, here? His face was familiar and after a moment I could place him. He'd been the target of Bee's anger at the recent gala.

"What? What is *she* doing in there?" Looking over his glasses he peered into the truck, backing away when he caught sight of my face.

"Tried to steal my wares. Your wares now, or it will be as soon as you hand over the chips."

The Lord shook his head nervously. "Oh no, I'll have no part of this, my friend. The deal's off - do you know who she is? A favourite of the High Seat, courting one of the ranked Lords. She has *friends*, Serraceuse."

"Dead people don't have friends," Serraceuse said in a bored tone. "You agreed to the price, Bolter. You're paying, whether you take the beast or not."

"She works with the Fae." His voice was urgent, shaking. "Some have even said she's met with a Guardian. I told you, the deal is off. You'll not get a thing out of me, you fool."

"Oh, I'll get it out of you alright." My eyes widened as Serraceuse turned his back on the man and pulled a gun from the front of his belt.

"No!" I cried, too late.

In one smooth motion, he swung back and shot the man between the eyes. The sound rang in my ears and sent shock waves through my body. Bile rose in my throat and my chest constricted until I couldn't breathe. Despite my horror, I couldn't tear my eyes away.

"Damned Talents." Serraceuse walked over to the body, kicked it, then started rifling through the dead Lord's pockets. "Can't dispose of them with style, can I? Bastards' got too many tricks up their sleeves, even if they're too dumb to dodge a bullet. No matter, I've got myself a new plaything, don't I?" He gave me a deadened smile, calmly slipping the gun back into his belt as if nothing had happened, then pocketed the few trinkets he'd found on the body.

"What do you want us to do with that, then?" One of Serraceuse's men spoke up behind him, sounding unenthused at dealing with a dead body.

"Throw him in the truck. We'll go down the river for a barbeque, yeah?" Serraceuse pulled out a wand and I flinched. "Oh, didn't expect that, did you? Lowly crim having a bit of Talent of his own? Deal with it."

As he spoke he traced a ward on the lock to secure it. Then, he pointed it at me. I felt the spell and my power swelled. The gun poking out of his belt made me hesitate, and I pulled away from the magic that would allow me to resist the spell he traced. If Serraceuse couldn't subdue me with magic... well, the alternative could be a lot worse.

Despite my intention, my gift flared inside me. I had to fight to keep it down, to let the trace wash over me, drown me in its effect. Somehow, I did both. The feeling of grogginess took over, but a thin tendril of my blocking ability reached out. My body slumped and my mind slowed, but I retained some kind of foggy awareness of my surroundings as rough hands pulled at me, then tugged at my belt. A hand dug in my pocket and pulled something out - my phone.

My sleepy mind nagged at me, saying it was important, but the spell had a tight enough hold that I couldn't move. Vaguely, I heard the muffled thump of something heavy being dumped beside me. The door slammed and darkness enveloped me. A moment later, just before I slipped into unconsciousness, sharp claws dug into my back. The pain seared my senses, waking me enough to harness my power and shake off the sleeping spell.

The engine rumbled and I lurched and swayed as the truck started to move down the uneven driveway. It stopped briefly before a screech signalled the rusty gate opening, then we drove off. My stomach dropped as we went down a hill, and I tumbled against iron bars as we lurched carelessly around a corner. Once, my fingers touched warm, damp cloth beside the cage and I jerked back with a sob, scrubbing the tacky residue off my fingers with my skirt.

When the truck finally stopped, I tucked the baby fiend inside my shirt and curled around it, pretending I was still under the power of the ward. The back door of the truck opened and I prayed they hadn't seen me flinch at the sudden noise. I was jostled as the cage scraped across the back of the truck. The fiend dug sharp claws into my chest as we slammed onto the ground.

Eyes closed, all I could do was prepare to face my worst nightmare.

Chapter Twenty-Three

"You want her out yet?" Jones called.

"Yeah." Serraceuse's voice moved farther away. "Look, someone left us a nice old barrel to cook her in." Shoes crunched, stopped, them a whoosh and a wave of heat billowed over me, washed away a moment later by the icy breeze. "Should've brought sausages. I love sausages."

Serraceuse had a voice like a knife down a windowpane. I'd landed face down so he couldn't see me squeeze my eyes shut in terror, or the single tear that leaked out. I breathed quickly, trying to calm myself before they noticed I was listening to them talk - talk about the pain they were going to inflict on me.

The lock on my cage joggled. "Uh, boss? You'll need to pop the lock."

Shoes crunched on dirt. The lock clinked again and the door swung open with a light squeak. Rough hands - different ones this time - grabbed me and hoisted me up, almost squashing the small creature tucked in my shirt. My lungs screamed as I held my breath to stop from whimpering. My heart pumped so hard I was sure the man carrying me would notice.

Very carefully, I opened my eyes, just a crack so they were still shaded by my lashes. He carried me over old concrete, broken by straggling grass. Graffiti decorated the ground and we passed an old drum packed with cold ash. The ground was strewn with rubbish. One of the worse sections of London, by the little I could see.

We stopped and Jones tossed me to the ground. The poor creature under me suffered a blow but stayed still and silent, only a flickering tongue on my skin to let me know he was still alive. Jones walked off and, terror of the unknown winning out, I risked a slight movement of my head to see what was happening.

I'd been left on the ground across from the men. The river gently lapped at the muddy bank just behind me, a that would normally calm me but today only served to further fracture my nerves.

Serraceuse, Ronson, Jones and another man stood by a second drum. Serraceuse poked at it with an iron bar. He held it up and spat on it, saliva hissing and sending up a thin ribbon of steam.

My stomach turned and adrenalin shot through me like fire. I didn't wait for a safe moment; I didn't sneak off. I panicked. Scrambling to my feet, I ran, blindly. A shout from behind made me turn, just for a moment - the wrong moment. A divot in the ground twisted my foot and I stumbled forward, trying to get my balance as I clutched at the wriggling fiend in my shirt. Startled, I realised where I was headed - straight for the wall that dropped down into the river.

Eyes blurred with tears, I whipped my head around, desperately looking for a way out. There were no buildings to hide in, no people to go to for help, and though my gift raged, it wouldn't stop bullets. As that thought flew across my mind, three shots rang out. I jumped, one arm wrapped protectively around the wriggling fiend I still carried in my shirt. Another shot went off a moment before I hit the water and more muffled booms sounded as I sank.

The shock of icy water pushed the air out of my chest and sent daggers of pain through my skin. My boots were waterlogged in moments, and I awkwardly kicked one off. The other stuck. Water dragged at the skirt wrapped around my legs, weighing me down. I kicked my legs desperately, lungs burning, and managed to bob up to the surface for a desperate breath.

Claws needled my skin as the drowning barrow fiend tried to climb clear of my shirt, and it bit into my neck for purchase. The pain made me cry out and water sloshed into my mouth. Still flailing in the water, I went under again before the fiend could escape. Fear and pain warred for my attention as my body screamed for air. The fiend clawed and bit until I helped it out, ripping my shirt buttons off to give it room to escape. It floated free, twisting and jerking in the water.

Out of air long enough for spots to start appearing in the darkness, I kicked with the last of my reserves and finally started to float upwards. My lungs strained and my limbs were heavy. Finally, I popped up like a cork, and held myself above water long enough to gasp a few breaths in. Something yanked at my hair, ripping my head back, then tried to climb on my head. Terrified, the barrow fiend had gone for the closest thing it could see - me.

Flailing in the water, I twisted around to see where I was. We'd been carried downstream a short way and there was no sign of our attackers. The bank was only a short distance away, but I had to get ashore, *now*. My legs burned and my arms were like lead, too weak to pull me out of the steady current that sucked us along. Helpless sobs wracked my body as I gulped in air and water all at once.

Taking a breath and hoping the fiend knew to do the same, I let myself sink again, taking a gamble. We weren't far from shore and I knew boats had gotten into trouble here. My feet kicked and flailed until they hit the soft, muddy bottom of the river. I tried to kick up, but one foot slipped. Using my arms to propel myself down again and trying to ignore the piercing in my scalp, I tried again.

This time I got it right, though with less force that I'd hoped. My thrust pushed me toward the bank, angling up for more air. When I broke the surface I was closer. Resting my legs, I pulled myself towards the sloping ground with my arms, weary, useless strokes that barely battled the current. I bobbed down again. This time, I hadn't gone far under when I hit dirt. That last push got me close enough to reach the bottom and I waded the rest of the way, feeling the weight of my clothes hanging down as I dragged my weary body to shore. Fingers numb, I fumbled at my open shirt, eventually just pulling it across my chest and hoping it stayed there.

Collapsing into sodden mud, I heaved and choked, spitting out water and slime. The barrow fiend dropped from its tangled nest in my hair, dislodging a few clumps as it fell. Still terrified that Serraceuse would catch up, I forced myself to wobbly knees to look around. The bridge was just a little way off. Masik would be there, he would offer protection. People, there were people there, too. They'd help, surely.

My head felt as soggy as my clothes and I didn't know how long I'd been floundering in the water. It took three tries to haul myself to my feet, and nearly toppled over again when I leaned down to scoop up the fiend. Biting wind tore through my wet clothes and my teeth ached from chattering so hard. Not happy in my shaking arms, the tiny fiend wriggled free, falling to the ground. It rolled in the mud for a moment, but followed as I started dragging my sorry limbs to find Masik.

When I reached the campsite of Masik and his tribe of homeless, it was empty. An old campfire still smoked gently, and the smell of something cooking filled the air. I dropped to my knees, exhausted and confused. Trolls never left their bridges. They must be close, surely?

"Masik?" My voice was weak and tremulous.

"Looks like he's scampered, my love. Never trust a troll to bail you out of danger."

Ronson's voice startled me and I screamed, turning to find him and Serraceuse both pointing guns at me as they advanced.

"Come on, let's do this quick. She's not getting a free pass, not after that little escapade. Tie her up." Serraceuse sounded vaguely irritated, voice still cold as a winter's night. "This bitch will send one hell of a message to the others."

Ronson tucked his gun in his belt and instructed me to lift my hands. Seeing no other choice, I obeyed. Ronson tied them together, the cord cutting into my skin. He threw me to the ground, then stood over me, gun drawn. Serraceuse poked an iron bar into the spent fire.

The bar glowed red, sucking in the heat as the smoke for the coals dissipated. The icy tremor in my body changed to one of terror as he drained the last of the heat out of the fire and into the burning weapon. Serraceuse turned to me, leaving a patch of cold, burnt ground behind him.

The baby fiend was gone - I hoped it was safe. My sideways vision wavered as I lay, face tacky with drying mud, too frightened exhausted to move. Focusing on my hands, on anything but Serraceuse's advancing figure, something caught my eye.

Somehow, the little Fae ring was still clean. It sparkled in the sun that streamed down, not yet high enough to warm my skin. A noise drew my focus back to the more distant Serraceuse, who pulled the now glowing metal bar out of the hot barrel to examine it. He spat on the end and at the hissing sound it made, my blood ran cold.

I flinched, drawing Ronson's attention. He kicked me, once, then placed a booted foot on my tied wrists, pinning me in the mud. My heart raced as Serraceuse turned to me and smiled. Short, shallow gasps tore at my chest as he approached, and a last wash of adrenaline flowed through me. Unable to hold back a pathetic whimper, I struggled, flailing about in the mud but unable to escape.

Serraceuse touched the iron brand to my bare flesh. Searing pain lanced my shoulder and I screamed, bucking and thrashing, a visceral need to escape taking over all logical thought. I channelled Talent - with nothing to trace with and no way of controlling it, the magic flowed towards the only source of concentrated magic it could find. The portal ring.

A howling sound rent the air. The sun flickered. The hot poker fell to the ground as Serraceuse's eyes widened, horror pulling his twisted face taught. Wrenching my head around, I saw why.

A portal to the Otherworld split the air right behind Ronson, a narrow slash that widened as I watched. Ronson tried to flee the widening sliver of empty space, stepping over me and kicking my leg in the process. He stumbled.

He caught himself, then barrelled backwards as a small figure launched through the air and hit him in the chest. On its own, the barrow fiend wouldn't have been able to overbalance him, but my limp body provided leverage as Ronson's heel snagged on my outstretched leg. Time slowed for me as he flailed, thrusting a desperate arm in my direction. There was time, I could save him.

I pulled back.

Ronson staggered, reeling, into the void of the portal as the barrow fiend jumped free. Though my mind reeled, I had enough presence to know what was coming, and that I wouldn't survive the stampede that was coming. Still, I curled into a ball, whimpering at the pain of movement as I covered my head with my arms.

Quiet. Not silent, but the sound of padded feet on wet mud was eerily soft. As the barrow fiends passed, their movement stirred up a chill breeze that tickled my arms. One or two leathery, bristled bodies brushed my huddled form, despite their efforts not to jostle one of their own. I felt that acknowledgement as they ran, mingled with a lust for blood so strong my mouth watered. Vengeance, for the one they lost. Fear, for her child. Resolve, to put an end to it. Though time stretched out, it was only moments until a terrified shriek split the air, cut off with sudden finality.

Stillness.

I lifted my head to see the pack clustered around something on the ground. Sirens wailed, penetrating the fog of my mind. Something small and dense nuzzled me, then shoved a blunt head under my arm. A bony plate pressed roughly against my head. Taking the message, I sat up, painfully aware of the damage I'd taken. I felt... closure. Was Serraceuse dead? Probably.

Despite the immense weight of my feelings, the overwhelming tiredness, the pain that flooded through me with every movement, I felt peace. It was done.

Chapter Twenty-Four

I didn't find out the rest of the story until later, as, once again, I lay in a hospital bed while Deirdre tended my wounds.

Masik, with that sixth sense that many of the Others possessed, had known that something bad was coming. After herding his people to another safe place he'd tried to get in contact with me, and sent one of his people to the local police station when he couldn't get in touch.

The poor young officer had a world of trouble trying to decipher a message that simply said 'Bridge is Door now, Lady'. Thankfully, she'd kicked the message over to the O.C.U., where it had eventually made its way to Greyson. He'd immediately known what it meant and rushed over.

Greyson and his team arrived to find me in Gibble's arms, untied but barely conscious, Lenny standing guard. My loyal dog had come to check on me after hearing the gunshot and realised that he had no chance against a locked cage. He'd immediately gone to Gibble for help. At least, that's what Gibble told me later.

As for Olfred... well, no one knew exactly how he'd made it there before anyone else. Gibble had found him sitting on the bank, lecturing my unconscious self on the perils of running headlong into danger. Though we were surrounded by some very large footprints, there wasn't a barrow fiend in sight.

Serraceuse's body turned up a street away, so badly mangled that the officer who found him had passed out at the sight. Ronson had disappeared; they were still looking, but I knew they'd never find him. The rest of Serraceuse's crew were tracked down soon after. It wasn't hard to spot two men dangling from a bridge, hogtied and held up by a thin strand of arachinum silk. Rumours abounded as to who would use such a rare and expensive material on two lowlifes, and they all pointed at the Fae.

There would be an inquest and I would be called to the stand, there would be no escaping that. Greyson assured me that temporary amnesia was common in crime victims, and that I shouldn't worry too much about my statement for now.

"He wasn't Talented, you know." Greyson looked at me over the paperwork he was filling out at the foot of my bed.

"What? He had magic, I saw him use it. The only way he could do that was if he were Talented, or... oh, of course."

"Yeah, half Fae. At least, that's what our delegate claims. We'll verify it later with genetic tests, but Umbers said it'd make sense."

"Oh?" I said, unsure if I wanted to know why he'd been talking to Harrod.

"Harrod couldn't dismantle the ward, the one at the warehouse. He said that'd bothered him at the time, but with everything going on he hadn't put two and two together. Seems Serraceuse got none of the looks and just a touch of Other magic, but a bloody good knack for wards."

The explanation did make sense, but I shuddered to think how badly things could have gone if he'd been born with more of the Fae genes showing through. Mortal-Fae couplings were rare. For once, I found myself exceedingly grateful for the fact.

"It's finally over, Em," Greyson said. "No more detective work, not for a while at least. Think you can keep out of trouble for bit?"

That brought a twitch of a smile to my lips.

"It would be nice to see you on a personal visit rather than a professional one for a change," Deirdre chided. "As much as I love my work, I'm much happier when it's not needed, especially on a dear thing like yourself."

"Dear thing? She just singlehandedly took out the most dangerous criminal we've ever been up against." Greyson looked downright affronted at her use of the term, then laughed as she rolled her eyes at him.

"No, it wasn't me. It was the barrow fiends. And the Guardian, she gave me the ring. I didn't really do anything, except get caught." I grimaced at my own ineptitude.

Greyson and Deirdre looked at me, agape.

"What?" I asked.

"Em, you *found* them." Greyson shook his head in wonder. "*You* tracked them down when my entire team couldn't find them. *You* saved the fiend, escaped from them once, and then you... what, called up an entire horde of beasts to trample them?" He chuckled, then added, "If that's what happens when you do 'nothing', I can't wait to see what your 'something' is."

Placing her hands on me, Deirdre trickled a little more of her healing power into my shoulder. "That's about all I'm able to do for now. You might have some stiffness in it for a while, and I haven't touched your poor scalp. That should heal quickly, though I've no *idea* how you even did that. If it's still bothering you in three days, come and see me."

Healing relied as much on the recipients' capability as the healer's. My exhausted, burnt-out state meant she wasn't able to completely fix my shoulder, but she'd done an excellent job notwithstanding. Reaching up to rub the spot, I could still feel some knotted scarring, but I could move my arm with only a little pain.

"Do take care, Emma." Deirdre leaned in to give me a warm hug. "Let your friends look after you for a little while. I might be able to fix bodies, but minds are a different thing entirely. You've more healing ahead of you, but time will help."

Harrod came to collect me not long after Deirdre left. As he helped me into the car, he asked if I was up to a detour on my way home. Feeling tired, but not wanting to spoil his surprise - it was obvious from the smile he kept trying to hide - I said yes.

Instead of driving to his house, we drove to mine. Expecting to see nothing more than a clean building site, when we pulled up the street I almost had to look around and check where we were. There, right in front of me, in the space that only days ago had been nothing but empty air and smouldering rubble, was my shop. It was beautiful.

"Harrod... *how*?" My mind reeled, and as I pulled myself out of the car I had to grip the door to keep from falling.

"Magic." He smiled at me and took my arm. "Come on. I moved all your things back while you were in the hospital."

My knees shook by the time I reached the door and I placed a hand on it, overwhelmed. Made of old silverwood and carved in the shape of a very large arch, it was not only beautiful, but functional. Even the tallest of my customers would be able to enter without having to awkwardly duck their heads. Above my hand, an intricate ward decorated the door. It was unfamiliar, but as I examined it, I noticed the circle wasn't quite closed.

"It's a Fae ward of protection. Unbreakable. At least, it will be once you finish it. We didn't want to get locked out before we were done."

"You organised this?" I asked, lost in wonder.

"Me?" Harrod chuckled and shook his head. "No, not by a long shot. I just helped a little. Barg was the main instigator but I think there were a lot of people involved."

I pushed against the door. As it swung open, smooth and sound-less, a sob rose in my chest. It was... indescribable. My builders had harnessed the magic of the Other, and I stood inside a shop that was at least four times the size of the plot of land it stood on, with a ceiling high enough that the whole shop seemed like an elegant ballroom.

The counter in front of me was made from mottled stone, polished until it was as smooth as glass. Running my hand along it, I walked around to examine the tall shelves behind, all stocked with finely crafted boxes for my teas. Glasses, cups and teapots adorned the lower shelves, all in different styles but somehow matched in an eclectic way. A stone sink with a pitcher of water beside it was set into the cabinets on the wall.

"No plumbing down here, but the pitcher will refill itself," Harrod explained. "The water is from some remote mountain spring, I believe. You should have everything you need to run a full service cafe, with a little staffing assistance."

My mouth was slack and words simply escaped me as I looked around. On shaking legs, I wandered in circles, looking over the shop. My shop.

Tables and chairs carved from heavy planks of raw oak filled part of the room, dotted with styled jars of glowing light. There were booths along one wall, and a long table against the front window.

As my eyes slid over it, I realised the view from that window was not of London. Instead, a field of purple grass and orange-leaved trees lay outside, a sparkling silver stream cutting through the landscape. One hand to my chest, I squeezed my eyes shut to force back tears.

"Harrod, that's... my dream..."

He shot me a quizzical look but didn't ask, and I didn't bother to try and explain. Tearing my eyes from the stunning scene, I let him pull me away to the small door at the back of the shop.

Dizziness hit me briefly on my way through, and I almost stumbled but for Harrod's hand on my arm. It led to a tiny room with wide steps leading up, and a door to the right. A peek into the side room revealed a casting room, sparsely furnished but surrounded by shelves for tea. Another ward, bigger than the one on the door but simple this time, covered the ceiling.

I pulled back and started up the stairs. Flutters of fear washed over me for a moment as I remembered fleeing my home, starved for breath and drowning in smoke. When I hesitated, Harrod simply stopped and waited until I was ready.

The stairwell was bright, lit by a skylight that showed blue sky through a glass pane at a dizzying height above us. Closing my eyes and taking some deep breaths, I tried to steady myself. Harrod pulled me down to sit next to him on the step, and placed an arm around me.

"Sorry, Em. You've been through hell and back these last few days, I should have waited."

"No," I said, gulping down a sob. "It's not just that. This... this is all so beautiful. Harrod, I can serve people tea while they're here, people can sit and drink it while they meet with friends and... it's *perfect*. I just can't help remember that last time I was here, right here, I almost died. I could have lost Lenny or Gib that night, too, I-" Fear shot through me. "Where are they? Where are-"

Squeezing my shoulder, Harrod hushed me. "They're upstairs waiting. They wanted to give you time-"

Without letting him finish I dashed upstairs, throwing open the door and rushing into the arms of Gibble, who waited just beyond it. Lenny cantered around, jumping up to lick my face as I laughed, head twisting away from the tickling sensation.

"Lady be liking the work that friends be doing?"

"Oh Gibble, it's just stunning. Show me!"

Harrod stood back while Gibble led me around my new home. Lenny gallivanted beside us, nudging open kitchen cabinets that were stocked with food and demonstrating how comfortable the new couch was by rolling on it enthusiastically, tongue lolling out with an upside down smile. The furniture was mismatched - dining chairs were interspersed with tall stools and a large, wide bench; the living room had an enormous arm chair next to a long couch and a small, elegant chaise. I realised why when Gibble, happy to watch me explore, sat down.

"Gibble! They made furniture just for you?"

"Not just chairs, Lady. Be going down the stairs and thinking of me."

Eyeing him, I did as he asked. Again the dizziness washed over me as I passed through the door, and when I looked down, I knew why. The stairwell wasn't... well, it wasn't quite *in* this world. I looked down not to the small room by the casting chamber, but to an enormous door. It opened to a single room, with a large pile of soft blankets scattered over a giant bed, some large chairs and walls lined with more books than I'd ever owned. Thudding steps behind me signalled Gibble's appearance.

"You live here now? That's wonderful!" As soon as I said it, I felt guilty. "Gibble, Serraceuse is gone. I'm safe now. Won't you miss the Other?" I forced the words out, knowing I owed it to him. As much as I wanted him here, I wanted him to be happy, more.

"If Lady be allowing it, Gibble would much be liking to have a place to be sleeping on this side of the port-gates. Be you willing for that?"

Dismayed that he even felt he had to ask, I threw myself at him again. He caught me without stumbling, patting my back as I squeezed him. "Gibble be thinking you be not minding then, Lady?" He chuckled, and we headed back upstairs together.

"The small chairs are for Barg, right?"

"Well, Barg and one other, Lady. Gibble will have to be explaining..."

～

"Oh, hello Master Tork. Your usual today?" Ellandra greeted the troll with a warm smile.

Tork eyed the demi-fae behind the counter who beamed up at him with innocent eyes. His normally surly expression softened and he handed over the chips without argument. "Tork want two box next week." Ellandra raised an eyebrow and he quickly added, "Please."

"Certainly, Master Tork. I'll let Lady Emma know to have them ready. You have a nice day, now." She waved a tiny hand at the troll, who gave her a respectful, yet slightly awkward half-bow and stomped out of the shop.

"Everyone told me trolls were cranky beasts, but Tork is just lovely," Ellandra said as she pulled a box of tea out and tipped some into a pot.

"You do tend to bring out the best in him," I said. I watched my new assistant pour water over the tea, then press her hands to the sides of the pot and heat it. Wondering for the umpteenth time how she did that without burning her hands, I set out a tray with some cups.

Ellandra had appeared on my doorstep the day I reopened. My surprise at seeing the demi-fae I had rescued from Serraceuse was only slightly less than when Gibble had shown me a letter from the Guardians, asking me to take her on as an apprentice.

Of course, when the Guardians 'asked' you something, you agreed, which is why my entire home had been built to accommodate not only myself, Gibble, Lenny and the frequently-visiting Barg, but my new assistant as well. They'd instructed Barg to make sure she had a place at my table, and Gibble told me there was another room in case she needed to stay the night. Despite my initial concerns over the arrangement, it was working out wonderfully.

"Why don't you take a short break, Ellandra? I can handle things for a while."

"Oh I couldn't, Lady Emma. The tree-god will be here shortly. He will wish to speak with you." Ellandra took up the tray of freshly made tea and gracefully glided over to deliver it to a table of hobgoblins that sat in one corner.

Not bothering to question her about Olfred, I simply took it for truth. It wasn't the first time she'd mentioned someone turning up, and she'd never been wrong. Sure enough, about five minutes later, he arrived and took a seat by the window, Lenny loping over to settle on the floor at his feet.

Carefully selecting a nice blend of lemonbalm and mint, I scooped some into a fresh pot, then stepped aside as Ellandra shooed me away.

"Please, Lady, go and sit. I shall bring you the tea as soon as it's ready."

Thanking her, I took a seat next to Olfred.

"I see them sometimes, you know," I said, eyes searching the picturesque scene for any sign of the barrow fiends. The fields and forest were empty, as they always were when people were around.

"Aye, that ye would. They be owin' ye a great debt, an' they no' be forgettin' it."

"Olfred, I've been meaning to ask you something. That day, when... everything happened, Greyson said you were one of the first there, even before the police. How did you know?"

"Well, it's no' tha' I didna trust ye had the ability te keep ye'self safe, lassie... I jus' didna think ye'd have the *sense*. I sent young Pearl, as ye named her, to watch over ye. Ye didna see her? She slipped back te me as soon as she saw ye in trouble wi' those louts. More's the shame I didna get there a mite earlier te save ye some grief from th' bastards." He looked me over sadly.

"Oh, Olfred, please don't blame yourself for that. If you'd come any sooner, I might not have been able to open the portal and it could have gone a lot worse. In fact, if-" I stopped, a thought occurring to me. "Olfred, what if I *hadn't* opened the portal? I'd already seen it happen, in the Other. Somehow the Guardian showed it to me before it happened. Could I have changed it?" Dread settled in my bones as I waited for his answer.

He looked at me closely. "Aye, lass, ye could have. What ye saw in the Other was just one o' many things ye could have seen, an' no' all o' them would have come te pass." He sat back, frowning. "It's no' the answer ye wanted, was it? Aye, Pearlie told me abou' the one tha' fell. Ye made a choice, lass. I might be one o' the old gods, but I canna tell ye if it were the right one." He put a dry, gnarled hand on my arm and looked into my eyes. "Only you can decide that. Dinna be tearin' ye'self up over it, though. It's done, and ye canna undo it. Dinna waste too much o' ye heartache over that monster, if he dinna be takin' beasts wha' dinna want te go with him, he would'na been there te get hurt, aye?"

Tears pricked my eyes. Throat tight, all I could do was nod. The guilt that lurked in the corners of my soul since that day had surfaced at his words, but I made myself think through what he said.

He was right - if Ronson hadn't been such an evil sod, smuggling animals, stealing babes from their mothers, he wouldn't have been standing on that river bank in the first place. If he hadn't been helping Serraceuse in his game of torture, he wouldn't have been right where the portal opened. Anger rose to war with the guilt and not for the first time, I pushed both down. There was no right answer, and I didn't have the courage to ask the question anyway.

Olfred left a little while later, and Barg dropped in to take Lenny for a walk. When the shop closed, I still sat at the window, so deep in my reverie I barely noticed Ellandra's farewell as she locked up and left me to my thoughts.

As I stared out the window into the now silver grass and red-leaved trees, movement drew my gaze. A herd of animals ambled in the distance, slowly walking along the tiny stream as a smaller pack member gambolled around their feet. The baby fiend, now three feet high and with a sleek coat like the older animals, reared upon to its feet and looked in my direction. As one, the pack stilled and turned to me. In a single movement they dipped their heads and pawed the ground once, then looked to the sky, mouths open.

Somehow, in the far distance, carried on the smallest trickle of a breeze, I heard the harrumph of the calling herd. It was the call of the barrow fiends to acknowledge one of their own; a call to one who was not then, but who had become one of their herd in spirit, if not in form.

I watched their display, sitting at the window, and I waved, and laughed through my tears as the youngest of the fiends shook his bony head, and entertained me with tumbles and jumps like a child showing off for his mother. My heart swelled, dislodging a tiny bit of the guilt that had taken up so much room. I watched the herd until they wandered off, knowing that no matter what I'd been through, it was entirely worth it.

* 9 7 8 C 6 4 8 9 7 6 1 1 0 *